ESCAPE FROM EXTINCTION

An Eco-Genetic Novel

Also by Frederic C. Rich

Christian Nation, a Novel

Getting to Green, Saving Nature: A Bipartisan Solution

ESCAPE FROM EXTINCTION

An Eco-Genetic Novel

FREDERIC C. RICH

Book design by Glen M. Edelstein

Published by Vector Books LLC
New York, New York USA

Hardback ISBN 13: 978-1-7346655-0-5
Ebook ISBN 13: 978-1-7346655-1-2

Publisher's Cataloging-in-Publication Data

Names: Rich, Frederic C., author.
Title: Escape from extinction: an eco-genetic novel/Frederic C. Rich
Description: New York, NY: Vector Books LLC, 2020.
Identifiers: LCCN: 2020909078 | ISBN: 9781734665505 (Hardcover) | 9781734665512 (ebook)
Subjects: LCSH Neanderthals--Fiction. | Genetic engineering--Fiction. | Eugenics--Fiction. | Nature- Effect of human beings on--Fiction. | Family--Fiction. | Science fiction. | FICTION/ Nature & the Environment | BISAC FICTION/ Science Fiction/ Genetic Engineering | FICTION/ Thrillers/ Medical
Classification: LCC PS3618.I33275 E83 2020 I DOC 813.6--dc23

Printed in the United States of America
First Edition

CONTENTS

Prologue

Gorham's Cave, Gibraltar
October, about 35,000 years ago

THE PERFECTLY ROUND MOON drifts over the water, centered at this moment in a jagged black frame as familiar to Pra as the contours of his mother's face. He emerged into this world from his mother's womb and from the womb of this cave he will now depart. Born into the dwindling Clan of the Tall Grasses twenty winters before, now he is alone.

Pra has ceased to feel cold. He watches the line of a shadow pass from just below his right knee, sliding down his shin as the bright disc arcs ever higher in the sky. Finally, the moon illuminates only his foot, which rests on the cave floor wrapped in the battered thick leather of a mammoth from the north. He closes his eyes and remembers his mother teaching him to make a boot, the bone awl puncturing a neat row of holes, his mother pulling the hide laces tight. *You must be sure*, his mother had said, *that the snow cannot enter where the pieces are joined. Do you understand?*

In the silence of the cave, Pra whispers to himself, "Yes, Mother, I understand."

The moonlight fractures into countless stars dancing across the surface of the sea. For his entire life, cold and hunger have pursued him, driving him south and west. Now, settled in this cave on a rocky peninsula surrounded by water, the taker of breath and life, he can go no farther. Each day Pra wonders whether it might be warmer on the other side of the water. Perhaps the beasts there are plentiful and give themselves freely. But only birds and fish can cross the water.

The sea terrifies Pra even more than the dark-skinned others, the newcomers who bewitch wolves to serve as their companions. These newcomers are strange people, unusually tall and lean, topped with small and oddly shaped heads. They and the wolves under their spell hunt well, leaving little for the clan to eat. Pra lost his mother and his father to the others, and then watched his sisters and the rest of the clan sicken and starve. He has been alone for three winters. Still, he wants to live.

A hacking cough and sharp convulsion in his gut pull Pra from his reverie. Looking up and out the mouth of the cavern, Pra remembers the time he saw an ibex standing placidly on the root mass of a large tree that floated across the bay. A persistent voice in his head had told him he could do the same. He did not listen. There had been so many voices in his head. But now they are silent.

Pra's eyes fall shut and his bulky hands drop to the cave floor. He is still. There is no sound other than his shallow breath. And then, with a long exhale, *Homo neanderthalensis* is no more.

Lake Hopatcong, New Jersey
May 1987

A four-year-old boy perches on the edge of a dock, staring intently at the water. His father, with the boy's younger sister, Mia, in his lap, sits nearby on the shore in a cheap aluminum beach chair whose brightly colored webbing seems too frayed to support such a large man.

The boy's fine black hair flops onto his forehead as he leans forward from the waist and grips the splintered wooden deck. His thin legs, which had been swinging, stop. An unnatural stillness descends on the normally fidgety body of the child, whose unblinking eyes seem trapped by some invisible image on the water's taut surface.

No one sees the boy, who cannot swim, pitch forward into the lake. He does not flail or splash, but instead drifts toward the muddy bottom, his lungs filling with water on his first inhale below the surface.

A small foot clad in a red sneaker is the first part of his body to reach the lake's bottom. But instead of landing gently in the muck, his toe strikes and punctures the bloated belly of a decomposing cow that had fallen through the ice earlier that spring. With a silent pop, the accumulation of methane bursts through the torn belly, creating a broad bubble that explodes toward the surface, bearing upward the body of the boy.

The father looks up to see his son shoot from the surface of the lake, fly through the air in a high arc, and land with one small bounce on the sandy beach at his feet. With a single cough, young Leo expels the water from his lungs and opens his eyes before his father even manages to rise from the chair.

This story had been told countless times. His father never tired of it. Leo supposed it to be true, but was never entirely sure.

PART I
ARCADIA

1
The Big Empty

MUIR O'BRIEN DROVE THROUGH the early-morning darkness with the radio off and the windows down. Two hours after leaving the shabby motel that looked like an oversize chicken coop, his truck passed through the last range fence and entered the far eastern edge of the sage desert. The dirt track faded to the corrugated shadow of a road, and in his rearview mirror Muir spotted a smudge near the horizon that signaled a distant dawn flowing westward. He pictured the long line of twilight, perhaps just about to leap the Rockies and flood the Snake River Plain. Within an hour, the tide of day would surge over the Columbia Plateau at his back and illuminate the wilderness of the Harney Basin.

Most people found the arid scrubby landscapes of the Great Basin to be unlovely, even alien. Muir, however, loved this place with no connection to the sea, which drained in only upon itself. The Oregon outback offered hunters antelope, cougar, bear, elk, and an abundance of other game. Coyotes were ubiquitous, predator to the jackrabbit and desert cottontail. And now, with the advent of autumn, the mule deer had returned from the upland forests to feed on the sagebrush of the high desert and the grasses in the rich marshlands below.

Muir parked his truck under a tree and started the long hike westward. Soon, the calls of quail, sage grouse, mourning dove, and chukar broke the silence of the dawn. The mourning doves sang with exuberance. Muir knew the first hard frost had been a signal for the birds to gather for their long migration. He heard in the birdsong the joy of a species doing exactly what its oldest and most fundamental instincts told it to do.

After the profusion of game, Muir considered the lack of people to be the best feature of "the Big Empty." One of the least populated areas in the lower forty-eight states, it was a place he could be certain of solitude. No roads. No loud-mouthed jerks in orange hats coming down the hill to spook his buck. This was a wilderness filled with an abundance of life that was there to smell, hear, and see, if you just stood still and paid attention. Only modern man could call it "empty."

Muir remembered the time when his wife, Meredith, had asked him why he felt compelled to hunt. He hadn't answered. And now he never would, at least not to her. Meredith died giving birth to their daughter, Lilith. Everything normal, the obstetrician had said. And then, on a Tuesday afternoon the previous November, Muir helped his happy wife into the pickup and headed to the hospital in Boise. By midnight, he had lost a wife and gained a daughter. He hadn't touched his rifle since. But yesterday, his desire to again be in this place finally overwhelmed the grief and protectiveness that had kept him at Lilith's side. He dropped the baby at his parents' house, told his manager he needed a day off, and pointed the truck west.

After walking for a half hour, Muir felt a slight throbbing in his temples and a sharpening of his pulse. He could hear the whisper of blood rushing through the artery that lay alongside his ear canal.

His father called the sensation "buck fever": a lurching shift of gears, a resetting of the nervous system, the ordinary part stilled and the other rising to kindle a latent primal self. It was like that moment before sleep, when a strange sideward slide marks the transition from conscious to hypnagogic thought, and a dream begins to emerge that is far more vivid than the muddle of fading consciousness. It was called a "fever," but only in its grip did Muir feel truly well.

Now, the first shallow shafts of sunlight grazed the slopes, warming the narrow aromatic leaves of sage and releasing their scent to drift in invisible currents up the canyon. Muir loved the mottled modest grays and greens of the scrubby terrain. He delighted in the sounds of the forest breathing: the distinctive rustle of leaves both dry and frosty, and the sound of air rushing over wings as an unseen woodpecker passed above.

Muir began the ascent of a narrow canyon by traversing its side-wall. With his rifle strapped to his back, he used both hands to scramble through gullies that last winter's ice had scoured clean and approached the scattered stands of western juniper at the top. Far below, the summer grass, parchment colored now, still waved, although stiffly, in a meadow tucked at the canyon's base.

The glow of dawn seemed to Muir to be designed for hunting. Like ultraviolet light revealing fingerprints invisible to the naked eye, the sun at just the right angle lit up the fur of the mule deer in an iridescent glow, revealing what at any other time of day would remain hidden amidst the cover of dense vegetation. Muir quickly spotted two bucks and three does high on the opposite wall of the canyon. Attracted by bitter rush, they emerged shyly from the shrubby cover into a clearing, their bodies etched against a white patch of shallow crusty snow, the isolated remnant of an early-autumn squall. He had a feeling it was going to be a good day.

Muir disdained the sophisticated range finders and spotting scopes that sportsmen refer to as "optics." He detested trail cameras. Of course, man was superior and always had an edge. That's why man was predator and the game was prey. But if predator and prey are too unequal, then the essential character of the hunt is destroyed. Too much technology, too much advantage, and it's just killing.

After spotting the deer, Muir reversed course and scrambled across the shallow canyon to approach the animals from the downwind side. Muir's dad, the man who thought it fit to name his son after a glacier, was never far from Muir's thoughts during the stalking phase of the hunt. Glaciers are cold, slow, and stupid, Muir used to complain. Glaciers are solid, deliberate, and dependable, his father would reply. You get what you see. That's the kind of son I want. And now his dad's words sounded clearly: *When you think you're going slow enough in the stalk, go half that fast. Remember, every step is a risk, every risk a possibility.* Muir's mind spoke to him in his father's voice. He was used to it. He slowed down.

As he crept from thicket to thicket downwind of the feeding deer, Muir saw that a four-point buck had wandered away from the rest of the group. Muir stood close enough to see the buck nuzzle away the thin crust of snow and nibble the vegetation below. Then, without any apparent provocation, the animal lifted his head to sort through all the sounds and smells of the dawning day and found something to cause him alarm.

At this moment in a hunt, Muir usually felt that the prey had been waiting for his arrival. It was in its nature to be prey to a superior animal. In this sense, Muir believed that the buck recognized and accepted the hunter. The instant the buck had stepped into the clear, the verbal part of Muir's mind shut down, overtaken by the older part of the brain, which knew what needed to be done and required no words to describe it. Muir felt only the comfortable certainty that he was doing a thing he was intended to do. With the deer in his sights, every movement of the animal seemed laced with meaning, as if the forces that governed life sat just below the ripple of haunch and twitch of nostril, ready to be revealed.

With a steady breath, Muir aimed his rifle just to the rear of the big buck's shoulder, the point that presented the best prospect for a clean shot and a quick kill. Without extraneous motion, he firmly curled his trigger finger. But in the instant before the crack of the shot filled the canyon, the deer leapt forward with a suddenness that seemed to violate the laws of gravity and inertia.

Muir spent a precious moment indulging in an expletive before regaining his focus. He noticed the deer glance at an uphill thicket. Quickly this time, Muir crouched and ran for an even denser thicket downwind of where he knew the buck, now invisible, would head. As Muir ran, he was aware only of the air on his skin, the spreading of his ribs as his chest heaved, and the unique nameless color of the lichen on the north side of the rocks.

Ten minutes later, when the buck cautiously emerged from the protection of the dense scrub, Muir, crouched deep in a thicket of stunted juniper, took his second shot. A solid lung shot, but not a quick kill. The deer stumbled, recovered, and then bolted downhill, with labored leaps replacing its previously graceful bounds. Within moments, Muir lost sight of the wounded prey. He summoned the image of a dying deer: the sudden dulling of the eyes, the final spasm of the flank muscles. This death was what he now owed the animal. It was his responsibility to follow it, find it, and kill it.

At first the track was clear. He spied two drops of bubbly lung blood, still tinged pink, stark against the dull yellow of a leaf. Muir knew the wounded buck would prefer to head downhill. It would seek the protection of the thickest brush. It would make for water, if there were any to be had.

Had Muir been thinking about time, he would have noticed the shortening shadows as the morning passed and the October sun reached its zenith not so far above the ridges of the Warner Mountains to the south. But instead, he was aware only of the shallow impression of a hoof in the moss, a freshly broken twig, a tuft of fur on the sharp end of a dead juniper branch, and the smell of blood and fear drifting downwind from the buck's lateral track across the slope.

The wounded buck had, as expected, sought refuge in the marshy lowland at the bottom of the canyon. From there, it entered an elbowed ravine between two ridges, the only exit from the rear of the canyon. Muir paused, momentarily uncertain whether his prey had in fact passed into the timbered plateau beyond. As he scanned the stand of ponderosa pine in front of him, jarring flashes of white plastic caught his eye. Muir removed his sunglasses and blinked. Doubting what he saw, he scrambled down a shallow rocky slope to the edge of the woods. But there they were. In the heart of the Big Empty, a vast place hundreds of miles from human habitation, Muir saw signs mounted on trees about every hundred feet:

Posted
Private Property—No Trespassing
Hunting, fishing, trapping, and vehicles strictly prohibited.
Violators will be prosecuted.
Arcadia LLC

It made no sense. Not here. Muir stopped short and drew a long breath. He had a decision to make. On one hand, respect for private property was a core plank of hunting ethics. You never entered posted property without permission. No exceptions. On the other hand, he had wounded an animal and could not rest until he finished the job. He squatted on his heels, drank from the water bottle, and considered his choice. When the water was empty, he had no doubt. His greater duty was to the wounded animal.

Half an hour later, Muir closed on the tiring buck. Its track led to a stand of ferns sheltered by a scrubby thicket, the ferns crushed in the center in the distinctive shape of a deer hollow. The buck had lain down, perhaps to die, perhaps to rest, but in any case had found the will to carry on. Muir knelt, placed both hands on the depression, and closed his eyes, remembering the larger elk bed, and that day with Meredith, the day Lilith had been conceived, only twenty months before, but in what now seemed like a previous life. When he opened his eyes to stand and resume the chase, he looked down and broke off a fern frond, closely inspecting both its front and rear.

"It can't be," he whispered to himself.

Muir held a master's degree in botany but still thought of himself as merely an amateur plantsman. There had been no money for a doctorate and no scholarship. And as far as he was concerned, without the PhD, you were just a guy who was interested in plants. He broke off another frond. The pinnae were offset from each other on the stalk, and the smaller rounded pinnules into which they were divided had a distinctive oblong shape, narrowing toward their tips, with lancet-shaped ends. But the thing that clinched it was the underside. On the back of each frond, he saw roundish pimples the color of juniper berries arranged in single rows on each side of the midrib. He knew of no living fern with these features. It seemed impossible, but if he was correct, then his deer had taken a rest in a type of fern that became extinct by the end of the last ice age, at least ten thousand years ago. Muir tucked the stems in his shirt pocket and refocused on the wounded buck. He knew he was close.

Five minutes later, Muir crossed a mostly dry stream bed and followed the track around a bend toward a pool of still water. The fresh prints suggested the deer had stopped to drink here, perhaps only moments before. He shouldered his rifle.

"Stop where you are," said a voice from behind him. "Put down the rifle and put your hands up. Now, buddy."

Muir turned around to see two men pointing assault rifles at his chest. They were dressed in black SWAT gear, with "Arcadia LLC" embroidered in green thread above each breast pocket. Muir put his rifle on the ground and raised his arms.

"My deer," he said. "I wounded a buck and have to . . ."

"Didn't you see that this property is posted?" one of the men asked.

"I did. But I wounded a buck, a four-pointer. He's only minutes ahead. I've got to take care of him. Please, guys."

"Sorry, sir. This is private property. There's no hunting allowed."

"Come on, guys, I've been hunting around here for a decade. There's nothing anywhere near here. What the hell is this? Who are you?"

"Sir, we're going to take your statement and drive you back to your vehicle. You may receive a summons in the mail."

Returning to a small ATV with some sophisticated-looking instrumentation mounted on the dashboard, the guards used an iPad to take Muir's picture and fingerprints and then handed Muir the tablet and instructed him to use it to complete a short questionnaire. They continued to refuse to answer Muir's questions. The three men rode in silence back to the spot where Muir had parked. It was the first time in his life that Muir had abandoned a wounded animal. He felt sick. When they arrived back at the truck, the two guards returned his rifle. Muir saw them in his rearview mirror, watching, as he drove away to the east.

Back at the motel, Muir lay in bed visualizing the wounded buck, dying slowly in the night due to his incompetence. He saw his father's face, with the familiar shadow of a squint signaling disapproval of a chronically underperforming son. Twice he got up to look at the fern fronds, more and more convinced that he had found a living stand of an extinct plant. He was determined to figure it out. And what in the world was Arcadia LLC, in the middle of nowhere, patrolled by guards with assault rifles? To fall asleep, he summoned up the sound of his daughter Lilith's laugh, and thought how happy she would be when he returned home to her tomorrow.

2
Polly and Leo

I am he. I sense it and I am not deceived by my own image. I am burning with love for myself. I move and bear the flames. What shall I do? Surely not court and be courted? Why court then? What I want I have.

OVID, *METAMORPHOSES III*: 437–473

"WELL, WHAT DO YOU have to say?" Polly asked, setting down her empty teacup. "About what happened."

"I'm very sorry that it happened," Leo answered.

"That's all? I'm writing an equation on the blackboard with my back to the audience. The crowd starts screaming. When I turn and look over my shoulder, I see a chap with a long knife jumping onto the stage, yelling, '*Allahu akbar.*' He was only a few yards away by the time the guard got his shot off. I was bloody terrified, and all you have to say is sorry?"

"What else do you expect me to say? I'm truly sorry you had to go through that. But it's hardly the first time. A lot of folks hate what I do and want to stop us, you know that."

"And that's supposed to make it better?"

Leo and Polly met for tea once each week in the library of their house on the outskirts of Portland, Oregon. Bleached birch paneling covered the walls. The books did not reside on shelves. Instead, Leo kept his collection of landmark works on the history of science in a sealed octagonal glass column at the center of the library. There, he explained to visitors, they were protected from dust and moisture and could be retrieved by a robotic device upon voice command. Polly had insisted on comfortable chairs, and the overstuffed green leather wing chair in which she sat struck an incongruous note amidst the cool techno-sleek of the room.

Leo drank a cup of Baihao Yinzhen tea, the optimal single cup, each day at the optimal time, 1:00 p.m. Years ago, Leo read that Song dynasty emperors had reserved this rare white tea for themselves. Investigating on Leo's instructions, SynBioData's scientists determined that it retained a higher concentration of antioxidant flavonoids than any other tea. This hardly surprised Leo. It wasn't that he had any faith in the medical acumen of Chinese emperors. But he did believe, as a prominent sign in the lobby of SBD headquarters proclaimed, "Civilization is a computer."

Much of SBD's early work had been based on the idea that human history could be seen as a vast distributed computing system processing countless empirical observations by individuals. No one person had any idea of the mechanism by which Baihao Yinzhen tea contributed to longer life or understood why one cup a day was the optimal dose. But, Leo believed, when that conclusion finally emerged from a millennium of human experience, it should be viewed as the result of a multigenerational blind trial, with more data points than any scientist could ever hope to muster during a single lifetime.

Polly had no qualms about this part of SBD's work, grounded as it was in history and culture. When the company was a struggling start-up based in the small Cupertino cottage she shared with Leo, Polly's work on computational analysis of large data sets had laid the foundation for the company's first breakthroughs. Now SBD was the world's largest corporation and had access to computers more powerful than civilization itself. The company's big hardware churned through every existing medical record, correlating symptoms, treatments, and outcomes with everything else discoverable about the patient. And it turned out that a vast amount was discoverable about each patient through the continuous mining of the patient's online activity, surveillance video, and GPS. When privacy advocates complained, Leo argued that other companies were allowed to gather and analyze all the same information for the purpose of selling you stuff, so why shouldn't SBD be allowed to do exactly the same thing with the goal of saving your life?

Changing the subject, Leo said, "I'm going on *60 Minutes* to get the word out on the pancreatic cancer story. Finally, it's something ordinary people can understand. We've been playing defense, Pol. I need to take back the headlines from Pastor Joe and all the other crazies who say I'm playing God. I'm playing doctor, not God. But until I get the politicians onside I can't . . . What I mean is that these people need to get out of my way so that syn-bio can realize its potential."

The previous year, just before its IPO made Leo the richest person in the world, SBD had contacted a hundred thousand people to tell them that its computers believed, solely from their online footprint, that they had early-stage pancreatic cancer. That morning, the company had announced that their big machines proved correct with respect to all but one of them, and that doctors estimated that four thousand of those people would have died but for the early warning. SBD stock rose to yet another a new high, and the net worth gap between Leo and the runner-up multi-billionaire widened once again.

"I'm happy for you, Leo," Polly said. "The pancreatic cancer demonstration is statistically incontrovertible." There were moments when Polly was able to reconnect with the pride she felt about SBD's early achievements and recall the joy of having Leo treat her as a full partner in his work. But she worried that now Leo's real love was the "syn" part of SynBioData—synthetic biology—work about which Polly felt more apprehensive than proud. As Leo liked to tell reporters, the design and fabrication of biological components and systems that do not already exist in the natural world was even more promising than the bio-data revolution that already had changed the face of medicine. Synthetic biology, he promised, would allow not only the prevention of disease through the elimination of the genetic mutations that cause it, but the creation and reshaping of life itself.

Leo and Polly now led largely separate lives, she as a mathematician who split her time between Oregon and King's College, Cambridge, and he as the peripatetic prophet for advanced biotech.

Polly was not ready to drop the subject of the most recent attack. "I can't believe it happened at King's. I'd always felt safe there."

Polly looked out the window at the fork in the Columbia River, visible far below the broad lawn immediately outside. She yearned for that lawn to be filled with sounds of children at play. Her children.

"You know, Leo, when I'm in Cambridge it sometimes feels like everything since I was a student there never happened. I can feel again like the Philadelphia girl falling in love with England. Falling in love with maths." She turned and looked again at her husband. "I can remember what it was like to be the girl who had never met you."

"There were flaws in the security plan," Leo said. "I looked into it personally and made some changes. You'll be perfectly safe when you're next in the UK. It won't happen again."

Polly had a good two inches on Leo and appeared even taller thanks to a halo of curly hair, still an assertive carrot red. She stood and started pacing.

"You know, Leo, did you ever consider that maybe not everything is an engineering problem that is capable of being solved? Or that maybe some of the things that apply to ordinary people, to ordinary lives, also might still apply to you?"

"Really, Pol? You didn't marry someone ordinary. I'm not one of those people lurking around in Plato's cave not knowing I'm looking at shadows. I'm the one who knows we're in the cave."

Polly sighed. "I married someone who had suffered like an ordinary person and had an inspiring passion to cure disease. I married someone who was smart enough to know that unbounded egotism is toxic."

"Toxic? Hardly. Egotism is just . . . honest."

Polly sank back into the leather chair and briefly rested her forehead in her hand. When she looked up, she resumed in a quiet voice.

"One thing I've never understood, Leo. Why did you bother to marry me? You don't need a wife. You don't think you need a friend, companion, or soul mate. So it wasn't that. You didn't want children. So why? What did you want with me?"

She looked up in the vain hope of seeing some sign of regret, embarrassment, or even mild discomfiture. But Leo appeared unperturbed.

"I'm not an ordinary man. I couldn't have an ordinary wife. You have one of the most insightful minds of your generation."

Leo paused.

"We both were misfits in our own ways, and I felt comfortable around you, Pol. I liked working with you. And I . . . admired you. Still do. You're a brilliant woman. Unique. Your achievements were . . . fitting. What more can I say? You were an appropriate match given the parameters I had identified. We made a good team."

Polly was accustomed to Leo's cluelessness about the feelings of others, but the awful truth of his answer rendered her speechless. For the first time in a long while, she allowed herself to wonder if her marriage could survive. Before Leo had a chance to notice Polly's pain, the door opened and Leo's personal assistant, Clip, entered the library without knocking.

Clip was no longer doing bio in a garage, but his clothing hadn't changed: yellow plastic flip-flops, a ragged pair of orange-striped pajama bottoms, and a stained black T-shirt bearing the words "Religion: Together we can find a cure." Normally she wasn't bothered by the superficial, but for some reason Clip's ridiculously careless dress irritated Polly.

Clip glanced at Polly, then back to Leo. Leo nodded.

"Hey, boss," Clip said. "Uh, I got you a meeting with that hacker in Seattle you wanted to see. Next week. I still don't think it's a great idea."

"I know. What else?"

"A really great report from Arcadia. Another hundred thousand acres, which brings us almost up to six million. And still not a peep from the locals. Nothing in the paper, not even loose talk in the bars in Burns. Nada. And they finally sent us the security report for last quarter. One bubba hunter chasing a deer got about two miles in from the east line. Nothing to worry about. Probably too fucking stupid to find the state forest."

"How do you know?" Leo asked.

"Know what?"

"That he's stupid."

"Huh? Well, I mean, these guys think it's fun to get dressed up and run around the woods killing defenseless animals. Uh, I don't know, but isn't that pretty lame?"

"The east boundary of Arcadia is 160 miles from the state forest. You think that he was too stupid to realize he was driving two hours longer than normal? Send me the report."

"Will do, boss," Clip said, turning to leave.

"And, Clip," Leo added, "go ahead and contact Professor Silva in Leipzig, the Neanderthal expert I told you about. Tell him I want a meeting. I'll go there."

"And if he asks what the meeting is about . . . you know, what you want?"

"Just say I want to see him. That'll be enough."

While Clip and Leo were talking, Polly's mind turned to the day she first met Leo, at the wedding of the beautiful daughter of a family friend to a promising young venture capital investor. At the time, she had dreaded all weddings. At this one, Polly had found herself seated next to an awkward young man who appeared as miserable as she did.

"I had to come," he had said defensively. "The groom invested in my start-up. No choice."

"Me too," she had replied. "The bride's mother is my mother's best friend. I hate weddings."

"Me too."

Hearing that the woman at his side was a mathematician, and under the influence of his first-ever glass of champagne, Leo had vented his frustration at the inadequacy of traditional statistical methods for use in high-dimensional biomedical data integration and analysis. Polly had casually suggested a tweak to the principal components analysis he had been using, and Leo had been impressed. This was something new for Polly. Every man she had dated had been scared off at the first glimpse of her intellect or passion for math.

Many glasses of champagne later, the two of them had sat on the steps while the rest of the party danced under a large tent. Polly had noticed that behind the thick glasses and ill-fitting suit was an attractive man. His olive complexion and glossy black hair seemed sensuously exotic to a girl raised in a sea of pale sandy-haired preppies. Leo, usually awkward and reserved around women, spoke passionately of his dream to transform medicine using big data.

"Have you heard of OI, usually called brittle bone disease?" Leo had asked.

Polly shook her head.

"It's a rare hereditary disease, caused by a genetic mutation. In a severe case, the bones lose their strength and just collapse, usually before a child is ten." Leo had stared at the ground. "My younger sister Mia had it. We were . . . close. For years I watched her just . . . her skeleton just fell apart. And after she died, my mother left us. Just walked away. I was eight. I guess she couldn't . . ."

Polly had reached out to put her hand on his arm.

"The day Mia died I decided that I would find a fix."

She had watched as Leo's face reset from a look of pain to one of uncompromising resolve. It was a look she would come to know well.

Polly's mother had warned her against marrying Leo. At the time, Polly attributed her mother's doubts to the prejudices of an old-school patrician from Philadelphia, prejudices that encompassed Italians, especially southern Italians, and Roman Catholics generally. But Polly was coming to realize that she, like so many daughters, had underestimated her mother. The woman's infallible social x-ray powers also extended to matters of character. Polly argued that Leo was a brilliant but vulnerable misfit who understood her own insecurities and needed her protection and support. She told her mother that every other man she met was threatened by her brain and alienated by her love of mathematics. With Leo, she explained, math was a shared passion that would provide a solid foundation to the relationship. But her mother had detected the seeds of an all-consuming ego lurking just below Leo's benign surface. Polly now realized that it was this ego that, with time and success, had come to harden the man who had seemed so hurt and vulnerable the night they first met.

When Clip left the library, Polly asked, "What's Arcadia?"

"I've been buying land in eastern Oregon. I call it Arcadia."

"Why?"

"Research."

"What kind of research? What are you up to, Leo? Why the secrecy?"

"Completely normal."

"You running the project personally through Clip? That's hardly normal. Leo, I've warned you before. Be careful. Those lab rats don't understand boundaries. It doesn't matter how shocking or immoral or disgusting, they will do it if they can. They will do it if for no reason other than because it's cool. And when the government and the rest of the world finds out, it's you they'll come down on. You know I'm right."

"Polly, it's wild land in eastern Oregon. It's ecology. We're doing research on plants. No designer babies, I promise. And I'm building a place for us in the same compound where the scientists are living and working. It'll be great to have a place to get away. You'll love it."

Leo's eyes drifted down to his wife's sensible wool skirt, which didn't quite succeed in disguising the pronounced curve of her broad hips. A pelvis adapted for childbirth.

"What's bugging you, Pol? Is this about children again?" Leo asked.

Polly's face and ears flushed.

"Sure, Leo. Must be. I've got the Fields Medal in a frame behind my desk, but whenever I'm a bit wound up, you think it must be all about my ovaries. Just another woman with her knickers all in a twist because her man doesn't want kids."

"But you still do, right?"

"I'm having children, Leo, with or without you."

Leo watched her slam the door on the way out. The door slam was a cliché. He disliked clichés. He glanced at his watch and found to his satisfaction that the short fight had not elevated his pulse, respiration, or cortisol. *Got to avoid those cortisol spikes*, he thought. It was one of his rules.

3
Garage Bio

Our future is a race between the growing power of technology and the wisdom with which we use it.

Steven Hawking, *Brief Answers to the Big Questions*

A WEEK LATER, CLIP SAT with Leo in the back of the white Land Rover that Leo preferred over black Suburbans, which, in Leo's opinion, virtually advertised that a VIP was perched within. Another vehicle with Leo's security detail followed at a discreet distance. The little convoy headed to an address in a dreary part of suburban Seattle, close by the airport.

"Tell me, Clippy," Leo asked, "what's the single thing that all people want?"

"Uh, more sex?"

"Close, but no. Not to die. Self-preservation is our strongest instinct."

"Uh huh."

"And here's the thing," Leo continued. "Aging's not inevitable. Other mammals live to two hundred. If people's number-one objective is to live, then why isn't longevity research the most popular cause on the planet?"

"Two hundred years?" Clip asked. "What mammal?"

"Bowhead whale. Mostly the same as our own DNA, but a few special maintenance and repair genes that we lack."

"Cool. But you know, man, I think most people either have accepted that they're gonna die, or they're in denial and they just ignore it, you know?"

"Exactly. When I started, lots of people said syn-bio was science fiction. But the real fiction is the absurd idea that aging is inevitable—that something about our biological architecture permits a century or so, but no more. That's bullshit. If the bowhead whale gets two hundred years, so can we—much more, in fact. It's just a matter of genetics. Why don't other people get this?"

"Yup, man. I know what you mean. Lots of idiots out there." Clip hadn't often seen Leo this emotional and thought about the first time he'd seen the clocks—small digital screens on the walls of the Portland house. Each displayed a three-digit number. Clip observed that over time the number turned both higher and lower. Eventually, he had asked Leo what it was. "My months to live," Leo had responded. "Computed in real time by an actuarial program, based on . . . lab work."

A few minutes later, the convoy turned off the state road into a sprawling subdivision. The scene reminded Clip of home. Everything about the place, he thought, was a kind of lie. Vinyl façades masqueraded as wood and brick. The landscaping was supposed to be "natural," but instead the kelly-green carpets that surrounded each house were the wholly synthetic product of a monthly drench of chemical herbicide and fertilizer. They called them "communities," but not a single child rode a bike or played in a front yard.

Starting at age twelve, Clip had gradually withdrawn from the life his parents had built in a similar suburb, retreating to a garage full of screens, servers, and centrifuges.

"Isn't it ironic, Clippy? I could hire any scientist in the world, any Nobel prizewinner, anyone. And yet here I am again, about to yank another kid out of his parents' basement or garage. And why? Because big bio is so fucked up."

"But aren't we big bio now? And don't get me wrong, when you found me, I was a hacker. You know, with an attitude. But this dude, boss, is supposed to be really bad news."

Leo ignored him. "Science was supposed to be all about the future, you know, feeding the hungry, curing cancer, not to mention all the cool stuff like space travel and flying cars. And what did we get? We got little boxes that are turning people into zombies. What the hell happened?"

"Leo," Clip interjected, "you know best. But what exactly do you want with him? I mean, what can he do for you that I can't? He worries me. People said he was doing some bad shit, maybe even working with pathogens. When one hacker pissed him off, he bullied the dude's little brother online and the kid committed suicide. Seriously, even hackers have a kind of code, Leo. And he was over the line."

"I can control him. He's a genius who takes risks, right?"

"Yeah."

"Well, that's why I need him."

The driver interrupted. "We're here, Leo. 3604 Lancaster Court."

* * *

The front door of the house opened before Leo had the chance to knock. "Mr. and Mrs. Grier?" Leo turned on his brightest smile, despite taking a dislike to the couple at first glance.

"You must be Mr. Bonelli . . ."

"Leo, please."

"Leo, then. Welcome to our humble abode. Do please come in."

The couple, both just shy of fifty but looking older, were not dressed for a casual Saturday at home. She wore what Leo surmised was her best dress.

"Is this your son?" the wife asked.

"No, ma'am. This is Clip, my personal assistant."

"Oh," said the man. "Well . . . welcome. It's a real honor . . . Leo. I mean, we both admire greatly your . . . you know, what you . . . do."

"My husband," the woman added, "means SBD. What a wonderful thing. With all you do for humanity, really, you're a saint. I mean, the people you've helped. And you know how tough it is for people like us. All the bills. The mortgage. College loans. We work so hard. Both of us. It's a godsend that you're here."

"Truly," the man added, "you've been sent by God."

"Thank you. But my business, actually, is with your son. We had an appointment. Is he here?" Leo's tone had turned cool.

"Yes, of course," Mrs. Grier replied. "But, how can I put this . . . our darling Oliver depends on us wholly. He confides in us and consults with us about absolutely everything. Wouldn't make a move without us. So . . . well, you know, if there's something you want or need, then my husband and I are the ones . . ."

"Leo, please tell me straight," Mr. Grier said, "is Ollie in some kind of trouble? We have no idea what he's doing down there—I mean we know it's biology, something about genes. About six months ago the FBI came. The agents wouldn't say anything to us but spent a long time downstairs with Ollie. Do you think he's in trouble?"

"Sorry," Leo answered. "I don't know anything about that. But it might be nothing. The FBI has a group that keeps its eye on biohackers, and given your son's reputation, well . . . It's probably nothing to worry about. Now, if I may . . ." Leo moved toward the basement stairs.

Dirty fluorescent fixtures hanging from exposed rafters washed the basement with a mustard-yellow light. Ants marched in an orderly line between a mound of discarded Chinese food containers and a crack in the concrete floor. Leo thought of the obsessively clean biolabs at SBD, entered through air locks and lit by meticulously calibrated bright white LEDs. And yet on the dozen or so folding tables along the basement walls, he was surprised to see the same equipment he would have found in any university molecular biology lab: a pure water distiller, a microcentrifuge, a UV transilluminator, a PCR thermocycler with an adjoining gel tank, another older-looking DNA amplifier, a bank of clear chillers and freezers, and a floor-to-ceiling rack filled with dozens of bottles containing solutions and chemicals. At the opposite end of the room, a stack of slightly rusted small cages, similar to the ones in which a child might keep a pet gerbil, housed scores of mice.

"Dude," said a young man wearing vintage Adidas sweat pants and a T-shirt, looking at Clip and completely ignoring Leo.

Clip nodded. "Never thought I'd see you off-line."

When the young man failed to respond, Clip spoke again. "So, man, I want you to meet Leo."

"Nice to meet you," Leo said, starting to extend his hand and then thinking the better of it. "Playg, right? Or would you rather I call you Oliver?"

"There's no Oliver no more. Name's Playg."

"Got it," said Leo. "Playg, you've got an awesome setup down here. Where'd you get all the gear?"

"The ODIN, at first."

Leo knew the scientist who founded the Open Discovery Institute, or the ODIN, to sell sophisticated kits for home bio. Formerly with NASA's Ames Research Lab, he had been called the "mad pirate king of biotech." His speech titled "How to Genetically Engineer a Human in Your Garage" attracted crowds at biohacker conventions around the country. Shortly after the discovery of CRISPR-Cas9, the revolutionary gene-editing tool, the ODIN started to sell the technology to thousands of enthusiasts.

"You have CRISPR?" Leo asked.

"Sure. eBay. Hundred and thirty bucks. Fucking insane, right?"

A reporter once asked Leo whether he was worried that any hacker with a hundred bucks could wield a tool that, like the find-and-replace function on a word processor, could be directed to find any specific sequence of DNA, neatly excise that sequence with a small pair of molecular scissors, and replace it with something else. A mouse embryo genetically coded to have a long tail—snip and patch, and now we have a mouse coded for a short tail. Leo had laughed and told the reporter that the kids in garages were just playing around with things like yeast, doing vegan cheese, and making lime-flavored beer. Not a problem. But even then he knew it wasn't true.

Playg saw the visitors examining some of the more sophisticated equipment. "Big labs," he said, "got the dough, and gotta have the newest thing. I get their castoffs real cheap. Reagents, enzymes, and antibodies—now that shit's expensive. But," he added with an ugly smirk, "I have my sources."

Clip looked uncomfortable.

"Can we see some of your work?" Leo asked.

"Whatever."

Playg first pointed to a microscope through which Leo and Clip saw a culture of benign bacteria that glowed with the bright colors of tropical fish, from which they now carried the genes for bioluminescence. He showed them a small vial of mustard seeds, sparkling as the result of the firefly gene inserted by Playg. Before Playg could move on, Clip stopped him.

"Shit, dude. Who do you think we are, the fucking PTA? That might work for throwing the morons from the FBI off the scent, but not us. Get real. I know what you can do. And if you can do it, you've done it. Show us the good stuff. That's why we're here."

Playg hiked up his sweat pants awkwardly and lifted his chin in the direction of Leo.

Clip said, "He may look like a gerk, but he's totally chill. He gets it. He's not like big bio. Leo says fuck the rules, they don't apply to people like us. Don't worry about Leo. Seriously."

"Sixty-two genes." Playg seemed torn between the urge to brag and his long-standing reluctance to discuss these things anywhere other than the darkest corners of the dark web. "I edited sixty-two genes in a pig embryo, deleting the ones that would be rejected by the human immune system, and editing the rest to look like DNA that people's white blood cells would read as human. I sent the edited embryos back to Singapore. Guy there told me the liver from one of my pigs was transplanted to a human and not rejected. It fucking worked."

Leo knew something similar had been tried at Harvard, but that the organs of the genetically modified pigs had not yet been approved for transplant into humans. No such niceties in Singapore. Good for Playg. This showed, as Leo had expected, that Playg's editing moxie was right up there with the top handful of scientists at Harvard and Stanford, perhaps better than anyone already on his payroll at SBD. And from this basement shithole. Impressive.

"I'm interested in longevity," Leo said. "Aging creates metabolic damage that I believe we can repair before it causes pathology. We can either rejuvenate senescent cells or knock 'em out. You agree?"

"Totally."

"You doing anything with hTERT?" Leo asked.

"Fucking right, I am. And forget drugs. Direct edit. Right into chromosome 19, an active copy of the hTERT gene." Playg looked very pleased with himself.

Leo had long been fascinated by the telomere, a cap at the end of every DNA strand that, like the piece of plastic at the end of a shoelace, keeps it from unraveling. Leo argued in his undergraduate thesis that, because the telomere is shortened with every division, it eventually loses its ability to protect the chromosome and allows the cell to malfunction and the body to age. SBD had bet heavily that hTERT gene therapy to restore the length of the telomere would prove one of the key strategies for life extension.

"And you used your own genetic material?" Leo asked.

"Yeah, an iPSC. Needed a fucking huge virus dose to saturate. That was a crapshoot, kinda scary. And six months later—my telomeres lengthened by .32 kb. That's about ten years of aging. So now I got the white blood cells of a seventeen-year-old. No side effects."

"I wouldn't have had the balls," said Clip, who knew that Playg was out there, but had no idea he'd gone this far.

"And that's not all. I'm gonna win the M Prize and show all the big shots how totally lame they are." This surprised Leo. He wouldn't have thought someone like Playg would be interested in something as conventional as the M Prize, which was for life-extension therapies that are proven in mice and potentially adaptable for humans.

"I'm using a double whammy. I genetically programmed a kill switch to get rid of senescent cells, then combined that with my hTERT therapy adapted for mice. Don't have the final results, but I can already tell the combined effect is exponential, almost 100 percent. That's doubled lifespan. Fucking big bio hasn't even come close."

Leo had heard enough.

"Playg. I want you to come work for me. You deserve better than this," he said, looking around the room.

"No, man. No way. This is how I work. I mean, I'm sure you got some sweet toys, but I don't do big bio. Can't stand rules. And I don't give a fuck about play money, in case you're thinking you can buy me."

"What do you care about, Playg? Have any other interests?"

"What, like other than bio?"

"Yeah. Anything. TV? Music? Gaming?"

"Nah. Never watched TV. Don't like music. It's all false. Only puppets fall for that crap."

"What about your parents?" Leo asked. "The money you'd make would change their lives. They seem to have a hard life."

"Yeah, as I'm sure they told you. They are total fucking stress puppies. Don't believe anything they say."

"Playg. Let me paint you a picture. I'm tracking every supercentenarian in the world. I've sequenced the genome of every one. I know everything about them—what they eat, how they fucked—whether they slept with the window open or closed. I mean everything. We're crunching the numbers now, figuring out what they have in common genetically, and what environmental factors may have led to epigenetic effects. I have teams working on every type of age-related damage that might cause pathology. If there's a better maintenance and repair gene anywhere in nature, I'll find it." He paused. Playg looked distracted. "And I've got a guy who figured out which gene allows salamanders to regenerate lost limbs. We're making synthetic copies of that gene and then editing it into human iPSCs."

That seemed to impress Playg. "Cool," he said.

"Eventually," Leo went on, "you'll be able to send us almost any cell from your body and we'll send back a replacement organ made to order. If an embryo tests positive for OI or any other heredity disease caused by mutation, we'll be able to edit out the mutation without any off-target effect."

Playg interrupted. "That's bold, man. I mean, human embryonic editing, they crucify you for that."

"You think that's bold? How about real syn-bio? You know Venter's wholly synthetic bacteria, which got him ridiculous publicity for creating self-replicating life from scratch for the first time? What was that, a million base pairs, just over a thousand cassettes of DNA each about a thousand base pairs long?"

"Yeah, I know," Playg said, "pretty lame."

"Well," Leo continued, "my guys are doing completely synthetic genomes now with a hundred million base pairs, and that's algae, not just a bacterium. I'm sequencing the genome of every extinct plant that's left a trace of usable DNA. You won't believe what we're doing with the restored DNA. And we're working bio apps of nanotech and AI. You've got to raise your sights. Who cares about the Methuselah Prize? Mice? Really? That's what you want to do with your genius?"

Leo saw that he had opened a crack in the young man's resolve. He thought about himself at that age.

"I get that you want to be respected for what you do. You need people to recognize how special you are. You want a place in history? Imagine if we give people another century of high-quality life. Imagine if we hack evolution and save the planet. You think anything ever will be bigger? And I'm offering you the chance to be part of it. I don't think you're a moron, but if you say no, that's exactly what history will call you. Playg, the biggest fucking moron of the twenty-first century."

"And," added Clip, "you'll get a cryo contract. In Leo's own cryo facility. So if you, like, have a car crash before we hack mortality, then you're guaranteed a really good freeze. No cryo tank colder. Man, think about that. It's your bridge to the post-singularity world. We're young enough, Playg, no need for us to miss it."

"Yeah. I know. I keep having this dream. I watch as big hardware maps every possible expression of a single gene. Then it models each expression against every possible environmental condition that could have an epigenetic effect. All in a few hours. It's awesome. I can't fucking wait until the machines are in charge."

"So, what about it?" Leo asked.

"Whatever, man. I could see leaving this pit. But no gerks, you know, big bio gerks. Can't deal with 'em. And no rules. And . . . I want my own whole genome next-next-gen sequencer. Just for me. Like, I get all the time, 100 percent of the time, no sharing."

"You got it, Playg. How 'bout next Monday? We'll send a truck for your stuff. Anything else you need?"

"The parents. You've got to get them off my back."

On the way out of the Griers' house, Leo dropped his previous pretense of politeness.

"Your son works for me now," Leo said. "I'll pay off your mortgage, your son's student loans, and any other debt you have. I'll pay you $500,000 in cash. If you try to stop him, if you try to negotiate for more, or if Oliver ever complains that you're bothering him, I'll destroy you both."

Leo walked out without giving them the chance to reply.

"Harsh, dude," said Clip as the white Land Rover pulled away.

4
Arcadia

After the Holy One created the first human being, Adam, He said: "It is not good for Adam to be alone." He created a woman, also from the earth, and called her Lilith.

They quarreled immediately. She said: "I will not lie below you." He said: "I will not lie below you, but above you. For you are fit to be below me and I above you."

She responded: "We are both equal because we both come from the earth."

Alphabet of ben Sira 23A-B (EIGHTH TO TENTH CENTURIES CE)

LILITH SQUEALED WITH DELIGHT as Muir plucked her from the floor, lofted her to his shoulders, and marched around his in-laws' living room, singing "Old McDonald Had a Farm." The toddler joined in at every moo, oink, quack, and baa. Being back with his daughter drove away all thoughts of extinct ferns and the mysterious Arcadia. He stayed for dinner with Meredith's parents but did not share with them any of the details of his eventful day in the Big Empty.

For the first year following his wife's death, Muir kept grief at bay through strict adherence to a routine. Each morning he fed Lilith breakfast and then dropped her off at his in-laws' on the way to work. He spent each weekday and every other Saturday at the wholesale plant nursery where he was director of horticulture. The firm's profits depended on his skill in coaxing rapid growth from perennials and shrubs, and his success in battling the spot, blight, mildew, wilt, and rust that could spread rapidly through an intensive monoculture and destroy a valuable crop within days. Muir took his job seriously and was good at it. His bosses and coworkers respected him, but few considered him a friend. The joke at the nursery was that Muir seemed to prefer the company of plants.

At five thirty each afternoon, he picked up Lilith from her grandparents' house and drove her to one of Boise's many small parks and playgrounds. Muir got strange looks from the other parents as he rehearsed for the tiny girl the names of the plants. "Oak," he said, pointing at the tree. "Birch." "Fern." "Daylily, or *hemerocallis.*" Lilith gurgled with happiness at this ritual and a week before had delighted her father by responding to his "oak" with "twee," her first word other than the usual "Dada" and "bye-bye."

Back home in the small craftsman bungalow that Meredith had loved at first sight, Lilith explored everything, crawling off at high speed. When Muir turned his back for a moment, the little girl disappeared, rummaging in a closet or decorating herself with kitchen pots that she seemed to think were hats. When she finally fell asleep, Muir had time to read, think, and mourn.

A week after returning home from his ill-fated hunting trip, Muir received a letter from Arcadia LLC informing him that the firm would not press charges for trespassing, but that if he were apprehended again on their land, they would prosecute. A few days later, an investigator hired by Arcadia called Muir and asked him to explain why he had been found so far inside the marked boundaries of private property. Muir, glad to have the chance to tell the whole story, this time mentioned his discovery of the extinct fern. The investigator, who refused to answer Muir's questions about Arcadia, quizzed Muir about his credentials as a botanist and asked whether he had shared with others news of his find.

Muir was astonished when the next call came from Leo himself, who asked if Muir could come and meet with him in Portland to discuss the fern. Muir said no, not because he disliked rich people in general, but because he reacted badly to anyone who projected a sense of entitlement. Muir always bridled when he felt he was being summoned. Eventually, though, his curiosity proved stronger than his pride. And now, Muir found himself boarding a helicopter with the richest person in the world.

"Like it?" Leo asked.

"What?"

"My helicopter."

Muir couldn't imagine what he was expected to say. He hadn't flown in many helicopters before and had little basis for comparison. And the truth was that Muir felt uneasy. He believed helicopters to be the most unnatural possible form of flight. Planes like birds stretched their wings and were supported by the air, but choppers thrashed and fought against gravity every second they were aloft. He didn't trust them.

"It's nice," Muir answered.

For the first fifty minutes of the flight, Leo stared out the window in silence.

"That ridge, you see it?" Leo jabbed a finger at the window as they approached a prominent ridgeline extending out of view to the north.

Muir nodded.

"That's it. The western boundary of Arcadia. In about ten minutes we'll be there."

Muir looked down at the conifer-green folds of the Cascade foothills, slowly eroding into the scrubbed flats and hollows of the Big Empty.

"Never seen it from the air," Muir replied.

"What you're seeing is the largest private land holding ever assembled in North America. I expect to reach six and a half million acres—that's ten thousand square miles."

Muir stared silently out the window.

"The famous King Ranch," Leo continued, "was less than a million acres, so mine is more than six King Ranches. And I'm buying more."

Muir turned away from the window and looked at Leo as if seeing him for the first time.

"Why?"

Although Muir asked the question Leo expected, Leo now hesitated to give the answer he had planned. Leo realized that he knew both everything (from the thick dossier back on his desk) and nothing about Muir O'Brien. At first, Leo's only interest in Muir had been to contain the possible damage from his discovery of the extinct fern. But after reading the dossier, Leo's instincts told him that the man also might prove useful. And now that he had met him in person, Leo knew his instincts had been correct. This taciturn man seemed to be grounded in a way that most of those around Leo were not. Leo tended to think of excessive integrity as a weakness, but in this case, he realized that Muir's character could prove a useful foil to the yes-men who surrounded him. So Leo resolved to tell Muir about Arcadia, or at least the few things about Arcadia that he was ready for Muir to know. Plants, Leo decided. No animals, and certainly not Neanderthals.

"Arcadia is a type of garden," Leo answered. "A very large and diverse garden. An experiment in biodiversity, if you will."

"It's not for hunting?" asked Muir, clearly surprised.

"I hunt there, but no, that's not what it's about. It's basically a wilderness restoration project. I'm going to show that we can restore a sort of high-functioning biodiversity not seen on this continent for over ten thousand years."

"So the fern . . ."

"We're taking all sorts of plants that, one way or another, were made rare or extinct when man appeared on the scene and reestablishing sustainable populations."

"I was right? It was a species of *Cladophlebis*?"

"Right. Superficially, it looks like dozens of non-extinct ferns. My people told me you've got 'the eye' for plants."

The chopper swooped low down the far side of a long ridge, revealing for the first time an enormous lake. The helicopter looped over the lake to give its passengers views in all directions.

"Lake Arcadia," said Leo. "I made it."

Muir spotted the great hyphen of a concrete dam spanning two low hills at the east end of the lake. From the drowned trees spiking above the water near the lake's perimeter, he could tell the lake was newly filled. The three large canals that drained the lake stretched to the eastern horizon, trisecting the scrubland of the Big Empty.

Muir leaned into the window, trying to make out what appeared from the air to be hundreds of oddly tiny patches of meadow dotting the shallow slope leading down to the western edge of the lake. Only when the aircraft descended farther did Muir recognize that these verdant dots were the thickly planted green roofs of low-slung structures that varied in size. Each building nestled back into the slope, with the roof at grade to the rear and a tall curved wall of glass rising above the ground on the downhill lake-facing façade. The whole complex was the size of a small town, but instead of conventional streets, rough tracks ran through drifts of intact forest and wild-looking scrub.

"The Village," said Leo. "Labs. Greenhouses. The people working on the project live here with their families. Everything they need is in the Village. There's no road, so everything comes in and out by air." Nodding toward an extensive construction project just below them, Leo added, "And my wife and I are building a house here."

The helicopter settled gently on one of five helipads arranged in a circle at the center of a broad open field.

* * *

An hour later Lake Arcadia and the Village finally disappeared below the ridge behind them as a small ATV, with Leo at the wheel, climbed a rough trail leading toward the timbered plateau where Muir's wounded buck had stopped to rest in a stand of ferns. When the track finally leveled out and the vehicle passed into the forest, Muir, largely ignoring his host, scanned the passing vegetation.

"There," Muir said, pointing. "You see? Just inside the edge of that clearing. The rocky soil we thought they liked, and just enough shade."

Leo pulled the ATV alongside a sickle-shaped stand of ferns. He watched as Muir knelt and then picked and closely examined a frond. Muir ran his hand through the plants, caressing their lacy tops, some of which had started to turn a reddish brown and others of which remained stubbornly green in contrast to the autumnal hues all around them.

"Where did you find them?" Muir said. "I mean, we thought they were lost long before humans came to North America. And most *Cladophlebis* species were tropical, but these clearly are hardy. It seems impossible . . ."

Leo stood over the kneeling Muir. "I didn't find them," Leo said. "I made them."

"Made them?"

"It's called de-extinction. Not really so complicated, but you need some sort of tissue sample to sequence the genome of the extinct plant."

"I'm confused. If you had a tissue sample, then it wasn't extinct."

"No, it was extinct, all right. But DNA lasts a long time when frozen, or in dry bones. In this case, my guys found some fern spores on the foot of a woolly mammoth frozen in the permafrost, which was enough to sequence the entire genome. That gave us the recipe for how to make a *Cladophlebis*."

"But there's a big difference between knowing the genome of something and being able to recreate it," Muir said.

"Right," Leo answered. "That's where genetic editing comes in. You've heard about CRISPR, I suppose? After we figured out the recipe for the extinct fern, we were able to determine what non-extinct fern is its closest relative. We then took a spore of the living fern, extracted its DNA, and then edited that DNA to be close to the DNA of the extinct fern. In this case there were only about three hundred base pairs that we had to change. The rest was easy. We inserted the edited DNA back into the nucleus of the spore, and up came the extinct plant."

"They're so beautiful," Muir said, still fondling a frond. "Think," he murmured, "of the possibilities."

"Exactly," said Leo, smiling broadly.

Back in the ATV, Leo headed north. Descending toward a rocky lowland, they crossed a temporary bridge over what looked to Muir like a newly dug canal, at least ten yards wide and not yet filled with water.

"Water," said Leo, waving his hand at the big ditch, "is key. Today it's mainly high desert. But during the Pleistocene, there was lots of water."

"But how?" Muir asked. "Where does the water come from? It's dry for hundreds of miles all around."

"Not completely. It's the Great Basin; it drains in on itself. The water's still here, underground, in the rock."

"Stop," said Muir. "Back there. Back up. I want to take a look." Muir jumped from the vehicle and trotted through a gap in the trees.

He knelt on the forest floor and touched the leaves of a seedling tree. Leo joined him.

"Amazing. Look at the leaf. It's got to be a *Ginkgo huttonii*, another plant we didn't think made it into the Holocene."

"You're right." Leo had been told that this one would be hard for even an expert to spot. "Tell me," he asked. "How'd you know?"

"See the leaf, just like our *Ginkgo biloba*, but straighter, somehow boxier. We know it from fossils found someplace in the north of England, I think. But I couldn't see the leaf from a distance. It was something about the attitude of the plant."

"Attitude?"

"Yeah, it's not really a professional term, but that's what I call it. How a plant holds itself, its overall presentation. You know how you can recognize someone from behind by their posture and how they walk? Kind of like that."

Leo recalled a comment from one of the letters recommending Muir for the doctoral program in botany, a hacked copy of which was in the dossier on Leo's desk. "An uncanny knack for plants," the professor had written. "He can tell how closely species are related long before the DNA results come back." Reading that was the moment Leo decided he wanted to meet the hunter who had stumbled into Arcadia.

"You know, Leo, I love plants. To see species that we thought were gone forever is such a privilege. To touch them, it's a joy. But . . ." Muir hesitated.

"Go on," Leo said. "I want you to understand what I'm doing. Ask anything."

Leo sat on the ground next to Muir on a patch of dried grass just uphill from the *Ginkgo* seedling.

"No plant or creature exists in isolation," Muir said. "Each evolved in partnership and conflict with others. Each one is uniquely adapted for a specific ecology."

"Of course."

"So your plants, these so-called 'de-extincted' plants, have been plucked from the distant past without their entourage—all the fungi, bacteria, other plants, and animals that made up their world. Maybe they'll survive, Leo, but I doubt they'll ever really prosper."

"Think of it this way," Leo said. "Fourteen thousand years ago the first humans crossed from Siberia into Alaska. They were brave enough to come south through a narrow ice-free corridor between two giant ice sheets. Can you imagine the courage that required? And when they passed the edge of the glacier into the ice-free parts of the American West, not too far from here, what did they see, Muir? Can you picture it?"

Muir silently scanned the vast flatlands to the north.

Leo continued. "Those people found an ecosystem that had evolved largely apart from the rest of the planet—a kind of evolutionary experiment, an alternative world. It would have been incredible, filled with mastodons, mammoths, saber-toothed cats. Vast herds of horses and camels. Scores of species of trees and plants uniquely adapted to that time and place. An enormous lake fed by glacial melt."

"Sure," Muir said. "That's my point. All of that is completely foreign to what we see here today. The poor fern may be alive again, but now it's a stranger in strange land."

"Maybe, but ask yourself why it died in the first place. Why did that original ecosystem disappear? There was no meteor, no new ice age, no volcanic eruption."

Muir frowned.

"*Homo sapiens* arrives on the scene and within two thousand years most of these species are gone. Thirty-four of forty-seven genera of large mammals, gone. The cats, sloths, lions, camels—all which flourished here for millions of years—gone in an evolutionary instant. That's why your fern is a stranger in a strange land, Muir. Not because of evolution, because of man."

"I get that, but so what? It doesn't change the fact that the fern is still a lonely traveler from a distant time," Muir said.

"It matters because we humans have some responsibility to fix what we screwed up. If we have the technology to restore some of the species we hunted to extinction, to restore the ecosystem that we destroyed, don't you think maybe we have an obligation to right those wrongs?"

Muir looked closely at Leo. Leo didn't strike him as the sort of guy who would put too much stock in moral obligations. Maybe he had misread him.

"So Arcadia," Leo continued, "is not just about bringing back a fern or animal here and there. It's the whole thing. Within the boundaries of Arcadia, I'm hitting the reset button on the human occupation of North America. Maybe this time we can get it right."

The two men climbed aboard the ATV, with Muir accepting Leo's invitation to drive them back to the Village. As the track crested a small hill, they again could see Lake Arcadia, which looked at that moment like a piece of the sky that had tumbled into the reddish embrace of the hills.

"Seems to me," Muir said, "like the impossible idea of a return to Eden."

"I remind you that in many traditions Eden is a walled garden, with a geometric layout and constructed canals. An engineering problem, really."

As the ATV bounced along the rough track, Leo regretted allowing Muir to drive. Leo did not like being a passenger.

"This isn't just about ecology, Muir. It's about humanity. It's not like the human genome is some kind of code that executes its instructions in a vacuum. Which genes are expressed, and even how they're expressed, depends totally on environment and experience. There's no control of human destiny without control of the environment."

Muir turned his head sharply to look at Leo, but didn't interrupt him.

"Cicero," Leo continued, "said a garden is 'second nature.' It's our chance at a do-over, having totally fucked up first nature."

"Seriously? You're saying nature is just some kind of complex equation that, with good enough computers, humans can solve?"

Leo turned his head. "Why not? However uncomfortable people find it, for the first time in human history we've got the technology to take control of evolution. Some call it 'directed evolution' or 'prescriptive evolution.' And I have the money to do it."

Muir stopped the vehicle in a small clearing, with young cottonwoods sprouting from a new wetland along one side.

"That's nuts." Muir was adamant. "I don't know much, Leo, but I know that ten thousand years of human history taught us that control of nature is always an illusion. *Always.*"

"Historically, perhaps. But transformative technologies allow us to transcend what we previously thought were limits."

Muir considered this with skepticism. But he supposed it was possible that someday a technology could come along that would turn upside down everything humans thought they knew about nature and their place in it.

Before he could respond, Leo said, "You smell it?"

"Elk," said Muir. "Recent."

"Grab a gun."

The two men set off on foot downwind of the elk. Muir pointed silently with his head to a gap in an old shrub oak, its broken twigs fringed with tufts of coarse hair. Neither man was used to hunting with another, but by unspoken agreement they assumed the natural rhythm of humans hunting in pairs. After twenty minutes, they knew they were close. While Muir continued to advance from directly downwind of the animal, Leo broke right, to the downhill side, flanking the prey. Sure enough, the elk, a bull wearing the light tan coat typical of autumn, bolted right, taking the easier downhill course, straight into Leo's line of fire. But Leo, caught off guard by the suddenness of the bolt and facing only the narrow profile of the animal approaching head on, missed his shot. The elk leapt with ease across what looked like an incipient slot canyon and bounded down a rocky slope into deep cover where both men knew they could not follow.

Leo and Muir did not talk as they headed back toward the ATV. Muir stopped and pointed toward a flattened patch of undergrowth. "Could have been his bed. Let's take a break."

The two men sat on the ground next to the elk bed, tucked in between a fallen tree and a dense thicket at the edge of a clearing. The location provided its occupant both cover and a quick escape. They drank from Leo's water bottle.

While Muir stared at the deep and lushly padded hollow, Leo noticed that Muir's sturdy torso appeared to deflate slightly.

"Reminds me," Muir said.

Leo stayed silent.

"I suppose you know that I lost my wife."

"I know," Leo said. "Never gets any easier, does it? My sister Mia died when we were kids."

"I'm sorry," Muir said. After a few moments, he chuckled to himself and added, "You know, Meredith never liked hunting, but one time she agreed to come along. I think she was relieved when we had a bad day and decided to make camp without having taken a shot."

Muir's smile faded and he gazed silently into the far depths of the surrounding woods. "That same day," he continued, "it was late afternoon when we came to a large elk bed, just like this one."

Leo nodded.

"She asked if I wanted to try it. She never looked more beautiful. The bed fit our bodies as if it had been made for us. I . . . I don't know why I'm telling you this. Sorry."

"No. Go on."

Muir looked down at the layers of vegetation lining the hollow.

"It was a cool day, but the grasses and pine needles felt warm, and that warmth spread through our bodies. It was the strangest thing, but we both felt it; kind of like a lava flow that burns everything in its path while at the same time creating new ground. We felt we were making love to the earth, as well as to each other. When we stopped, it was dark and the moon was high in the sky."

Leo appeared pensive.

"Later, we found out it was the time we conceived our daughter, Lilith. Nine months later, Meredith was gone."

5
Gamete Fusion

LEO OPENED HIS EYES without moving the rest of his body. The slowly sharpening focus seized his attention from the rapidly fading loop of an early-morning dream. He gazed upon his outstretched left arm, wrist and palm up, perfectly still against the subtle white stripe of the sheet. He admired the sight of his translucent skin stretched tightly over the long wave of smooth muscle and sturdy cross-hatching of tendons. The skin also revealed, just below the surface, a roadmap of veins, fractal and faintly purple.

Leo rolled to his right and observed his sleeping wife. He did not know her body as intimately as he knew his own. He studied the line of her breasts, visible under the sheet. Polly never had been conventionally beautiful. After Leo became famous, journalists wrote about Polly's plain appearance and lack of fashion sense, as if these were somehow more relevant than the fact that she was the first female to hold the Cambridge professorship previously held by Isaac Newton and Stephen Hawking. Thinking about the evening before, Leo felt a faint awakening of lust, but this faded quickly.

When he returned to the bedroom with the breakfast tray that the maid had left in the hallway outside, Polly was awake. The sleepover had gone off without a fight and his wife still seemed mellow.

"Morning, Pol. Sleep well?"

"Very."

Leo set the tray on the bed next to his wife, who was now seated upright, supported by an oversize pillow. She poured coffee for both of them, staring closely at her husband.

"You look younger," Polly said. "Last night I thought it was just the lighting. But even now, in the morning light, I could swear you look younger."

"That's nice," Leo said, turning his back. "It must be my new workout."

Polly pulled the breakfast tray closer and poured herself more coffee.

"Why do you never tell me the whole truth anymore?" she asked.

"What do you mean?"

"We both know that's not it. What the hell have you been doing, Leo?"

"No big deal. There are some SBD therapies that haven't yet gone to clinical trial. I decided to try some of them."

Polly knew him too well to be shocked. "What therapies?"

"You really want to know?"

Polly nodded.

"There are three. hTERT, of course. I used a saturating viral dose to deliver an extra gene to manufacture hTERT. Telomerase production increased exactly as predicted, and I achieved about two decades reversal of telomere shortening on my leukocytes. My white blood cells are twenty years younger than yours. No side effects."

Leo paused, expecting Polly to be impressed with this news. Instead, she stared at her coffee, scowling.

"Second," Leo continued, "are senolytics. I've been on three non-approved drugs for two years, both intended to clean out nondividing cells. The results are dramatic. My load of senescent cells has decreased by 20 percent, and this in turn seems to have slowed down degenerative aging in the surrounding tissues."

"You said three."

"Yes, well. Parabiosis." He held up his hand. "Before you disapprove, let me emphasize that there is absolutely no adverse effect on the young people involved."

"Leo, I don't even know what that is." Leo, who was standing next to the bed, shifted his stance and started to pace.

"Sharing of the blood. Remember those studies where a young mouse shares its blood with an older mouse—their circulatory systems are stitched together so the younger blood circulates through the older mouse. We don't know whether it's just repair or genuine de-aging, but the older mouse gets younger in almost every possible way: rebuilding muscle and organ cells, enhanced growth of brain cells, everything. Some other companies are doing young plasma transfusions. But my guys think that you need actual parabiosis—sharing—for the best results. Once a month I make a stop in Mexico. It's just like dialysis, except the blood that comes back is from seventeen-year-olds. The metabolic effects are immediate and dramatic. Didn't you notice the clock? My months to live have been trending up."

"Oh, Leo. That's truly ghastly. My God. Those poor children. What if the press finds out?"

"They're not children. And, as I said, there's no effect on them whatsoever. I get a few hours of young blood bathing every cell in my body, and then the blood goes back to them. A week after the session, their own blood chemistry is back to normal."

It took a moment for Polly to sort through her thoughts. She knew there was a long history of self-experimentation in science and was hardly shocked that Leo could not resist trying some of SBD's experimental longevity treatments. But the thought of Mexican teenagers sharing their blood made her skin crawl.

"Leo, since we're together, I thought perhaps I should tell you that I've decided that now is the time to have a child."

"*You've* decided?"

"Yes, I've decided. With sperm that's not yours, unless of course you change your mind and want to be the father. You know I would welcome that. But if you don't, then I'm going ahead anyway, before it's too late. It's what I want, and it's too important to me to sacrifice in the interests of our marriage, if that's what this is."

"It's a terrible idea. I could stop you, you know." Leo paused, staring at the floor. "But if it's what you need to do . . . It's your body."

Leo had never told Polly, or anyone else, that the idea of conventional reproduction filled him with dread. As Leo's study of genetics had progressed during and after graduate school, he became privately obsessed with the odd idea that conventional conception should be seen as the destruction of the self. Meiosis, the process by which sperm and egg are created, shuffles your genes and then rips asunder each chromosome, literally destroying the genome that makes that individual unique. And gamete fusion—the merger of sperm and egg—dilutes the genome of each parent by half. Leo was incredulous that this violent obliteration of the individual was sentimentalized as essential to marriage, epitomized by D. H. Lawrence's wrongheaded view that marriage must be a combination and not simply an annexation. For Leo, annexation was the only type of marriage he could tolerate.

Leo turned, entered the bathroom, and closed the door. Polly heard the sound of the shower.

Sipping her coffee, Polly remembered with fondness the first few years of her marriage, when she and Leo worked as partners to build the business that eventually became SBD. They had no income other than dividends from a small trust fund from her grandmother, which paid the rent on the tiny cottage in Cupertino with a sloping back porch furnished with mismatched rockers. Polly spent half her time on the postdoc research and papers needed to advance her academic career, and half her time side by side with Leo writing the equations that would allow those early programs to look for medical insights in vast data sets of seemingly irrelevant information. Leo at the time was a sort of charismatic prophet, indifferent to money and obsessed by his mission to revolutionize human health and longevity by turning conventional medicine on its head. She had been swept up in his idealism and his vision. They ate cold pizza for breakfast and drank coffee all day. She was happy because she was in love, although some part of her knew even then that their feelings were not entirely mutual.

Polly thought about the day she discovered she was pregnant. She hadn't told Leo about her missed period. After a week, she bought a cheap test kit at the local drugstore. When two red stripes appeared on the strip, her elation was offset by concern about how Leo would take the news. They had never discussed children. She decided to sneak away for a blood test before saying anything to her husband. On the day the doctor confirmed the pregnancy, she waited until they were having their daily glass of Mateus on the back porch. Leo quickly overcame his shock and was all business. Neither of them had intended to become pregnant. It was a mistake. A child would get in the way of their work, especially now. Maybe later. In any case, better to take care of it right away.

Two days later, Polly agreed. She could have said no, but she didn't. At the end of the day, the abortion had been her decision. She didn't blame Leo.

Polly listened to the sound of the shower through the bathroom door. Perhaps, she thought, Leo's continuing antipathy to having children represented a rare instance of self-awareness. Perhaps a man with such an ego and singular sense of purpose really could not be a father. On the other hand, she thought, people change. Leo's shell of ego had hardened gradually around a damaged and vulnerable heart. The man she fell in love with was an awkward misfit, still not reconciled to the twin tragedies of his childhood—his sister's death and his mother's abandonment of her family. Math teaches you to deconstruct a problem and solve complex equations one part at a time. *The issue here*, Polly thought, *is how to break through the shell.* A child might do it, slowly melting away the bonds of ego. But in Leo's case, it might also take a hammer blow, a shock that broke through directly to his old hurts and fears.

* * *

Feeling the almost scalding water pummel his shoulders, Leo shut his eyes. After his mother left, his father never spoke of her again. She was excised so completely from their lives that Leo sometimes wondered whether she had really existed. No one hired by Leo could find evidence either that she was alive or of her death. Memories of his father washed across his mind. On a day Leo remembered with cinematic clarity, his father—then a captain—stood in the wheelhouse of a tug, scanning the horizon and never once making eye contact with the child seated cross-legged in the bow. The child watched as the crew joked with each other in Italian but became silent in the presence of his father. Leo stared down at the sea, mesmerized by the ever-changing bow wake. In his memory, he stared and stared at the waters of the Hudson, searching.

6
Hacking Evolution

Men have become like gods. Isn't it about time that we understood our divinity? Science offers us total mastery over our environment and over our destiny, yet instead of rejoicing we feel deeply afraid. Why should this be? How might these fears be resolved?

Sir Edmund Leach, Reith Lectures, BBC, 12 November 1967

EXTINCTION IS NO LONGER forever. Thank you."

With these words, Dr. Adri Chatterjee ended her briefing to reporters about the just-concluded symposium of geneticists and ecologists titled "Revive and Restore." About thirty reporters sat in folding chairs on the terrace of the National Geographic Society's white-striped modernist headquarters in Washington, DC. A small group of placard-carrying protestors, so far quiet, watched the proceedings from the steps below. Leo stood alone off to the side, with Clip and Playg lounging together on a low wall a few yards away.

"Why are we wasting our time out here?" Playg complained. "Fucking National Geographic, really? Like where my grandmother got her science? What the fuck?"

"Outside of the hacker world," Clip answered, "these guys are the best. Leo thinks they can help."

"Help with what? I thought you said Leo had balls. Everything we're doing in the lab, man, is fucking pathetic, boring, lame. And now this."

Next to the diminutive Bengali American speaker, a lanky scientist from Cornell, the geneticist José Vargas, stood silently. Behind him, a younger man shuffled impatiently from one foot to the other.

Chatterjee pointed to a reporter for the first question.

"I understand, Dr. Chatterjee, that this is an impressive technology and that bringing back extinct animals would be appealing to lots of folks. But what's it for?"

Chatterjee had fielded this question dozens of times.

"Sir, I'm glad you asked that question. Let me tell you a story. The great northern tundra has been absorbing greenhouse gases for hundreds of thousands of years, and the permafrost under the tundra is what keeps those gases trapped there. There's now so much carbon locked up in the permafrost that if it were to melt and that carbon were released, it would be the equivalent of burning all the world's forests two and a half times over. That's how important it is. And unfortunately, the bad news is that the permafrost *is* melting."

"Why?" another reporter called out. "And what does that have to do with bringing back extinct animals?"

Chatterjee smiled.

"I'm getting to that. For a long time, what we now call tundra or taiga was a lush grassland known as the 'mammoth steppe.' This was an amazing ecosystem, host to vast herds of antelope, deer, horses, and mammoths. But at the end of the Pleistocene—that's the end of the last ice age roughly eleven thousand years ago, just yesterday in geological terms—the herds vanished, probably hunted to extinction by humans. These animals were vital to maintaining the permafrost, because they both compacted and scraped away the deep winter snows, allowing the winter cold to refreeze the ground below. When these animals went extinct, no other species performed this service, and the permafrost, very slowly at first, started to melt. The mammoth was what we call the 'keystone species,' the single animal essential to this particular ecosystem."

Chatterjee paused again to make sure the reporters were keeping up.

"So you ask why do de-extinction . . . well, if we can restore the mammoth to the tundra, it will slowly turn back into mammoth steppe, the permafrost will stop melting, all that carbon will stay out of the atmosphere, and global warming will be reduced. You follow? And what's more, our colleagues in Russia have already set aside an enormous reserve in eastern Siberia and are ready to start restoring the grasslands as soon as we can give them some of those new almost-wooly mammoths."

"It sounds like *Jurassic Park*," another reporter shouted out, "and we all know how *that* ended."

Chatterjee laughed with everyone else, but her narrowing eyes revealed her impatience.

"We hear that a lot. But this is completely different. Let me be clear. The dinosaurs went extinct sixty-five *million* years ago, when we humans weren't even a twinkle in evolution's eye, so dinosaur extinction can't be blamed on us. And you're right—bringing dinosaurs back would not end well, mainly because the planet today is nothing like the planet when dinosaurs flourished; they just wouldn't fit in. And one more thing: you know that scene from the movie where they show the mosquito trapped in amber, with the blood of a dinosaur supposedly still inside after sixty-five million years? That's totally bogus—DNA is recoverable for a few hundred thousand years, but not millions. Unlike *Jurassic Park*, what we're all talking about today is a real technology. In 2003, some of my colleagues in Spain brought back an extinct bucardo, that's a type of ibex, or mountain goat. She didn't live long, but she was born."

"It's exactly like *Jurassic Park*," one of the protestors yelled. "Exactly like *Frankenstein*. If we don't stop it now, it will come back to bite us, every one of us."

Chatterjee responded politely, "You'll have your turn, sir."

A reporter picked up the line of questioning. "OK, so if it's not blood in an insect in amber, then how did they do it?"

"Here's one way I explain it to my kids, who seem more comfortable with the digital world than the biological one. Let's say you have the 2.0 version of an app on your phone—that's like the DNA of an animal alive today—and you want to turn it back into version 1.0—to revert to the extinct animal. First, you'd need to figure out what the code was for version 1.0—for extinct animals we get that by analyzing bits of bone or frozen tissue. Then, you edit the version 2.0 code to put it back to the way it was in the first version. You then reload the edited code back on your phone—this is the step where you insert the edited DNA back into the nucleus of an egg cell. And presto, your phone is now running version 1.0 of the app—you've recreated the extinct animal. That's one of several ways real-world de-extinction works."

Playg leaned over toward Clip. "She may be a fucking big shot, but you know what this is? It's hacking. The famous professor is only a hacker like me, and she's hacking evolution. Think of how *that* could fuck things up. Wish I'd thought of it."

The lanky Cornell geneticist stepped forward. "Yes, well, that's *how* it works. But Dr. Chatterjee neglected to mention the critical ingredient: money. Thanks to Pastor Joe and his friends over there," he pointed to the protesters clustered behind the seated reporters, "the federal agencies that provide so much of our other funding are not funding our work on de-extinction." Turning to stare directly at Leo, Vargas added, "So we rely on private capital and philanthropy."

"Always comes back to the green stuff, man," Playg said to Clip.

"Always. They say they want to save the fucking world, but that's total crap. They want dough."

"Not everyone," Clip answered. "Leo doesn't need more money. He really believes in what he's doing."

"Really, dude? Talk about drinking the Kool-Aid. You're a hacker. Can you hear yourself? You've been lickin' his ass way too long, man."

The younger man behind Vargas came forward and pushed his way awkwardly to the microphone. "I'm Abe," he said. "Abe Myers." His loud vest and clashing tie seemed to signal a cultivated eccentricity. "Do you all know the most dramatic extinction story in history? 1794—a single flock of two billion passenger pigeons flew over Shelbyville, Kentucky. It took two hours for the flock to pass over the town. They were *the* keystone species for North America. But only 150 years later, in 1941, the last one, Martha, died at the Cincinnati Zoo. Every single other individual out of this huge population of billions and billions of individuals was shot, netted, or hunted to death."

The young man, obviously emotional, paced back and forth behind the lectern, his whole body expressing his anger.

"And you know what happens when you lose a keystone species? All hell breaks loose, is what happens. Think it doesn't affect you? In 1998 we were able to link the soaring levels of Lyme disease with the disappearance of the passenger pigeon. And now, now we can fix this. I'm going to bring them back. I don't know if it'll take ten years or forty years, but it doesn't matter. It will happen. They were so beautiful . . ."

Vargas put his arm around the younger scientist's shoulders and interrupted. "Thank you, Abe."

Chatterjee pointed at the leader of the small group of protesters, who had been waiting patiently with his hand raised. "Pastor Joe, in the interests of hearing from all sides, is there something you'd like to ask?"

"There is."

The handsome cleric, who never wore a collar, stepped forward and smiled broadly for the cameras. Joseph O'Malley was the very model of the next-generation televangelist. The forty-year-old from Queens dressed like a banker from Manhattan but spoke with an accent that would have placed him somewhere just west of Kansas. His passion was politics, and he was as sophisticated a practitioner of the political arts as he was skilled at theological tautology. Raised in the church of his Irish ancestors, he narrowly escaped a Catholic seminary in terminal decline and showed up unannounced at the doors of Liberty University in Lynchburg, explaining that he had no money but was prepared to renounce his Catholicism and devote his life to building the Godly Kingdom in America. And he had done just that. His cable show, *All in for Jesus*, the first also to stream directly to the smartphones of the faithful, had made him a star. His nearly two million Twitter followers ranked him well above the next-most tweeting pastors, the Pope, Joel Osteen, and Rick Warren. And now, just weeks before, he had announced his candidacy for Congress.

"You see, folks, Americans have always thought of the creation as sacred, something permanent and unchanging. A glimpse of the majesty and eternity of God. So what, exactly, gives you people the right to change that which the heavenly Father has created?"

Chatterjee answered. "Pastor Joe, surely you understand that there's nothing permanent or unchanging about nature. Just the opposite. Nature is all change all the time, constant evolution through mutation followed by natural selection. *That's* the system your God gave us. And as to whether mankind has any right or place interfering? All I can say is that we've been bending nature to our will for more than ten thousand years, when we bred dogs from wolves, grains from grass, and all sorts of livestock. Mankind has already proven himself a skilled creator of life."

Joe swept away these points with a dismissive wave of his hand.

"All those things were just a nudge that nature could take or not, using plants and animals that nature allowed to breed with one another. That was working within God's plan and God's rules. Using Dr. Vargas's editing prowess to put the genes of a jellyfish into a soybean is something different—the nature God designed for us does not permit that. When you edit DNA you're rewriting God's rules. Do you think, Dr. Chatterjee, that you can do better than the one who is omniscient? Because if you do, I think this would be a grave concern to every Christian. Most Americans would join us in putting a stop to it."

Shouts of "Amen, brother," rose from the crowd of supporters. They waved their signs for the assembled media, "Stop Playing God" being the most common.

"Pastor Joe," Chaterjee replied, "you know I respect your right to believe what you wish in the realm of the spiritual and supernatural. But here on Earth, there's no reason at all to privilege DNA in its current form—static DNA is most certainly not part of biology, or God's plan, if you want to call it that."

Vargas stepped forward. "Let's take an example: A mutation that would allow the body to shut down the growth of breast cancer. It could happen tomorrow, or it could take a million years. But if it happened, that mutation would be as 'natural' as anything else in our genome, and evolution would embrace it and spread it throughout the population. So if I can identify that mutation now, hurry the process along, so to speak, and save millions of lives, don't you think any merciful God would be all in favor of that?"

The youthful Abe Meyer, who had been fidgeting like a second grader, interrupted, speaking to the crowd in a strong voice and again ignoring the microphone.

"And why can't you see that what I'm doing is actually atoning for what surely should be a sin in any religion—the extermination of one species by another. Help me understand—your God creates the passenger pigeon, then he carefully packs a pair of them off on the

Ark to escape the flood. And then we come along and exterminate all five billion of them. What does your God think about that? And now we find that the nature your God gave us includes all the tools we need to bring that species back. Are we supposed to ignore the tools he gave us? How could using those tools possibly be contrary to the will of a deity?"

Joe waited a few beats before answering, deftly allowing the emotional temperature to cool and the assembled crowd to refocus on him. "You've heard, young man, about pride? The deadliest of the sins, which sends a corrosive trickle of hubris to slowly erase the soul. You may think that with your test tubes and chemicals you can control the future of the planet and of humanity. This is the particular blindness and curse of the sciences. A hubris warned against by the ancients, not to mention by our Lord in the Bible."

Vargas, who had subtly rolled his eyes during Abe Myers's short diatribe, stepped forward to answer. "Yes, and a wise warning it is. But with respect, the ancients could not have envisaged our technology. None of the religious traditions reflects knowledge of basic genetics and evolution. If they did, I think the teachings would look quite different. The fact is that today we can bring back extinct species. We can teach machines to drive cars. We can outwit cancer. These are completely natural developments in the long story of human history. They're the inevitable consequence of the way our brains have evolved. We could no more turn our back on them than we could stop walking or using our opposable thumbs."

All eyes turned to Pastor Joe. He smiled warmly and spoke as if addressing a child. "Do you agree, sir, that you cannot fully control what you don't fully understand?"

"Of course."

"And do you think, Professor, that you fully understand the great mystery of life on this planet, where it came from, how it works, and where it's headed?"

"No, not completely."

"Then your dreams of usurping the role of God, taking control of nature, and even redesigning man, are the real delusions here." He turned directly to the reporters, the smile gone and his mouth now set in a look of determined toughness, sending a ripple through the crowd of protestors, the amiable mood morphing into what could have been a prelude to violence. "That's all I have to say, except that we'll be watching you very closely."

With a quick smile Pastor Joe defused the tension. "And, friends, please join our campaign at JoeForOhio.com. We need your help."

The press corps ignored the three scientists, still standing awkwardly on the terrace, and clustered around the cleric. His team already had unleashed a barrage of tweets, determined to have Pastor Joe's objections, and not the "Revive and Restore" message itself, be the story.

Clip and Playg walked over to join Leo.

"He's a fucking moron," Playg said directly to Leo. "Why don't you crush him, man. Just take him out. Why stand there and listen to this crap?"

"Jesus, Playg." It was Clip who responded. "Leo knows what he's doing."

Leo turned to Playg. "He's actually a genius, Playg. Another news cycle stolen from science. He'll win his election and he'll go far."

"He's a fucking imbecile," Playg muttered under his breath, not willing to concede the point.

* * *

Leo, Clip, and Playg reentered the building and walked down a long corridor to a small windowless conference room where Professors Chatterjee and Vargas waited. Leo greeted them with warmth and complimented them on the day's program.

Playg sprawled in a chair far from the rest of the group and stared at his phone. Clip sat down next to him. Leo had not introduced them and noticed both professors staring at Playg. "My assistant," he said nodding at Clip and ignoring Playg. "Anyway, that Pastor Joe," Leo continued. "Impressive. You've dealt with him before?"

Chatterjee answered. "Yes. Not always in person. He sends out small groups to demonstrate or harass whenever we appear in public. So far, he hasn't gotten much traction. I really don't think he will with de-extinction and re-wilding—it's a bit hard to understand and far away from the things that really get folks riled up, like designer babies or bringing back extinct hominins."

"He might even serve a purpose," Vargas added. "Not all of our colleagues are as careful as we are, Leo, and knowing he's out there helps keep them honest. We can't afford another Gelsinger or He Jiankui."

"Who're they?" Playg whispered to Clip.

"Really? You don't know?" Clip replied. "Gelsinger was an eighteen-year-old kid. 1999, I think. Got gene therapy during a clinical trial, and the docs fucked up big time. He died. Real messy. They stopped all trials. Set back gene therapy for years."

"That's lame. What'd they expect? There's no progress without people dying."

"Yeah, well, the Chinese professor, He Jiankui, didn't kill anyone, and he kept two infants from getting AIDS. But he crossed a line—germ line edits to an embryo—and he's now in a Chinese prison."

"Really?" Playg asked, looking concerned. "I thought the Chinese were more chill than that."

Leo had been staring at Vargas, as if to find, behind the impassive façade, a clue as to whether the man had really meant what he said about Pastor Joe.

"I disagree. He's a dangerous man, José. Never make the mistake of believing your enemies are doing you a service." Before Vargas could respond, Leo continued. "Good thing he hasn't got a whiff of our latest iPSC breakthrough."

The two professors leaned in, tantalized at the prospect of being tipped off about a new product launch from SBD. Leo looked at Vargas. "GenRescue was a great deal for us."

Vargas smiled, but couldn't completely disguise the pain of having sold his start-up to SBD at a price that, in retrospect, had been far too low.

"It won't surprise you to know," Leo added, "that the real value was in the iPSC."

When Leo first heard that Vargas had figured out how to induce ordinary skin cells to behave like stem cells—those with the potential to turn into any other type of cell, such as liver, bone, sperm, brain—he immediately grasped the implications. With so-called induced pluripotent stem cells, iPSCs, there was no more need for harvesting of stem cells from aborted fetuses. One of the major political impediments to advancing genetic research, solved.

Leo continued. "We're launching a service for same-sex couples to have children with genetic material from both partners, just like a heterosexual couple. Say they're lesbians; one of the women supplies the egg as usual, which of course carries her DNA. The other woman provides a skin cell. We treat it to achieve pluripotency and then induce it to turn into sperm, which carries her DNA. The sperm fertilizes the egg in the normal way, and *voilà*, we have an embryo with genetic material from both parents, even though both are women. The dream of every gay and lesbian couple in the world. We're rolling it out for about two hundred grand a pop."

Vargas refused to be baited. "You're right, Pastor Joe's not going to like that one very much."

"I don't give a damn," Leo said. "I think you two need to be bolder. Sequencing is improving at four times the pace of Moore's law. You think that religion or morality can keep up and provide useful guidance? We can't afford to listen politely to his medieval nonsense. We need to hit back."

"Leo," Adri Chatterjee replied, "you know that José and I see it that way, but we've got to be cautious. We've got to play by the rules, even if they're stupid. If we don't, the whole thing gets shut down for a generation."

"I don't agree. With respect, putting the wooly mammoth back on the Siberian tundra is great, but it's like putting a Band-Aid on a melanoma patient. Want to know what *my* vision is?" Leo stole a brief glance at the numbers flashing on the face of his watch. "All over North America, not just mammoths, but every ice-age mammal that humans hunted to extinction: wild camels and horses, the American cheetah, mastodons, the ground sloth, giant beaver, short-faced bear, dire wolf. All of them, and the plants, of course. Why? That's what evolution gave us. That's the web of life that's sustainable, adaptable, and thus resilient. That's what it will take to start over and correct what *Homo sapiens* did when they arrived."

The two professors glanced at each other, uncertain whether Leo was serious.

"Leo," Vargas answered, "even if we could do all that, which we can't right at the moment, aren't you forgetting the key problem? Almost six hundred million people inhabit North America. You want giant ground sloths wandering across interstate highways? Cheetahs hunting in suburban subdivisions? It won't happen."

"It could. Only 20 percent of North America is intensively developed. At least 50 percent can be considered sufficiently wild. But of course we've got to demonstrate first that it works."

When Chatterjee and Vargas had nothing to say, he continued. "SBD has a project that I call Arcadia. A large piece of uninhabited land . . . very large. I'm piloting techniques to restore the hydrology, scrub toxins, diversify mycorrhizal fungi, and reestablish the levels of mycoplasma-related endobacteria that prevailed before human arrival. I've already de-extincted hundreds of species of ice-age plants and reintroduced them to the wild. It's time for animals."

The academics were stunned. "Why haven't we heard of this?"

"Not ready for prime time."

Adri Chatterjee stood up and with deliberate casualness asked, "Leo, would it be OK if we spent a few minutes alone?" Leo looked across at Vargas. "No," she added. "*With* José. But just with you." She nodded toward Chip and Playg at the end of the table.

"Oh. Sure," Leo said.

Playg left without acknowledging anyone in the room. Before leaving, Clip stood and smiled at the two professors. "It was an honor to meet you, Dr. Chatterjee, Professor Vargas."

When the door shut, Chatterjee said, "I think I recognize the surly one. Is he the biohacker who calls himself Playg?"

Leo looked surprised. "He is. How could you possibly have recognized him?"

"From his picture. About six months ago, the FBI came and showed me his picture. Asked what I knew about him. Asked me to review transcripts of chats and texts, to help them understand what he was up to."

"Oh," Leo said. "The government is now monitoring lots of these garage-bio kids to be sure they're not into anything too dangerous. I knew they'd come to speak with him before I hired him. He's the real thing, Adri. Unconventional and unpleasant, perhaps. But smart, and he's got the gift in the lab. Just needs direction."

Chatterjee hesitated. "Leo, God knows you can take care of yourself. But I think you should know. He's seriously bad news. I know kids say all sorts of things to each other online, but this stuff was angry, classic sociopath. And the stuff he said he was doing . . . driving pathogenic traits through populations of benign bacteria, for example." She paused to let this sink in. "Sure, it could have been bragging, but even so, pretty troubling. You'd better be careful."

Leo showed neither surprise nor concern. "Yes, of course. I greatly appreciate the warning, Adri. I do." He paused. "So, back to Arcadia. SBD has been doing all the editing for the plants. But for mammals, you guys are the best. You can do it better and faster. Will you help? I want ten species of extinct North American megafauna to start. Any order you like. Twenty individuals of each species, with sufficient diversity to support breeding. Your two labs collaborate, an unlimited budget. It costs what it costs. The overhead from these grants will keep your labs humming for the next decade."

Chatterjee asked, "And this Arcadia. Is it protected? I mean, contained? No people around?"

"As remote as you can get in the lower forty-eight. No possibility of public blowback."

Chatterjee stood. "No possibility? Now you *are* sounding like *Jurassic Park*. Don't do it, Leo. It's too soon. I'm sorry, gentlemen, I don't want to be part of this conversation."

Vargas stayed in his seat. When she saw that her colleague was not prepared to leave, she walked to the door. "Don't worry, I didn't hear a thing. Nice to see you, Leo."

When the door closed, Vargas looked straight at Leo.

"No hominins," Vargas said. "You know all that I said about Neanderthals was just PR, right?"

"Of course. Nothing to do with that. Just think, you've been talking about re-wilding for years. Now you have the chance to do it right. Diverse populations. Environment carefully calibrated to their needs. They'll have every advantage. If re-wilding can work anyplace, it's there."

"And we play by the rules, right?" Vargas said. "No cutting corners. We do this straight up, following all the guidelines. Is that agreed?"

"Absolutely."

"OK, Leo. I'll do it," Vargas said. "I think I'll do *Camelops hesternus* first. To see the big camel back in the American West, now that would be something."

7
The Glacier

Glaciers move in tides. So do mountains. So do all things.

—John Muir, *Letters from Alaska*

As the pilot banked the boxy red floatplane to starboard, the bulky headphones worn by Leo and Muir crackled to life. "Just below is where the glacier used to end. It was a tidewater glacier, the face was right here, fronting on Glacier Bay."

At home Muir had a photograph, given to him by his father, of the glacier as it appeared when John Muir first visited in 1879. Now, looking down, it was difficult to imagine a great ice wall where only a tongue of water lapped in the gap between the two mountains.

"Thirty miles to go," the pilot continued. "The water we're flying over, we now call it Muir Inlet. But before, everywhere you see water, all was ice."

Before Muir's strange visit to Arcadia, he anticipated that he would have little in common with a man perched at the very top of the 1 percent. He had expected to dislike Leo. But he didn't, and for reasons he did not understand he had revealed to a near stranger a thing so intimate that he had never before discussed it with anyone other than his deceased wife.

Muir was not so naïve as to believe that Leo's apparent interest in friendship was uncoupled from an agenda. He knew that men like Leo didn't bother with the "little people" unless there was something they wanted. And so, when his cell phone rang and Leo invited Muir to join him on a visit to Alaska, he wondered what exactly it was that Leo wanted. Nonetheless, this time, despite all his misgivings about Arcadia, Muir didn't even consider playing hard to get. He told Leo that seeing the Muir Glacier had been a lifelong dream.

The glacier, which previously split to flow around and past a rocky promontory, now had retreated so that it merely embraced the knobby mountain like a giant pincer. The pilot flew up the east fork of ice, revealing a pitted and fractured surface that made landing or hiking impossible. He then flew low back down the west fork, landing into the wind on the placid surface of the Muir Inlet, away from the tongue of floating ice at the base of the glacial terminus. As the plane taxied to a shallow pebble beach, Muir studied the glacier's face, which was a disappointing dirty white, not the crystalline blue of Muir's imagination.

"You sure I can't talk you guys into coming back with me?" the pilot asked. "Doing this without a guide, even for just one night, is not a good idea." They had discussed this. Leo had been insistent that the two of them should hike alone, and Muir acquiesced, figuring they couldn't get in too much trouble in just one night. They planned to take a short hike up the ridge to the east of the terminus, camp for a night overlooking the glacier, and return down the next morning.

"Thanks, we're good," Leo said. "See you tomorrow at noon."

After a dry landing off the plane's pontoon, each of them hoisted a small pack that included a quarter-dome tent. Muir carried a .375 Ruger Hawkeye Alaskan rifle. The two men headed wordlessly toward a steep trail visible at the far side of the rocky beach.

The landscape at the lower elevations had not yet begun to recover from the glaciation that snuffed out all but microbial life. The rocky scree was barren, except for the occasional smudge of gray-green lichen in the shadow on the north side of a rock. The stone at this level was remarkable for an almost sensuous rounding and polish, without any of the fractured surfaces and jagged edges that the eye expected in any such expanse of rocky mountainside. Only in the far distance, at heights well above the last century's glaciation, could they see trees, mostly spruces. Muir pointed out the dying understory of transitional alders that had fixed nitrogen from the air and created the more fertile soils in which the spruces could reestablish themselves.

The two men hiked without conversation, climbing to a point only a few hundred feet above the top of the glacier. The superficial lichens and algae were now joined by a low-growing moss. The moss, whose minute stalks were invisible to the eye, gave the impression that a spongy yellow-green felt had been randomly scattered on the pebbly ground. It was rare for Muir to be the one to break the silence. He knelt on the lee side of a small boulder.

"*Actaea rubra*," he said, pointing to a tiny plant emerging from the narrow joint between a boulder and the ledge rock on which it sat. Leo stopped and knelt next to him.

"Baneberry," Muir continued. "All it needed was a few crumbs of decayed organic matter, a crack pulling in water by capillary action, and protection from the wind. Of the billions of seeds and spores passing by in the air, this is the one that dropped in the crack." Muir chuckled. "It's ironic. Baneberry is quite poisonous. Six berries are enough to shut down the respiratory system of an adult human."

After a few more minutes of hiking, it was Leo who spoke. "Your baneberry is a great illustration. DNA without environment is nothing."

"Meaning what?"

"Meaning that the traditional account of genetics is incomplete. Meaning that it's the experience of the genome, its interaction with the environment—both in the present and over many generations—that matters. Genes are in a constant conversation with the world."

"So?" Muir seemed distracted, more interested in the increasing numbers of cushiony dryas and other pioneer plants.

"So, if SBD focuses only on genetics, it does only half the job. One of my scientists likes to say that you can take the most perfect genome and set it down on the moon and nothing will happen. DNA might be whizzing around the universe on comets and asteroids, but it only comes alive and functions properly when it's got the right environment around it. *That's* why I needed to do Arcadia. Genetics is only half the story. Environment is the other half."

"Every biologist gets that," Muir answered. "DNA is everywhere. What's rare is habitat." He pointed across the valley. "We're high enough to start seeing the mountains. Not sure, but maybe the near one is Mt. Cooper? See it?"

The summit now visible behind the western ridgeline looked like the jagged hump of an albino camel, hiding shyly in a broad valley.

Leo glanced to his left for a moment and then resumed walking. "With Arcadia I'm going to show that we can engineer a habitat perfectly calibrated for a super-diverse and resilient biotic community, including humans."

Muir stopped to pee, facing downhill and aiming at a pocket of barren scree.

"Urea," he said, turning back toward Leo. "Nitrogen, potassium, and phosphorus. In a month, it'll be green." And, before starting up the trail again, he added, "To be honest, Leo, I'm almost as afraid of your engineering the environment as I am your reengineering DNA."

The two men hiked for another mile or so, along a trail that became increasingly steep and narrow, before Leo responded.

"I understand your fear, Muir. All the greatest achievements of humanity were accompanied by apprehension and doubt. Here's the thing: somewhere along the way random mutations gave us intelligence. From that moment on, our destiny was set. Because the unavoidable fate of intelligence is to make choices, to take responsibility, to take control. We can no more turn our backs on the powers that our intelligence grants us than a panda can give up eating bamboo."

Muir, having experienced the perils of turning an ankle when help was far away, walked with small and careful steps.

"Fear," he responded, "can hold us back, but sometimes it can keep us alive." And, after only a few more steps, he added, "And that intelligence you say fates us to take control? Doesn't it also allow us to choose to let evolution take its course without our intervention?"

Leo began swatting at the small insects that had started buzzing around their faces and ears as the vegetation became denser.

"Really? Is that what you choose, Muir? If Lilith had a disease that could be cured by a genetic mutation, and you had a choice to wait and see if that mutation appeared randomly, or to give her the gene modification she needed, which would you choose?"

"Leo, I don't want to argue. You know more about this than anyone on the planet, and I'm just a plantsman. But you asked. And my gut tells me that 'directed evolution' is a terrible idea. What I love most about nature is that we *don't* control it. Look around you. What do you feel? You feel like you're an ant, a spore drifting in the wind. That's the point. Nature teaches us humility."

Leo, who was walking in front on the narrow trail, stopped and turned to face Muir. His tone turned impatient. "Do you hear yourself, Muir? You're just repeating clichés and slogans. It's ridiculous to think that nature, which is cruel and random, is somehow the only measure of what's good. You might as well just say that I shouldn't 'play God.' It doesn't mean a damn thing. Maybe I was wrong about you." He paused. "Maybe there's a reason you don't have your doctorate."

Muir's ears flushed pink. "And I guess I misjudged you too. You may very well be just another selfish asshole who's been blinded by his money." Muir rarely lost his temper, but Leo had picked at a sore spot. "It's only because of your billions that you think you can control everything. You . . ."

Muir froze in midsentence. The two men had stopped a few paces before the mountainside trail took a sharp curve to the right. Muir saw it first. A massive light tan bear, with the distinctive shoulder hump of a grizzly, lumbered around the curve, stopping less than two yards behind Leo's back. Seeing the two men, the bear reared up on its hind legs in surprise and lifted a paw to take a swipe at the creature just in front of it.

"Bear, get down. Duck. *Now,*" Muir shouted.

Leo fell forward to his knees, glancing over his shoulder as the bear's paw swished only inches above his scalp. He tucked his head, gripped his knees, and curled into a defensive posture on the narrow trail. The uphill side was nearly vertical, the downhill side too steep for either bear or man to make an escape.

As Leo fell forward, Muir reached back to remove the rifle slung over his left shoulder, but found the gun's strap tangled with his backpack. While Muir struggled to free the rifle, the bear fell forward, pinning Leo under its body. Muir, one hand still trying to free the rifle, lunged forward, unleashing a volley of staccato kicks to the recumbent bear's muzzle in an effort to distract its jaws and claws from shredding the man pinned underneath. Moments later, one of the bear's claws swiped across Muir's retreating shin, tearing his pants and drawing blood.

As Muir fell backward, the bear rose slightly, preparing to lunge forward. This created just enough of a gap under its belly for Leo to roll away to the side. On the second roll, Leo tumbled over the trail's downhill edge, sliding about twenty feet on his stomach before his left foot hit a small outcropping of rock, breaking the fall. Leo balanced with one foot on the knob of rock and clutched at the steep stony slope with his fingers.

The bear, ignoring Leo, lunged forward at Muir. Muir again tugged hard at the rifle with both hands. This time, his fall having dislodged the strap, he was able to swing the gun forward to the front of his body. The .375 bullet did its job and the grizzly fell in place. Muir staggered to his feet and shot a second bullet into the animal's skull at nearly point-blank range.

Hardly pausing to catch his breath, Muir slipped the pack off his back, pulled out the quarter-dome tent, and cut loose the guy lines designed to hold the tent to the ground. Knotting two lines together, he stood searching for an anchor. The tree line was still well above them and no rock was large enough to support the weight of two men.

"You OK?" he shouted down to Leo.

"Can't . . . much longer," Leo answered between ragged breaths.

"Hold on. I'm coming down."

Muir knelt next to the bear, which he figured must weigh about eight hundred pounds. It would have to do. Securing one end of the rope to the grizzly's hind foot, he looped the line around his back and rappelled the twenty feet down to where Leo was so precariously perched, a knob of stone all that stood in the way of another hundred feet of free fall.

"Keep your foot and weight on the rock," Muir said. "Lift your hands and grab my waist. When I say 'ready,' slowly release your foot from the rock and begin to climb with me."

Twice during the climb, the bear's leg abruptly shifted from the weight, causing them to lurch downward. Each time, Leo's legs lost their grip on the rock, leaving him hanging on Muir's waist and Muir straining to hold the weight of both men.

A few minutes later, the two men clambered over the edge of the narrow trail and flopped to ground, exhausted. After recovering his breath, Muir tore a strip from his shredded pants leg and used it to bind the wound on his shin, which he saw was superficial.

Leo lifted his head from the ground briefly and turned to Muir. "Thanks. Really."

"No problem."

Leo rolled to his side, stared down the precipitous slope, and then closed his eyes, still breathing heavily. Muir waited for several minutes, but Leo's eyes remained shut. Eventually, Muir spoke softly. "We need to set up camp before dark. We need to go."

They proceeded up the trail, with Muir in the lead, this time holding his rifle at the ready. As the afternoon wore on, there were no signs of another bear, but they were plagued by an airborne stew of ferocious bugs. Swarms of mosquitos performed a seemingly coordinated blitzkrieg against any patch of uncovered skin. The incessant buzzing and biting added to the hikers' dark mood.

"Here," Muir said, nodding toward a flat patch of rock below a small ledge that would protect them from the wind. They set up camp with only the minimum required conversation. Each of the men took a pouch of chicken chili and retired to his tent to eat the cold food alone.

* * *

When the sun rose from behind the mountains to the east, a curtain of illumination slowly descended across the opposite ridge. It was one of those moments when nature indulges in extravagant showmanship, producing an effect that in art would seem gaudy, but in her hands sets the standard for transcendent beauty. Leo was up first and prepared a pot of coffee on a tiny camp stove. When Muir emerged from his tent, Leo handed him a tin mug, and the two men sat facing west, transfixed by the show.

The patches of snow on the dome-like mountain dividing the two arms of the glacier, which had appeared dirty the afternoon before, now glowed with a side-lit purity. And the glacier itself, lurking in deep shadows, had been transformed from ice white to steel gray. So liquid were its contours, so convincing its appearance of flow, that the brain rebelled at the thought that the glacier was a solid thing, expecting instead that at any moment the surface would resume the undulations and torpid flow of molten rock.

After allowing him a few sips of coffee, Leo said, "Muir, about yesterday. What you did was incredible. You saved my life by risking your own. What can I say?"

"Don't say anything. I acted on instinct. Anyone would have done the same."

Leo laughed with a bitter edge. "I'm not sure who you hang out with, Muir. But the anyones around me couldn't have, and probably wouldn't have, even if they could. And what I said yesterday, before. I shouldn't have. And I didn't mean it. Really. I'm sorry."

"Forget it. And what I said, I was totally out of line. I don't know what came over me."

The border between light and dark descended slowly down the opposite ridge, illuminating the mountainside inch by inch. The pockets of snow circling the summit now shined like pearls in a necklace. The rock flank that yesterday appeared barren was revealed by the solar spotlight to be awash in glowing chlorophyll from algae and mosses.

"Beautiful," said Leo.

"I really only feel free in the wilderness," Muir said, giving the answer he had been reluctant to share when his wife had asked why he hunted. After another few minutes sharing the unfolding scene, Muir added, "Leo, tell me you don't see magic here."

"Sure," Leo answered, "I do. But I also know why. My brain is awash in chemicals because of my genes and how they program my body to react to this particular stimulus. They do this because over countless mornings our ancestors thrilled with relief that the sun chose to return for another day."

"You know," Muir said, "when my wife died, a friend sent me a poem. It had a line I've never forgotten, 'a forest for love and a river for grief.' I sat for days along a wild stretch of the Snake River, and hour by hour I could feel the grief shrinking, being contained to the point where there was room for Lilith, room for living." Muir turned away from the view to face Leo. "When your sister died and your mother left, you must . . ."

Leo interrupted. "I was only a child. Not the same." Before Muir could answer, Leo continued, "We'd better head down. But before we go, I want to ask you something. I want you to come work for me. I want you to run plant conservation at Arcadia. We're collecting genetic material from endangered and extinct species from all over the world. SBD's gene bank is now the largest, double the size of the American Museum of Natural History, which has been at it for over a century. More than enough material for a PhD and a lifetime of study afterward."

"Really? Why me? There are many others far more qualified."

"There are, at least on paper. But you're the one I want. I have a gift for spotting talent. I've made lots of unconventional choices along the way, and I believe they're one of the reasons for SBD's success." He paused to see if that was explanation enough. "You've got your own gift, Muir. And now I know I can depend on you. Arcadia is my baby. I know you'll take care of it."

"I'm flattered. But you know that I have real doubts about some of the things you're doing there."

"I know. But nothing is set in stone. This is your chance to influence what gets done and how. And think of your daughter. You and she will live in one of the most beautiful and protected places in the world. I'll hire people to help you take care of her. She and the other children at Arcadia will have the best education money can buy, all for free. I'll pay for college. Think of it, Muir, all your responsibilities satisfied, all your worries solved, leaving you to do what you love. You can get your doctorate."

"Thanks, but I can't," Muir said. "Meredith's parents in Boise are the only family Lilith has, other than me. I don't want her to be separated from them."

"You can take a copter whenever you want, on SBD's dime. That's not a problem."

Muir stood, still feeling the peace that only came when he was many miles from civilization. He gazed down at the glacier and thought of his father. His dad's two-week visit here had been one of the formative events of his life. He said the glaciers had taught him the perspective of geological time, and the ability to see the solid and static as fluid and dynamic. After a moment, still staring at the glacier, Muir spoke.

"I'll do it."

8

Was ist der mensch?

The field of philosophy . . . can be brought down to the following questions: 1. What can I know? 2. What should I do? 3. What can I hope for? 4. What is man? The first question is answered by metaphysics, the second by ethics, the third by religion and the fourth by anthropology. Basically, however, all these could be counted to anthropology, because the first three questions relate to the last one.

IMMANUEL KANT, *LECTURES ON LOGIC* (JÄSCHE, 1800)

ACTUALLY, LEO, THE TRUTH is I'm not really so interested in Neanderthals. What really interests me is humans. You know Kant's question, 'What is man?' That's what I'm working on. And I mean of course the scientific answer, to finally replace the speculations of religion and philosophy."

Leo was surprised to hear this from Rafael Silva, the man who had sequenced the complete genome of *Homo neanderthalensis* using only bone fragments. He should, Leo thought, have been very interested in Neanderthals. Neanderthals were the reason Leo had traveled to Germany and was now sitting across the table from the eminent professor.

Two days earlier, in his office at Arcadia, Leo had walked into Clip's lab and announced, "Clippy, we're going to Leipzig. Tell Playg he can come too." The next evening, Leo's jet left Portland bound on a nine-hour flight to Leipzig, during which Leo retreated to his private room to sleep. Clip watched movies and chatted with the stewardess. Playg ducked into the lavatory every couple of hours to smoke a joint, having disabled the smoke detector with a Styrofoam cup.

Arriving in the former East German city at noon, Leo asked the SBD driver to take them directly to the Max Planck Institute for Evolutionary Anthropology. Clip stared out the car window, fascinated by the old Soviet Pavilion, which appeared to be a cross between a Mormon temple and a fascist railroad station. Its incongruous steeple, still topped by a red star, had shed much of its original gilding. Only a block later, the Planck Institute came into view, a far more graceful structure with a gently curved façade topped by a glass cap that seemed to float above the building.

Professor Silva greeted the visitors from Oregon in a small seminar room. He wore wire-rim glasses on a lean face that reminded Leo of Stephen Hawking. Leo asked him to explain his surprising assertion that modern humans, and not Neanderthals, were his main interest.

"Think of it this way. Every trait we share in common with, say, *Homo erectus* or *Homo habilis* can't be what defines man because they were shared with other species, and thus are not unique to *Homo sapiens*. So how do we go about finding out what *is* unique to man? What is it that makes humans human?"

Clip chimed in. "Obviously, you need the closest relative. The delta between that species' genome and our own is what makes humans human."

"Exactly. Our closest living relatives, the chimps and bonobos, are really quite distant in an evolutionary sense. Thus the need to sequence the genome of our closest cousins, the Neanderthals. It's the differences between their genome and ours—differences that are truly unique to man—that tells us what man is."

"And the answer?" asked Leo.

"Well, turns out we're not so special, at least quantitatively. Out of a genome consisting of roughly three billion base pairs, only about a hundred thousand base pair positions are different. It turns out the genetic recipe for making a modern human is not so long."

"Professor, can't we look at it the other way around?" Clip asked. "I mean, you're also saying there aren't so many edits needed to make a Neanderthal."

"That's not what this is about. The interesting thing isn't the differences in the genome, it's the differences in the phenotype—what *traits* are uniquely human? One thing is clear, it's not the story we've told ourselves for years. It's not intelligence or language, for example. Neanderthals had both. And, by the way, not all of the differences run in our favor. Humans lack a gene Neanderthals had that allows wounds to heal faster. We're only at the very beginning of correlating the differences in the genomes to actual traits. But eventually, it'll give us the full picture of what it is to be a human."

"Dude, what the fuck is the point of that?" Playg had been looking bored and distracted, fidgeting in his chair, and not even trying to put on a façade of deference to one of the most respected scientists in the world. The Brazilian professor gave the young man an incredulous look, and then addressed Leo.

"In answering 'what is man?' we expect to illuminate some of the greatest mysteries of the human genome. The ALU sequence, for example, or the role of genetic dark matter."

Clip interjected. "Professor, I've read you've achieved fifty times coverage from a 130,000-year-old toe bone. It's an awesome accomplishment."

Silva smiled. "Remarkable, yes? In our public tours we ask them to imagine a thousand copies of *Bleak House* having been shredded in a wood chipper. You don't have an intact copy of *Bleak House* to refer to, but you somehow have to take all those fragments and figure out how they fit together to make a single book. And of course that's not to mention the fact that scrambled into the mix together with the Neanderthal fragments are the DNA from the hands of the anthropologist who dug it up, the museum curators who cared for the skeleton, and even, despite all our efforts, DNA from the janitor who cleaned the lab the night before."

"I'd like the boys here to see your lab and meet some of your team," Leo said. "Would that be possible?"

Two postdocs arrived to escort Clip and Playg to the lab, leaving Leo and Silva alone in the professor's office.

"My question, Rafael, is whether your work on ALU and dark matter is adequately funded. If it's not, I can help."

Silva looked relieved. "Leo, it's not. And I couldn't be more thrilled that you understand its importance."

"Write a proposal," Leo said. "You'll get what you need. The only condition is that your results are shared with SBD before publication."

Silva was effusive in expressing his appreciation. In a way that suggested that the business part of the meeting was over, Leo waived off the thanks and asked, "And what about your work on other extinct mammals. That continuing?"

"Not really. We did the mammoth, ground sloth, and marsupial wolf, and also the Tasmanian tiger, before turning to Neanderthals. I really focus on hominins now."

"Are you following Chatterjee and Vargas? I was at 'Revive and Restore' in DC a few weeks ago. What do you make of what they're up to? After all, your work in large part made it possible."

"Their work is driving some great technical advances, especially in editing. No question. I don't really have a problem with it. Not sure I entirely buy the ecological argument, but it really doesn't matter. If some of the traits that we lost when the ice-age mammals went extinct could be useful, then let's bring them back. Why not?"

"I find the ecological argument pretty convincing," Leo replied. "But we shouldn't bring these animals back unless we have someplace to put them, someplace they fit in." Leo paused, in part to see if word of Arcadia had leaked out to Silva. When Silva said nothing, he continued. "But to be frank, one or two megafauna aren't enough. We need to scale up and do more. More complex animals, and de-extinction feats that will really capture the imagination of the public."

"Hmm. Could be," Silva replied, "but my advice is to go slow. You remember what happened in 2010, when my Neanderthal genome paper came out in *Science*? Same day, I was doing a lecture in your country, at Vanderbilt. The paper had been released only hours before, but already there were threats against my life. The university insisted that two armed guards accompany me everywhere. You would know better than I, Leo, but these people have real power. Not only in America, but also here in Europe. Their goal is to shut us down. Shut down all of it."

"Why you?"

"Why me? Because of the Neanderthal. It undermines everything they believe about the uniqueness of man—man being made in God's image, or, even if they're not creationists, modern humans somehow as the final climax and end point of evolution. And they think my work is the first step toward Neanderthal de-extinction. They say it's a slippery slope."

"And isn't it?" Leo asked. "Aren't they right about that part?"

The Brazilian cocked his head, surprised. "Absolutely not. Just because we know the recipe for making a Neanderthal, it doesn't mean we should. And besides, de-extincting a Neanderthal almost certainly can't be done right now as a technical matter."

"You think Vargas is wrong?" Leo asked. "Remember when he told the *New York Times* he could bring a Neanderthal to life with present technology for only $30 million?"

"Yeah, and a few years later he also told *Le Monde* that he was confident he would see the birth of a Neanderthal baby in his lifetime. Vargas is a genius at publicity and raising money for his lab. But sometimes he goes too far. Remember what happened next?"

"What, after the interview in France?"

"Yeah. Later that year, in one of the London tabloids, a picture of a pleasant-looking Neanderthal and that headline, what was it? Something like 'Cornell professor seeks mom for cloned cave baby'?"

The two men laughed.

"And you know what?" Silva added, "José told me he heard from hundreds of women who wanted to volunteer."

Leo turned serious. "Rafael, I have to say, I think José is right about one thing. He says that deciding *not* to proceed when we have the technology to do it may seem like the safe course, but that too is a risky decision. We're being offered a way to increase human genetic diversity that could end up saving the species. He's right. Neanderthal cognitive abilities and other traits could prove important."

Silva stopped smiling. "It's a red flag to a bull," he said. "An unnecessary distraction. We don't know the phenotypes associated with most of the edits we'd be making, and we can't do it without making potentially catastrophic editing errors. And that matters, Leo, because we're not talking about a mountain goat here, we're talking about a hominin—a sentient, intelligent type of human. Besides, you'd never be allowed to do it in the US or Europe. Even China; look how they reacted to He Jiankui, and that was for a legitimate medical purpose. So why get people all riled up?"

"It's a big world," Leo said, realizing that he would not get what he wanted here in Leipzig.

Silva shook his head. "Remember this, Leo. We should never lose sight of the distinction between what a scientist can do and what a scientist ought to do."

Leo answered without hesitation. "And my view, my friend, is that 'ought' is not the province of science—only 'is' and 'can' and 'will.'" Before Silva could answer, Leo continued, "But enough of that. I'm eager to see your labs."

Silva led Leo through a maze of hallways while the two men gossiped cordially about former colleagues of the professor who now worked for SBD. Finally, Silva opened a plain stainless-steel door and ushered Leo into a large lab lit mainly by natural light from a bank of windows along one side of the room. The walls and ceilings were painted a high-gloss bright white. Counter-to-ceiling white shelving hosted ranks of sparkling beakers and other glassware. The well-groomed techs wore immaculate white lab coats. Clip and Playg, incongruously unshaven and dressed in bright colors, stood with a group of scientists clustered in front of the window to watch some sort of commotion outside.

"And what is happening here?" Silva asked.

"Another demo," one of the techs answered in a British accent.

A group of about twenty protesters milled around the road in front of the institute building, carrying placards and shouting. The group took up a rhythmic chant in German, "*Du bist nicht Gott. Du bist nicht Gott.*"

"It means, 'You're not God,'" Silva explained. "We get this almost every week."

Leo peered out the window and was bemused to see that one of the German demonstrators held a sign with a picture of Pastor Joe. He locked eyes with the man, who abruptly turned to the side and hurled a softball-size piece of paving stone directly at Leo. Silva and the lab techs all ducked as the stone bounced off the plate glass with an alarming crash. Leo did not flinch. He looked down at the stone thrower with a smirk.

On the plane heading back to Portland, when Clip was in the lavatory, Playg sat down next to Leo. "He was a fucking wimp, man. Typical big bio, all that shiny equipment and not using it for shit.

Sure, sequencing the caveman genome, that was slick. But you heard him, now he's not doing squat. I know what you want, Leo, and you and I both know you won't get it from him." Leo leaned back in his large leather seat. Playg leaned forward. "But I know where to go, man. I know who will do it."

9
Agnes

MUIR SHUT THE DOOR to his house, closing the chapter of his life that had been both the most joyous and the most painful. He was not a man who invested his emotions in objects. It was just a house, and he and Lilith were now leaving it to make a new life.

Lilith fussed and cried when the SBD helicopter rose noisily from the tarmac at Boise's airport, but she soon settled down and pressed her nose to the window. The first time Muir had flown to Arcadia he had sat awkwardly across from a stranger knowing almost nothing about his destination. And now, crossing into Oregon from the east, he was heading back to Arcadia to work for the same man, with whom he now shared a peculiar sort of intimacy.

When the copter settled gently onto the pad, a solitary figure stood off to the side, clutching her wide-brimmed straw hat against the wash of the rotors. Looking through the aircraft window, Muir guessed she was about forty. She wore a crisply pressed cambric-blue cotton dress with a square neck and pleated skirt over a plain white blouse. Her smile was as warm as her dress was severe. Muir guessed correctly that this was Agnes, the nanny hired to care for Lilith.

A month before, someone from SBD called Muir to tell him about the woman they had selected. She was a registered nurse with a background in pediatric medicine. About a dozen years before, she had been recruited to serve as nanny to the four children of a Portland family made rich by a fortuitous tech investment. This family had given her enthusiastic references. SBD's investigators reported that Agnes had separated from her husband after three years of a childless marriage. She switched from nursing to the nanny position shortly after the divorce. She had not dated since assuming her position, and did not drink or use drugs. She attended a Presbyterian church a couple of times a month, but there was no evidence of fervent religiosity or any particular ideological conviction. Did Muir approve? He did.

When the rotors finally drifted to a stop, Muir descended the steps with Lilith in his arms.

"Mr. O'Brien, I'm Agnes. And this must be Lilith."

Shaking her hand, Muir insisted that she call him Muir.

"May I?" Agnes scooped Lilith into her arms. The little girl stared at her face, sniffed curiously at her chest, and then sweetly rested her cheek on Agnes's shoulder.

An Arcadia security officer, far friendlier than the pair who had intercepted Muir during his first visit, drove the three of them on an electric cart through the Village to a low-slung concrete structure tucked back into a rocky slope. Its thickly planted flat roof appeared from the end like a bushy eyebrow perched over the curving glass façade that overlooked Lake Arcadia. Although scores of similar structures were clustered around it, dense planting ensured privacy. Before entering the house, Muir stopped and gazed at the long lake and slowly inhaled the sage- and pine-tinged air.

Inside, the house appeared plain and modern, foregoing any attempt to compete with the beauty of the sweeping lake views that dominated most of its rooms. Agnes explained that she occupied a separate apartment at the rear of the house, with a direct entrance into Lilith's bedroom from her own.

"Want to see the playroom, sweetheart?" Agnes said.

Lilith squealed with delight as they entered what looked like a nursery school classroom. Multicolored soft foam cubes were stacked neatly on a bright carpet, woven with the letters of the alphabet. Lilith, staring at the dozens of other toys arranged carefully in all corners of the room, struggled to be released from Agnes's arms. Agnes set her down and the little girl dashed from toy to toy, exploring this newfound cornucopia of treasure. The first time she fell, Agnes moved forward to help and comfort, but the little girl picked herself up without a whimper and carried on her exploration.

"Mr. Bonelli is an unusually generous man, but," she said, lowering her voice, "he doesn't really understand very much about children. As you can see, it's all a bit too much. Too much for a single child. I explained that to Mr. . . . to Leo, but he insisted that we leave it as is for your arrival and allow you to decide."

Agnes chose a small stuffed elephant and put it in front of the girl. Lilith tilted her head and considered the object. She then turned away, choosing her own toy, a simple wooden puzzle. Ignoring the two adults, she sat and worked with a determined squint to fit each piece into the appropriately shaped hole.

"I'm sorry," Muir said. "She doesn't like to be told what to do. You'll find she's a real handful."

"Nothing to apologize for," said Agnes. "She's just a child." They watched as the little girl solved the puzzle, dumped out the pieces, and started again.

"She's so beautiful, Muir," Agnes said. "Her skin tone is . . . well, not quite what I would expect. Was her mother . . . ?"

Muir was taken aback, as few people had the presumption, or perhaps it was the courage, to raise a subject that might imply uncertainty about the racial or ethnic identity of his daughter. He laughed to assure Agnes that he did not consider this to be an awkward subject.

"Her mother's family was Welsh, and of course the O'Briens are Irish. So out comes Lilith looking nothing like either parent. Go figure."

Agnes again studied the little girl. "Lots of things skip a generation or two, you know. It must have been quite a mix to create such beauty."

Agnes turned back to face Muir, suddenly efficient, even brusque. "Muir, I want you to know that I will love your daughter and I will protect her as if she were my own. You must never doubt that."

Muir seemed embarrassed. "Of course, Agnes. I don't doubt it, and . . . and I appreciate it very much. This is all quite new for me."

"OK, then." Agnes sat down on the floor next to Lilith. Muir walked out to the terrace, emerging just as Leo and Polly, riding together in the same electric cart, pulled up in front of the house.

Leo shook Muir's hand rather stiffly and introduced him to Polly. Leo, who had not told Polly about the bear attack and how Muir had saved his life, now worried that Muir might mention it, provoking an argument with Polly. He didn't know that Muir had decided he could never again mention the incident, lest Leo think he was being reminded of a debt.

"I'm so grateful to both of you," Muir said. "This is a new start for Lilith and me."

Polly smiled and shook Muir's hand.

Hearing the arrival of Leo and Polly, Agnes emerged from the house with Lilith in her arms. When Muir didn't say it, she did. "Mr. . . . Leo—and Polly—I want you to meet Lilith. Lilith, darling, say hello to Leo and Polly."

The little girl looked directly at the two adults, smiled, and waved her pudgy hand. Polly smiled warmly and planted a kiss on her cheek. "Hello, sweetheart," she said. "Welcome to Arcadia. It'll be so nice to have more children around here."

Muir noticed a slight hardening of Leo's face. Muir and Agnes exchanged glances. "Time to clean up after the trip," Agnes said. "Let's go inside, shall we, dear?" When she entered the house with Lilith in her arms, the little girl twisted around, still staring and waving at Polly.

Leo turned to Muir. "Muir, everything OK? House OK? You approve of Agnes?"

"Leo, the house is perfect. My gosh, the view. The playroom for Lilith, really, thank you. And Agnes seems wonderful."

"Great. You'll see, you'll come to love it here. Everything is calibrated for . . ."

Polly interrupted. "It is beautiful, but you must forgive my husband, Muir. He will try to reengineer your life if you let him. He can't help himself."

Before Leo could respond, Muir said, "I'm dying to see the lab and meet the botany and hort teams. To get to work."

"Then come on," Leo said. He slid into the driver's side of the cart and beckoned for Muir to join him. As soon as Muir swung his feet inside, Leo floored the pedal and the vehicle sped silently away.

Polly was left standing in front of the house. She could see Agnes and the little girl through the large window. She took a step in that direction but stopped. She then turned and watched the cart carrying her husband and Muir speed up the hill. She became acutely aware of her hands hanging awkwardly at her side. Moving with jerky indecision, her hands first found the pockets of her skirt, then crossed over her chest, and finally dropped again to her thighs. With a deep breath and slight thrust of the chin, she started walking slowly up the hill.

10
100,000 Nucleotides

When you see something that is technically sweet, you go ahead and do it, and you argue about what to do about it only after you have had your technical success. That is the way it was with the atomic bomb.

—Robert J. Oppenheimer (1954)

DR. SHEN," LEO SAID, "I just want you to know that I think you've been treated terribly unfairly. Really, what they did to you was just inexcusable."

Leo could not have chosen a more public place for this most private conversation. The Fullerton Bay Hotel thrust pier-like into Marina Bay at the heart of Singapore, a blue-tinged glass box that gave an impression of complete transparency. Guests passed down a long arcade, the reception desk at the far end framed in a sort of black proscenium arch. Along the edges, bathed in light from a high slanting wall of glass, Singapore's elite sipped *kopi* or scotch while gossiping, transacting business, or both. Leo had a rule: Sneaking around is what attracts attention; do your business in public, and people will think you have nothing to hide.

The professor seated on the black armchair across from Leo once had been China's leading geneticist. He was convinced that, had he been working in the West, his long string of innovations would have led to fame and riches. But in the Chinese academy, the nail that sticks up gets hammered down. The more his research advanced, the more jealous his colleagues became, and the more the hated bureaucracy scrutinized his work. All this came to a head when Shen identified the genetic mutation responsible for osteogenesis imperfecta, a fatal bone disease commonly known as OI, and modified human embryos in an attempt to correct the mutation. It was a technical triumph but the last straw for the Chinese government, which was not prepared to endure the inevitable accusation that it was engaging in eugenics. Shen was fired by his university and banned from conducting genetic research in China. Having no other way to continue his life's work, he emigrated with much of his team to Singapore. He was luckier than his colleague He Jiankui, whose modification of embryonic twins to protect them from the AIDS virus landed him in prison.

Leo admired the scrappy little city-state of Singapore. It represented the perfect balance between order and freedom, showing the world that a high degree of collective responsibility for the public welfare was possible without stifling innovation and entrepreneurship. It was no surprise that a scientist like Shen would be tolerated, even supported, in Singapore.

"Mr. Leo, sir, thank you for your understanding. It means a great deal to know that you appreciate and endorse my research."

"Any serious scientist thinks the same," Leo answered. "But for me it's also personal. Did you know, Dr. Shen, that my sister Mia died of OI when I was seven?"

"Oh, Mr. Leo. I am so sorry. It is a difficult death, especially for a child."

"Yes. You can imagine, when I found that you had started your embryonic editing with mutations in the COL1A1 and 2 genes, well, it seemed like destiny for us to meet."

"Indeed so! We Chinese have an expression, it is *yuanfen* that has brought us together, without a doubt."

"You can understand why I—in particular—was astonished and disappointed that your important work was not valued in China. Of course, there are details that must be worked out as we start editing embryonic cells, but it seems to me that the academicians there just must not see the big picture."

"You are right, sir. That is it."

Leo put down his coffee cup and leaned in. "They don't get that after four billion years of evolution by natural selection, we've entered the era of intelligent design. The future of life on the planet, especially human life, is now whatever we decide it should be. Do you think I go too far?"

"No, I agree," Shen said, scanning the lobby nervously.

"Expecting someone?" Leo asked.

Shen turned back to Leo and grinned awkwardly. "Sorry. I am often followed. Even here."

"What are you working on now?"

"You may remember that back in Guangzhou the number of surviving embryos in which the edits were successful was disappointingly low. Too many off-target mutations. I am very proud to say that our numbers have improved greatly, only a 2 percent failure rate now. Still too high, of course, for therapeutic use. I have no doubt that we will get there, but our funding is not adequate. Mr. Leo, sir, I need money."

Leo liked the frankness of the Chinese.

"Is the Singapore government supporting you?"

"No."

"Then . . ."

Shen again turned to look over his shoulder and stared for a few moments at a Chinese couple who sat down on the other side of the room. In a lower voice, he answered, "We have our own source of funds."

Leo waited in silence for the explanation.

"Mr. Leo, you know, I suppose, something about Chinese parents? Our typical customer harvests between ten and twenty eggs from the wife. These are fertilized in vitro by the husband's sperm. The resulting zygotes are sent to our lab here. We sequence each and send a report. Of course it includes known hereditary diseases and the simple things, gender, hair and eye color, and so forth." Shen hesitated, and then continued. "You may be surprised how much more we can now tell them: intelligence, athletic disposition, that kind of thing. Expressed in terms of probability, of course. They choose the zygote they want, which is returned to China and implanted in the woman's womb. We charge each couple about $200,000 US."

"Impressive. And I suppose some of those parents come back and ask for edits?"

"Of course they do. And why not? It's only natural. Let's say zygote number 12 has all the traits the client wants, except, say, for height. They come back and ask if we could just edit that one thing, to fix the height." Shen laughed nervously, then sighed. "As you know, height is a polygenetic trait, so it may be a while before we can fix that."

"But if you could make the fix, would you?" Leo asked.

Shen's chair creaked as he shifted his weight and crossed his legs.

"I'm sure you agree, Mr. Leo, that human embryonic editing is inevitable."

Leo nodded.

"It will start with single-gene disorders. Then we will move on to polygenetic disease, and in time the accuracy of our edits will mean that the risks are no greater than those of many other approved therapies. You agree?"

"Of course."

"So it really comes down to heritability. To the germ line question," Shen continued. "It is totally, what's the word . . . hysterical, to say that every time we edit a germ line cell we are somehow permanently changing humanity. It is just not so. It would be no different from any other germ line mutation—natural selection will decide whether or not it is a good thing for humanity."

"Right," Leo said. "Once the accuracy is good enough, or at least it's a level of risk that someone is willing to tolerate, would you do an edit on a viable embryo?"

"Of course I would like to. But . . . no, not quite yet. There would be too much pressure, even here in Singapore." Shen looked squarely at Leo. "I need money, Mr. Leo. I hope that is why you are here."

Leo did not react.

"I want $3 million a year, no strings attached. You give it to me and SBD gets an exclusive license on my OI therapies and any other therapies that result. If you do not do this, Mr. Leo, I will have to try to make the same deal with one of your competitors."

"Really?" Leo said, briefly annoyed.

As the professor waited, Leo sat back in his seat and stared at his coffee, as if considering the matter.

"Is $3 million really enough?" Leo leaned forward. "Professor. I'm impressed by your work. I know how expensive it is to run a lab of your sophistication. I hope you might agree to accept $5 million. And also to help me with one or two other little projects that might come up from time to time."

Shen looked warily at Leo and then broke into a smile. "OK, then, five."

While their coffee was being refreshed, the two men chatted about their mutual admiration for Singaporean culture.

"Mr. Leo," Shen said when the waiter had departed, "one more thing. This has to be our secret. No one must know that you are paying me or the amount. If the Chinese government found out . . ."

"Of course, I had assumed as much. I'm good at keeping secrets."

"And one more thing. Forgive me for asking, but I was surprised that the request for this meeting came to me through a man like Hop."

"Hop?"

"He's the acquaintance of your Mr. Playg. A young Malaysian. It is true that I have used him for one-off assignments, but his reputation . . . well, it presents certain complications . . ."

"I understand," Leo interrupted. "These youngsters bring a certain energy to our field that I find our more established scientists sometimes lack."

Again Shen scanned the room nervously. Leo wondered if his paranoia might be indicative of some broader personality disorder. Paranoiacs could be dangerous.

"What I need to know is whether you contemplate that Hop, or Mr. Playg, or, well, others like them, will play any role in the work we do going forward, because my position here in Singapore is somewhat delicate . . ."

"No, not at all. You won't see or hear from them again. Not to worry."

Leo, who had flown nonstop the eight thousand miles from Portland to Singapore, abruptly felt that draining away of energy that was symptomatic of jetlag, a problem to which he had assigned a team at SBD and which, to his frustration, they had failed to crack. For now, Leo—like any other long-haul traveler—downed the rest of the coffee in his cup and hoped he would not make a serious blunder, especially as the critical part of the meeting was yet to come.

"Have you been following what's happening with de-extinction?" he asked Shen casually.

"Oh yes. Most interesting. An innovative use for editing that should help to drive the technology forward."

"Have you been doing anything in this area?"

"Our team is focused on the human genome. But modification from the non-extinct to the extinct genome is exactly the sort of editing at which, if I can say this without being immodest, my team is the best in the world. Someday China will rue what it has given up."

"You're not being immodest. And how about the Neanderthal? That's a hominin genome, a type of human. Right in your sweet spot."

Shen again shifted in his chair and moved closer to Leo.

"It is something I have . . . thought about. It might be an interesting first step, to prove up the editing on a hominin other than *sapiens*. Only one hundred thousand nucleotides if you start with the human genome. I can do that today, assuming we had the money to at least double the size of our team. And a few months from now, I will be able to do it with an order of magnitude better accuracy."

"That's the key, I think," Leo said. "How much better?"

"My team is already using CRISPR with less than one error per three trillion base pairs. I am convinced that very soon we'll have virtually no off-target mutations. So yes, I think we could do it. And do it better and faster than Chatterjee, Vargas, or any of the others in your country."

"No doubt," said Leo. "And what about the ethical side? You have any concerns about doing a hominin such as the Neanderthal?"

Both men looked up as a large group of German-speaking tourists stopped right next to them, pointing excitedly out the windows at the casino across the bay, which resembled a giant boat hull held aloft by three skyscrapers. After they passed down the arcade, Shen answered the question.

"It would have to be done correctly. A Neanderthal would be intelligent. You would need someone committed to providing an appropriate place for it to live, and probably also make more than one so it had companionship. To eliminate questions about the risks of it reproducing, I would give it an uneven number of chromosomes, you know, so it would be sterile, like a mule. And you would obviously need to allow it some degree of self-determination if it survives to adulthood. But . . ." He paused. "I do not see any issue regarding the decision to bring it into existence in the first place.

After all, Mr. Leo, none of us gives permission to our parents to bring us into the world."

"Quite right."

"And, I should have said, I would not actually start with human DNA as the base genome to be edited. It would seem to the world too much like human cloning, which would be unnecessarily provocative. Instead, I would start with chimp DNA, which is mostly the same."

"Really?" Leo asked. "That's a lot of additional DNA to edit. Neanderthals are so much closer to humans. I always assumed you'd start with a human."

"Using chimp DNA would be harder, no doubt, perhaps ten times more edits, but it would be doable. Besides, if you went with human DNA, whose genotype would you use? Who would allow themselves to be, in essence, duplicated as a Neanderthal? No, it's really unthinkable. If someone does it, they will start with chimp DNA, I am sure of it."

"I see. Perhaps you're right. If it's OK with you, Professor Shen, I might want to . . ." Leo hesitated to find the right word, ". . . pursue this further. Would you mind if I got back in touch?"

Shen smiled warmly. "But of course. Please do."

"And I know," Leo added, "that I can count on you to keep our conversations in absolute confidence?"

"Of course."

Leo decided there was no reason to stay the night in Singapore. He headed straight back to the airport. He wouldn't mind the long flight. There was a lot to think about and Leo did some of his best thinking on planes.

11
Parthenogenesis

Did I request thee, Maker, from my clay
To mould me Man, did I solicit thee
From darkness to promote me?

MILTON, *PARADISE LOST*, QUOTED ON THE TITLE PAGE OF MARY SHELLEY, *FRANKENSTEIN; OR, THE MODERN PROMETHEUS*

DESPITE THE CONTRACTIONS, NOW in their third hour, Amina was the calmest person in the small bedroom of her Andalucían farmhouse. This was her eleventh delivery in as many years. There were the five children with whom she and her husband Hamid were blessed. And since her dear Hamid had passed, she had given birth as a surrogate mother about once a year, each time bestowing the blessing of a child on a new couple. Amina Ayala loved how she looked and felt with a child in her womb. Rising at dawn to feed the animals, she felt a special solidarity with the does, ewes, and sows who, like Amina, were pregnant more often than not.

In addition to her favorite midwife, Amina permitted the baby's biological parents to attend the birth. The midwife now worried that the baby's head was not yet in the ideal position. The parents, simple farmers from a village in the next valley, looked anxious. Amina knew that everything was fine and told them all to relax. Surrogacy remained illegal in Spain, so arrangements were informal, with women like Amina taking on couples from surrounding towns and villages. Amina's reputation for smooth pregnancies and easy births extended throughout the region, resulting in a long waiting list of potential clients. The modest fees paid for her services had allowed her to keep the farm after her husband's death and pay for the hired man whose help was needed until the children were older.

Amina's instincts were correct. Within the hour the baby, her head perfectly positioned, emerged smoothly. The midwife snipped, cleaned, and swaddled, and handed the baby to its genetic mother. Amina did not look at the newborn, but instead fixed her own gaze on the face of the mother. She never tired of seeing the ecstatic joy that was her gift to the other woman. She watched for that moment when the miracle of maternal love rose from somewhere deep within and attached itself to the tiny creature handed to the woman only moments before. The parents, with tearful expressions of gratitude, left the room and returned home. Amina usually returned to her chores on the farm within a few days, feeling empty and daydreaming about her next pregnancy.

The Ayala family had farmed this hillside patch of the Andalucían countryside for many generations. Its soils weren't the most fertile and its ancient olive trees weren't the most productive, but—as Hamid told his children—this place is in our blood, and our blood is in this place. The house and farm buildings, once bright stucco white and now a mottled gray-brown, clustered midway up a small hill. A sweeping field of sunflowers painted the foreground bright yellow, and rows of olive trees, like beads draped carefully over the spine of the ridge, striped the dry soils with a muted green. In pens close to the house, goats, sheep, and Amina's beloved black pigs sought the shade of almond and fig trees. Thus it had always been. No irrigation. No cereal crops. No organic certification. No hoop houses growing exotic berries and fruits for city folks. The man from the bank that held the mortgage drove up the hill in his black Fiat several times each year. He didn't know about Amina's surrogacy income and could not understand how the widow of Hamid Ayala was making ends meet. The bank wanted its collateral modernized, but Amina was determined not to change a thing.

One morning, about a month after her most recent delivery, Amina's son ran excitedly to the barn to tell her they had a visitor from America.

* * *

The A Wing of the medical center at Arcadia was off-limits to all personnel without a special pass. Only a handful of employees knew that A Wing hosted a sterile birthing room, clad in a special composite of stainless steel developed by SBD for its resistance to contamination. Imaging equipment and monitors surrounded the hospital bed in the room's center. The facility's designers had started with the gear found in a state-of-the-art obstetric intensive care unit and then added a half dozen other pieces of diagnostic and therapeutic equipment custom-crafted for the extraordinary circumstances of this pregnancy. A one-way glass wall allowed the occupants of an adjacent room to observe the proceedings. In addition to Professor Shen, nearly a dozen doctors, nurses, and technicians in surgical scrubs stood around the table. Agnes, similarly dressed, stood at the side of the bed and held Amina's hand.

Everyone in the room that day had been carefully vetted by Leo, and none more so than Amina herself. SBD's team had surveyed the average percentages of Neanderthal DNA in populations around the world, attempting to disentangle the influence of the Denisovans, another ancient hominin that mated with *Homo sapiens*. The team found dozens of Neanderthal DNA hot spots, but none more promising than Spanish Andalucía, where a few individuals were found to possess three times the normal range of 1.8-2.6 percent Neanderthal DNA, and where genomes were unusually diverse due to the area's history of occupation by Carthaginians, Romans, Vandals, Visigoths, and Moors. No one knew whether this would affect the odds of the embryo taking and growing to term, but all agreed it couldn't hurt. So SBD agents arrived in Andalucía, did their homework, and learned about Amina's reputation as a surrogate. Amina and two other women agreed to come to Granada for a day of medical testing. The team was thrilled with what the tests revealed about Amina: 5.85 percent Neanderthal DNA, a pelvic inlet large enough to pass a head nearly 40 percent larger than that of a normal human infant, soft ligaments that allowed the four joints of the pelvis to fold as easily as an elbow, and back muscles like those of a boxer. They really had no idea what challenges this delivery would present, but if any *sapiens* woman could handle such a birth, it was Amina Ayala.

Initially, Amina was reluctant to leave her farm and family. But Amina agreed to an extended stay in Oregon after Leo's people made it clear that, if she did, the farm's future would be secured and her children's education fully funded.

It was not an easy pregnancy. From the earliest days, Amina felt that something was off. The fetus fussed and Amina's body seemed to struggle uncharacteristically to accommodate its presence. Six weeks before the due date, she developed symptoms of an immune system reaction, which the team suppressed with drugs. After that, they required her to spend most of her time in bed. Agnes, who spoke serviceable Spanish, came to visit every afternoon and encouraged Amina to tell her all about the farm and children. These chats, together with pictures sent daily by her family via Facebook, made her confinement in this distant and strange place tolerable.

And now, finally, her labor started. Hers were typically fast and easy, but these contractions had begun over twelve hours ago. The doctors, huddled around the various monitors that circled the bed, repeatedly adjusted the position of her pelvis using electronic controls and small hard foam wedges. After the obstetrician announced "twelve centimeters," he told Amina to push. Usually a few hard pushes were all she needed. But this time, she was told to push only when instructed, and to take long rests in between.

After a couple of hours of this, the doctor in charge nodded toward the glass and said, "Now." Leo had ordered that, in the absence of a medical emergency for which their help was needed, the assembled team should not be permitted to see the child that emerged. Within seconds, only Agnes, still holding Amina's hand, Shen, standing to one side, and the obstetrician, peering between her legs, remained in the room.

When the baby finally emerged, he reminded Amina of the almost five-kilo giant she had brought into the world a few years ago. The doctor was facing her as he picked up the infant from between her legs. Amina saw him recoil before he quickly turned away with the infant in his arms. Taking the child, Agnes said, "Yes, Doctor, some babies are downright ugly, but they're all beautiful in the eyes of God, and their parents don't love them one iota less. Nor do I—he's an angel."

When the wrapped baby was settled in a high-tech cart and wheeled into the adjacent laboratory, Agnes turned to Amina. "Don't worry, dear. He's perfectly normal, a healthy baby boy. You did great." Then, turning toward the one-way window, she asked in English, "So, Leo, what shall we call him?"

The intercom crackled to life and Leo's disembodied voice came out of speakers in the ceiling.

"His name is Ned."

12
What Child Is This?

His flesh, his bone; to give thee being I lent
Out of my side to thee, nearest my heart
Substantial Life, to have thee by my side
Henceforth an individual solace dear;
Part of my Soul I seek thee, and thee claim
My other half . . .

MILTON, *PARADISE LOST* IV, 482 488

THE ALARM ON HER phone reminded Polly that it was time for her weekly tea with Leo. Looking up from the draft of her paper on the P vs. NP problem, Polly shifted her gaze to the verdant stand of ferns outside her office window and smiled. She now spent most of her time at Arcadia in a private office that faced away from the lake. She had been surprised and touched when Muir offered to create a special garden designed to be viewed from her desk.

"I want to do a math garden for you," Muir had said. "But frankly, I don't know where to start."

"How about the Barnsley fern?" Polly had suggested.

"Oh gosh, I can't believe . . . um. Polly, I confess, I've never heard of it."

Muir had looked so upset that Polly couldn't help laughing. "And why would you? It's not a plant, it's a computer-generated pattern resulting from a type of fractal equation known as an iterated function system. And it looks exactly like a fern."

"Oh." Muir smiled broadly. "OK, then. I'll research it and see if I can find a plant that's close."

Two weeks later, Polly had returned to her office to find a sweeping stand of *Asplenium adiantum-nigrum* newly planted outside her window. On close inspection, she was amazed to find that the fronds closely matched one of the mutations of the Barnsley fern fractal. She found them beautiful, and not only because the complex geometry of the plant could be described by a simple equation.

Leo's weekly meetings with Polly were now held in the main room of their house in the Village at Arcadia. Leo had positioned two club chairs by a glass wall that framed sweeping views of the lake. He now spent little time at the house in Portland, and Polly also preferred to come to Arcadia between her periodic stays in England.

"Pol, I hope you don't mind my asking, but have you had any luck? I mean, your decision to have a child." Just over a year had passed since Polly told Leo of her intentions.

Polly tried hard to give the impression that the emotionally fraught topic was nothing more than a household detail. She did not want Leo to sense her despair.

"No luck. And, to be honest, I'm out of options. I've tried every fertility strategy and therapy. And," she added, staring straight at her husband, "the sperm of a dozen different men."

Leo took a sip of his tea. "SBD has some experimental techniques. Would you like to . . ."

"Thank you, but no. Some things are just not meant to be."

A few moments later, Clip entered the room. Seeing Polly, he said, "Sorry, if this is not a good time . . ." Clip's dress had improved. He now wore jeans and a T-shirt, sneakers instead of flip-flops, and had abandoned the woolen watch cap.

Polly gave him a smile. "No problem, Clip. Come in."

Clip handed Leo a single piece of paper, which Leo signed and returned. Clip left the room.

"It's nice to see him grow up a bit. Maybe you weren't entirely wrong about Clippy."

Leo did not respond.

"But, Leo, someone's got to tell you. Everyone here loathes Playg. Everyone. I just don't understand how you can . . ."

Leo interrupted. "He's gone."

"Gone?"

"Gone. I fired him last week. He's moved to Malaysia. You'll never see him again."

"Let's hope. It was a mistake from the beginning, Leo." Leo didn't answer. Polly, knowing her husband, suspected he hadn't changed his mind, but rather that Playg must have served his purpose and thus was no longer needed.

And Leo decided not to tell her that FBI agents had come to SBD's Portland offices to interview Leo about Playg. The agents had intercepted coded messages between Playg and another hacker describing techniques for the modification of a mosquito to carry the same genes that enabled toxigenesis in bacteria. A bite from the modified insect would be lethal to humans. Although there were legitimate scientific reasons for this type of work, the agents feared terrorism. Leo assured them that this was not work sponsored or sanctioned by SBD and fired Playg the next day. Two days later, the FBI informed Leo that upon receiving their subpoena, Playg fled to Malaysia.

"Another thing, Leo," Polly said. "What's going on in A Wing at the medical center?"

"What do you mean?"

"You know exactly what I mean. It's on lockdown. They wouldn't let me in, told me I had the wrong kind of pass. We were partners, Leo. There was a time when you told me everything."

Ned had not left the laboratory complex since his birth, but Agnes visited A Wing daily, giving rise to rumors that a child was somehow involved in the mystery. Polly was determined to find out what was going on.

"An experiment," Leo answered.

"Don't dodge the question. There's a child. Why else would Agnes be involved? What in the world have you done?"

Leo set down his cup. "Well," he said, "you know we've got a long track record of doing plant de-extinctions. And now the same genetic editing improvements and cloning technologies are starting to bear fruit with higher-order organisms."

"Animals?"

"Yes, including animals. Arcadia's had success with some smaller mammals, and others, with our support, are working on the wooly mammoth and some other keystone species."

"For God's sake, Leo, are you really telling me that Agnes leaves Lilith and goes daily to the medical center to visit small mammals?"

"No. We've made a rather dramatic leap forward."

Polly started shaking her head slowly back and forth.

Leo finally looked her straight in the eye. "*Homo neanderthalensis*."

Polly froze. "What? A Neanderthal?"

"Yes. The complete Neanderthal genome was sequenced years ago. A geneticist in Singapore has advanced his editing to the point where it's practically error-free. I had him do the edits in Singapore, all perfectly legal. The zygote was implanted in a female surrogate, who gave birth to a healthy Neanderthal child right here in Arcadia."

"And the child . . ."

"His name is Ned."

"Was normal—I mean, other than being a Neanderthal? No editing errors, no mutations, no birth defects?"

"Too early to tell for sure, but nothing we've been able to discover during the past six months. He appears perfectly healthy."

"Dumb luck, Leo. Without trials . . ." Polly stopped short and rose from her chair. "Wait a second, what genome did you use as the base? It was from a chimp, right? Please tell me it was from a chimp."

"Pretty close. Why does it matter, when what comes out is a Neanderthal?"

"My God, tell me you didn't." The color drained from her face.

"Didn't what?"

"You used your own DNA, didn't you?"

Leo was silent.

"Oh my God, you did. Why should I even be surprised? Of course, it would have been absolutely irresistible. So the child is you, with the traits of a Neanderthal." She paused. "A freak with traits that disappeared forty millennia ago. How could you be so absolutely bloody stupid . . . so . . ."

Leo, who was watching the wind agitate the surface of the lake, interrupted.

"Probably more like thirty thousand years, not so long, really. And he is hardly a freak. After all, we've already seen a child with the DNA of three parents, you know, the mother, the father, and the woman who provided mitochondrial DNA instead of the mother. We'd better get used to it, Pol, pretty soon there'll be dozens of new models for reproduction."

But Polly was not listening. Instead, she was thinking about the infant child, confined to a laboratory in A Wing.

"He's a *baby*, Leo. He may not be *sapiens*, but he's a sentient, intelligent, emotional being. You can't keep him locked up in your lab like a mouse or a chimp. When people find out it'll be the end. Mark my words, Leo, the end. They'll shut down SBD, take your money, and send you to prison. Is that how you want to live your life?"

"He's not living like a lab rat. Agnes is looking after him. He'll be raised with Lilith and the other children. Educated, assuming that proves possible."

"And loved?"

"He'll have what he needs. I'm sorry you don't approve, but you're smart, and after a while you'll get it. It'll be fine. I've got to go, I'm late."

Polly remained seated as he left the room. As the door shut, she started to cry. Thoughts and worries tumbled across her mind in an uncharacteristic jumble. Polly didn't know whether she wept for herself, her husband, or the poor creature in A Wing.

* * *

Leo walked briskly across the Village toward the botany lab where Muir had his office.

Muir had refused a separate office, opting instead for a desk in a quiet corner of the large shed that housed the main tissue-cultivation lab. Instead of a window, his desk faced a wall of shelves covered with scores of small pots, each of which nurtured the seedling of a de-extincted Paleolithic plant. When he wasn't staring at the screen on his desk, he studied these fragile specimens with a sense of wonder undiminished by familiarity. The air in the large shed, although filtered for pathogens, retained the sweet smell of moist soil.

Freed from the normal constraints of budget and planning, Muir had engaged scores of paleobotanists from around the world and promised generous remuneration in return for sources of ancient plant DNA. Seeds and spores, frozen tissues, partially fossilized rinds, plant matter found in frozen animal feces and cadavers—all streamed into Arcadia. If material was identified as belonging to a taxon that was believed extinct and that might contribute to the genetic diversity of Arcadia, the paleogenetics lab set to work sequencing the genome and identifying the extinct plant's closest living relative. Once the modifications necessary to recreate the defining traits of the extinct plant had been identified, the main genetics lab set to work. At the end of the process, seeds, spores, and live tissues were delivered back to Muir's team of botanists, first for propagation in the nursery, and then for establishment in the wild.

When the seedlings of these plants first emerged, with leaf shapes, stem colors, textures, flowers, barks, and habits not seen on the planet for ten millennia, the result seemed to Muir to be a joyous miracle. His gut still led him to doubt that interfering with the natural course of evolution was wise. But as the specific so powerfully trumps the general, Muir's love for each resurrected species gradually displaced his doubts about the ambitions and tools that brought them to life. Once a plant existed, Muir argued to himself, it was entitled to a shot at survival. He came to believe that nurturing these resurrected life-forms, and solving the complex puzzle of how and where they fit into the ecosystem of Arcadia, was what he was meant to do.

Muir looked up to find Leo sitting down in the chair in front of his desk.

"Everything good?" Leo asked.

"Good," Muir replied. "On track. No new issues."

"Finding time to work on the dissertation?" Leo asked.

"Some. I have a weekly Skype with Professor Lewis on Fridays," he said. "In other words, a lot gets done on Thursday nights after Lilith is in bed."

Muir referred to his dissertation topic as "bottoms up." His thesis was that ecologists focused too much on the keystone species at the top of the ecological pyramid, whereas the right way to understand a robustly sustainable ecosystem was from the bottom up. Start with the soil bacteria and the mycorrhizal fungi necessary for plants to absorb nutrients. It was a theory he insisted on applying at Arcadia, where he asked the geneticists to give equal time to the ancient bacteria and fungi that, he was convinced, his resurrected plants would require in order to thrive.

"Lilith good?" Leo asked.

"Flourishing. But of course she misses Agnes."

"Oh?"

"After school. Agnes used to be there the whole time. Now Agnes is gone for a few hours every afternoon. You know, over at the medical center."

"Yes. I've been meaning to tell you. It's important to me that you understand."

"Understand what?"

"You've had your doubts about de-extinction, but now that you've seen it in action, you've got to admit, it's the most hopeful thing that's ever happened in the field of conservation biology."

"Maybe. But it doesn't mean we don't still have to be careful."

"Careful, perhaps. But not timid. That's the thing, Muir. You get excited about an extinct type of *Ginkgo*. But not the general public. We need something bolder, more exciting, something that makes people understand just how much we can do."

Leo paused. At the far end of the large room, about a half dozen workers in green aprons leaned over trays of seedlings, taking photographs and tissue samples. They stood too far away to overhear the conversation.

"Muir, what's the single biggest difference between the Paleolithic and now?"

"Difference? In what respect . . ."

"Multiple hominins," Leo continued. "The genus *Homo*, the keystone of keystones, whose brains would have a greater impact on nature than the dinosaurs, than anything that ever lived on the planet. The difference is that back then there wasn't just one type of human. We had the Denisovans, Neanderthals, *sapiens*—and there were probably more—all different types of humans wandering around at the same time, all with big brains, probably with different cognitive abilities and skills. Can we really restore the integrity of the planet without them?"

Muir remained silent, unsure of the implications of what he was hearing.

"What I'm saying is that *sapiens* didn't exterminate just the wildlife; one way or another we also got rid of the other types of humans. The other humans weren't deselected by evolution; they were deselected by us. So, to really undo the harm we've done, we need them back."

"You can't be serious."

"I want you to know, Muir. There's a baby in A Wing, a *Homo neanderthalensis* baby."

"You . . . you made a Neanderthal?" Muir had heard the rumors about A Wing but assumed that Leo had perhaps edited a human embryonic cell, presumably to eliminate a hereditary disease.

"Yes. Yes, I did."

"That was a mistake, Leo."

"He's completely healthy," Leo replied.

"That's not the point. It was wrong."

"It wasn't. His brain was the same size as a *sapiens* brain at birth, but it's already growing far more rapidly than in a human child. Think of what he might be. Think of what we'll learn. I'm disappointed in you, Muir. I expected your understanding and support."

Muir stood. "I don't understand, and I certainly don't support what you've done. I . . . I need to think about this." Muir's face betrayed the struggle to control his anger. "I think you should leave, Leo . . ."

Leo, his face flushed, stood and walked away. As he left the building, his watch blinked red to indicate a perfect storm of physiological anomalies. Skin conductivity, cortisol levels, respiration, blood pressure, and heart rate, all in the red zone.

PART II

NED

13

Ned's Journal, January 23

ON JULY 23 I'LL be 15. Last year Muir gave me this journal for my birthday and I still haven't used it. He hasn't asked me—Muir is too cool to do something like that. But still, I don't want to hurt his feelings. So here I am.

Today Muir told me that Sam, the giant armadillo from the nursery, was released to the wild. The first. I hope he makes it. Not like the family of ground sloths who all died. That was a bummer.

My friend Ting from the hort lab won the crew race on the lake. It was fun. He took Lilith and me to the diner afterward to celebrate.

I don't know, is this what you're supposed to write in a journal?

When he gave the journal to me last summer, he said I should write about my memories and also things that are important to me now. Well, why not say it? I love Lilith. I can't believe I just wrote that down. She doesn't know. No one knows. I think about her all the time and want to be with her. I saw Ankur Patel looking at her funny in math class today, and I didn't like it. He's a jerk.

What else is important to me? Other than Lilith? Agnes and Muir. My dad, of course. I want to see the world outside of Arcadia. Lilith goes out. So do all the kids, mostly to see their relatives. Dad says we don't have any relatives, which seems strange. But it doesn't matter. I still want to see outside. It's so unfair that he won't let me.

Do other people really write their most secret thoughts and feelings in their journals? I really can't quite believe they do.

OK, that's a start. Muir asked me yesterday what I wanted for my next birthday. I want to see the outside. Dad never asks what I want for my birthday, but maybe I should tell him.

All for now.

14
Kissing Cousins
(Ned, Age 5)

DURING THE YEAR FOLLOWING Ned's birth, Muir's relationship with Leo remained strained. But in time Muir's initial revulsion at the concept of hominin de-extinction—just like his doubts about the wisdom of bringing back ice-age plants—had abated, crowded out by his growing fondness for the little Neanderthal boy. The act that brought Ned to life may have been immoral, Muir thought, but the child, an utterly beguiling child, could hardly be blamed for his own existence. Eventually, Leo and Muir resumed their occasional hunting trips.

Polly responded to the news of Ned's birth by moving from the house she had shared with Leo to her own quarters up the hill on the fringes of the Village. She still returned to Arcadia between the short semesters spent performing her duties as a fellow at King's College, Cambridge.

Leo released Ned from A Wing about a year after his birth and delivered him into Agnes's care. She moved with Ned to a small house located right next door to Muir's. Agnes still looked after Lilith. As a result, for the past five years, Lilith and Ned had spent the better part of every day in each other's company.

The kindergarten classroom at Arcadia's primary school was as colorful and bright as any other, but there were differences. When SBD's architect was designing the structure to accommodate the children of Arcadia's growing population, Leo reminded her that kindergarten meant a garden for children and instructed her to blur the boundary between indoors and out. And so the normal pint-size tables and chairs were scattered in a greenhouse-like room, normally open on two sides, among a miniature landscape of tiny streams, ponds, patches of meadow, and small trees. Each child tended his or her own small bed of flowers and vegetables. Turtles, frogs, chipmunks, and even defanged snakes wandered freely.

As this was still an SBD facility, big hardware observed, recorded, quantified, and analyzed everything that happened at the school. And nowhere more so than the kindergarten in which Ned was a student. From behind mirrored glass, two paleoanthropologists observed the scene in front of them, taking notes the old-fashioned way while SBD's computers analyzed the video in real time, comparing Ned's behavior to every study ever published about *sapiens* children of the same age.

The little boy they observed was not so little. Ned stood at the same height as the other children, but everything else about him was larger. By age five his skull had reached the same size as that of an adult human and was still growing. He resembled a dwarf rugby player, prematurely broadening in the chest and hips, with slightly bowed legs. He wasn't fat; the word people used was "sturdy." His teacher called him, with affection, our little Eskimo.

But more than this, it was Ned's extraordinary face that caused people to take a second look when seeing him for the first time. The face that had so startled and repulsed the doctor who attended his birth—an oddly triangular shape, broad at the crown with a virtually nonexistent chin, the skin wrinkled and dusted with a thin reddish-brown fur—had resolved into something quite different. Now his face was fair as any Scandinavian's, framed by a shaggy mop of coarse reddish hair. From the front, the boy's head still appeared almost v-shaped, with a skull that was broad from ear to ear, across which you could detect the beginnings of the brow ridge that would eventually cap his wide-set eyes. A thick nose presided over a set of unusually large teeth. Seen from the side, his forehead sloped back sharply and the recessiveness of his chin exceeded the normal range of variations in human morphology.

People meeting Ned for the first time tended not to focus on any of these unusual features, but instead were captivated by his enormous eyes: bright green, round, and set far apart, like the headlights on a car. He looked at everyone he met with a distinctive mixture of intensity and warmth. And below those eyes, his smile was broad and generous.

Ned and two other children sat on the floor in a circle, with bright red wooden blocks piled in the center. The teacher explained that they were going to build big cubes out of the little blocks.

"OK. Jessica, sweetheart, why don't you go first? Please divide up the blocks so each of you can build something. Make sure you have some, and Ned has some, and Max has some. OK? Please go ahead."

The little girl leaned forward and with a big sweep of her arm pulled all the blocks in front of her. She started to stack the blocks, but the teacher interrupted.

"Not yet, dear. We're not building yet, we're just dividing up the blocks." She pushed the pile back into the center. "OK, Max. Your turn. Please divide up the blocks so each of you can build something."

The little boy didn't hesitate. He pawed the pile toward himself and then, sensing that perhaps Jessica had not gotten it quite right, presented a single block to each of the other two children, retaining the rest for himself.

"That was nice, Max. Thank you," the teacher said, pushing the blocks back to the center. "And now, Ned, your turn."

Ned stared at the pile as if trying to count. Then, seeming to realize that was too difficult, he leaned forward and pushed blocks one at a time to each child in the circle, as if dealing cards, repeating each time, "One for Jessica, one for Max, one for Ned."

"Very nice, Ned. Thank you. And now that you each have blocks, I want everyone to use your little blocks to make a big cube. Do you all remember what a cube looks like?"

The children nodded. To make a big cube from the little cubes, each child required twenty-seven blocks. The pile in front of each of them contained twenty-six blocks.

"OK, then. Let's start."

At roughly the same speed, each child laid down nine blocks in tic-tac-toe formation, and then repeated the pattern on the next layer. Max was the first to complete the third layer and realize that he needed another block. He leaned over and grabbed a block from Jessica, inserted it to complete his cube, and smiled at the teacher. "I win," he said.

Jessica kept working, but then appeared crestfallen when she realized that she was two blocks short. Ned, having observed all of this, took two of his blocks and handed them to Jessica, who finished her cube. When Ned realized that he was now three blocks short, he simply nodded at his unfinished cube and turned to the teacher for guidance.

Behind the one-way glass, one of the paleoanthropologists put down his pen. "And that," he said to his colleague, "is why Neanderthals are extinct and we survived."

The other scientist, smirking, said, "And that, my friend, is why the world *sapiens* have built over the past ten millennia is so fucked up."

Agnes entered the classroom and shot an annoyed look at the one-way glass. "Come on, that's enough testing for today. They're children, for goodness sake, just let them play."

* * *

One late-spring afternoon, Agnes and Muir sat on the terrace in front of Muir's house, sipping iced tea while they watched the children play in the small meadow to one side.

Ned and Lilith had become inseparable. Although Lilith was nearly two years older, Ned's accelerated development meant that by three he had caught up in almost every way, and now, at five, he appeared at least seven. Lilith was as slender and long-limbed as he was squat and square. Each had found in the other the only companionship they appeared to require. Lilith was close to no other girls and maintained a standoffishness, bordering on hostility, to all boys other than Ned. Muir, anxious that Lilith become better socialized with a larger group of children, had invited three other girls for the afternoon.

Down in the meadow, Ned and Lilith were on their knees whispering to each other, giggling over a design Ned had made using pebbles and twigs. Ned lifted his head and said to Lilith, "They're coming."

"Who?" Lilith asked.

"The other kids."

"How do you know?" she asked.

"I smell them," Ned said. Leo's tests had revealed that Ned's nose hosted about sixty million olfactory receptors, ten times more than *Homo sapiens*, and—perhaps more significantly—that his brain devoted much more neural real estate to the detection, memory, and analysis of olfactory inputs. His enhanced sense of smell was complemented by a significantly wider field of peripheral vision. He almost always won at Freeze Tag.

"Let's play Red Light, Green Light," Ned said when the other children arrived. This was a game at which the children were more evenly matched. "Who wants to be the stoplight?"

Lilith volunteered, and for the next hour the children shrieked with laughter as they dashed toward Lilith, endlessly stopping and starting as she called out, over and over, "Red Light," and then, "Green Light."

"I never tire of watching children at play," Agnes said.

"You're in the right line of work, then," Muir said. "For some of us, it gets a little stale after the first hour."

"Do you realize, Muir, how lucky Ned is to have Lilith? He needs her; without Lilith, he'd be one lonely little boy. But, of course, he needs a father too."

"He's got Leo," Muir said, earning a frown from Agnes. "And you know I do what I can."

Agnes looked up sharply toward the group of children playing. Her peripheral hearing—the ability to keep one ear on the children while having an adult conversation—was almost as acute as Ned's peripheral vision. She had heard Lilith say, "What's wrong, Ned?"

Ned froze in place and turned pale. When Agnes arrived at his side, he whimpered, "Dogs."

Agnes turned around to see Polly appear at the top of the hill with her two Basenji hunting dogs, Hudson and Beckett, on long leads.

"Not to worry, dear, Polly will keep the dogs at the top of the hill, and you can come sit with the adults. OK?"

Agnes took his hand and walked him to the terrace where she had been sitting with Muir. Lilith ran ahead.

"Why not sit on Muir's lap, darling? OK?"

Muir hoisted the boy to his lap and draped one of his thick arms over the boy's shoulder. He could feel the child shaking slightly. "Don't worry, buddy. I've got you," Muir said.

Polly walked slowly down the hill without her dogs, while the other children continued to play without Ned and Lilith. Polly walked her dogs every afternoon around this side of the Village and every few days stopped to visit with Agnes and, if he was not at the lab, Muir. The Basenjis were unshakably loyal to Polly, who doted on them and spoiled them with every luxury. When they were only puppies, she had brought them with her for the first time, thinking the puppies and children might enjoy some time together. As they approached, Ned screamed. He dropped to the ground, curled into a small ball, his whole body convulsing in fear. Polly continued to visit, but from that day on she secured her dogs far up the hill before proceeding down toward the house.

"Afternoon, Agnes. Muir." Polly looked at the boy in Muir's lap. "Don't worry, Ned, the doggies are far away." The child smiled weakly.

"Sweetheart, why don't you go inside and read your book," Agnes said. Ned hopped off Muir's lap and ran into the house holding hands with Lilith.

"How are Hudson and Beckett?" Muir asked. "Such handsome dogs. Are you ever going to let me take you and the dogs hunting? I'm sure they'd take to it right away. It's in their genes."

"Thanks, Muir. I'm sure the dogs would love it. I'd like it too." It occurred to Polly that not once during their marriage had Leo ever invited her to accompany him on a hunt.

Polly gazed past Muir toward the house. "Ned is such a strange boy. Do you think the dog thing is a type of autism? I'm sure Leo's had him tested. Maybe Asperger's?"

Agnes answered. "No, we're quite sure it's not that. Lots of us have phobias. Some come from childhood experience, but some appear more deeply seated. Something about his . . . roots may make him terrified of dogs."

"How will he live, Agnes?" Polly asked. "I know he's just a child now. But he can't stay in Arcadia forever. How will he get on? He's so different, and the world is so cruel."

Muir answered. "The world will just need to accept that he's a different kind of human. We've got lots of time before Ned has to cope with what's beyond the boundaries of Arcadia."

15

Ned's Journal, February 14

I REALLY SCREWED UP. AGNES helped me pick out a box of Valentine's Day cards from the store. The cards had a chipmunk—I really like chipmunks—and Agnes said the chipmunk had adorable eyes. I've always given cards to all the girls at school who were my friends, because Agnes said this was polite. This year, when I gave the card to Lilith she got angry. I remember exactly what she said. "You gave me the same card as Amber and Julie? Really, Ned? We're in high school, and you gave me a card with a stupid chipmunk?"

She's right. I'm an idiot. I can't do anything right. And now I feel a knot in my stomach that won't go away. I need Lilith to forgive me.

OK. You know what the real problem is? I'm UGLY! There, I said it. So unfair. With the exception of Amos and Steve, all the guys in my class look like they're supposed to. The way girls want you to look. They're tall and thin and walk around in a way that shows they know they're cool. And I'm going to be short and thick and awkward FOREVER. I hate the way everyone acts when they first see me. They try to hide it, but I can see. They all think they've never seen anyone more funny-looking. I can hear what they say. I don't know why, but people whisper stuff thinking I can't hear, but I can. I heard Ankur Patel call me a freak. He's such a jerk.

Agnes says I'm wrong about being ugly, but she would. But once when I said something to Muir about it, he didn't say I was wrong. He said, "Forget it." I remember that now. "Forget it." I think he meant it was true but I shouldn't care. Well, I do care.

All for now.

16

Sarah

(Ned, Age 7)

LEO SAT IN A comfortable chair by his office window and opened a folder containing a selection of letters and printed emails. The twenty reviewed by Leo each week—never more, never less—were selected by an algorithm that "learned" which ones Leo was most likely to want to see by analyzing all the previous letters to which he had chosen to respond. Mostly, the correspondents asked for money or access to experimental therapies. The desperate and the dying fixated on internet rumors that SBD had discovered, or was on the verge of discovering, breakthrough treatments for their particular condition.

As he flipped to the next letter in the folder, written in a neat looping script on expensive stationary, the words "osteogenesis imperfecta" leapt from the page. OI, known as brittle bone disease, was the genetic condition that killed his sister.

Dear Mr. Bonelli,

If there is, as I have read, an experimental treatment for OI, I beg you to admit my seven-year-old daughter, Sarah, to the trial. Is there a childhood disease crueler than osteogenesis imperfecta? Sarah has dozens of fractures. Her spine is slowly crumbling. Do you have any idea what it is like to watch the one you love most in the world assaulted relentlessly by the mere force of gravity and collapse before your eyes? Although wracked by pain, she maintains a warmth and optimism that is heartbreaking. We have nothing to lose, so risk is meaningless. I have no god to whom I can pray. You have the power to help. I put my daughter's fate in your hands.

Leo stared out the window for a few minutes, lost in memory. He scrawled "find out more" across the top of the letter and returned it to the folder.

*   *   *

A month later, Lilith and Ned ran up the hill to Agnes, who sat on the terrace knitting.

"We're thirsty and want some lemonade," Lilith said.

Agnes gave her a disapproving look and Ned immediately intervened. "May we please have some lemonade, Agnes? Please?"

"That's better. Of course. Wait here, I'll be right back."

After Agnes returned from the house with a pitcher and glasses, the three of them sat drinking and looking out at the lake. Ned seemed focused on a sound, presumably a bird, that Agnes and Lilith could not hear.

"So, children," Agnes said, "Ned's dad needs your help."

"OK," Ned said.

"There's a little girl—seven, exactly your age, Ned—and her name is Sarah. She's sick, and Leo and the doctors in A Wing are trying to help her. You know that sometimes when you're sick it's scary, and you can get lonely? Well, Sarah needs to have some friends. Would you like to go visit her?"

"Sure," Ned said. Lilith looked skeptical.

"OK, then. Let's go."

When Agnes and the children arrived at A Wing, they found Sarah Moore perched in a strange-looking wheelchair, the back of which was tilted back almost forty-five degrees. Crescent-shaped cushions, like those that people use to sleep in airplanes, surrounded and supported her head. Long sandy-blond hair framed a pale face and shy smile.

"Hi," Ned said, approaching as if to shake her hand.

A nurse standing next to the wheelchair put out her hand and Ned stopped. "So, children, before you can play, you need to know the rules. You cannot touch Sarah, OK? And no roughhousing, no bumping into her chair."

"So how can we play, then?" Lilith asked.

"I know," Ned said, "how about cups?"

When Leo entered the ward an hour later, laughter filled the room. A pile of brightly colored disposable plastic cups rose on the tray of Sarah's wheelchair, with all three children blowing madly to get them to fall over as Lilith added a red cup to the top of the pile. The pile didn't fall. When Ned carefully balanced a blue one at the apex of the shaky structure, Sarah gave a big blow and the cups tumbled to the floor as she shrieked with delight.

Seeing his father enter the room, Ned smiled broadly. "Hey, Dad. We have a new friend. Her name is Sarah. I really like her."

Leo's smile froze as he took in the scene. After a moment, he asked, "Whose idea was it to play cups?"

"Mine, Dad," Ned said. "I thought it would be fun for Sarah."

Leo turned away to hide the pain on his face. His younger sister Mia also had been his best friend. The two children, inseparable, walked hand in hand to and from school every day. When she started having fractures, Leo insisted on coming with her to the hospital, every time. When she was confined to bed in strange contraptions designed to support her spine, he spent every spare hour at her side. Leo's father had believed that store-bought toys were an unnecessary extravagance. So Leo had become proficient at adapting household items as playthings. As Mia had become more and more fragile in the last months of her life, lightweight plastic cups were the only safe toy. Leo improvised dozens of cup games to keep her entertained. Now, when he remembered his sister, he saw her six-year-old face, eyes bloodshot from crying, framed by the bright colors of cheap plastic cups.

Leo turned back and watched Ned, who had started another game. Of course, it easily could be a coincidence, Leo thought. But the mysteries of heritability were profound, and Ned was a modified clone. For the first time Leo saw through the outward appearance of his son and was gripped by the conviction that he was looking at himself.

Since the sick girl and her mother arrived at Arcadia, Leo had come every day to sit at Sarah's side. Sometimes they talked, and sometimes they sat in silence as Leo went over and over in his mind his plan for curing the child. The easy part was correcting the mutation in the COL1A1 gene; that had been demonstrated by Dr. Shen and licensed to SBD. The challenge, as with all gene therapies, was the vector—how to deliver the editing tool to the patient's cells. The traditional load of adenovirus was out of the question; the risk of immune system overreaction was too great. Using the AAV8 virus as a vector was doubtless safer, but some members of his team were pushing a new technique known as CRISPR-Gold, in which the Cas9 protein (the editing tool), together with guide RNA to direct the tool to the mutation and donor DNA to correct the mutation, all are wrapped around a gold nanoparticle. Leo would need to make the final decision and was determined to get it right. After all, what were all his achievements worth if he couldn't now save Sarah Moore from suffering the same fate as Mia? He was confident of success.

* * *

Several days later, Leo, working at the standing desk he kept in a small office outside the main genetics lab, looked up to find Arcadia's chief of security standing at his open door. Calvin Wei, a first-generation Chinese American, had come to SBD from a military career in cybersecurity. "Got a second, Leo?"

"What's up?" Leo answered.

Calvin closed the door behind him as he entered the room.

"It still surprises me, Leo. You hire some of the smartest people in the world, and what, they think our big metal doesn't scan their texts and emails? Or that some encryption they download for free can make a difference?"

He handed Leo a manila folder. "Seth Levine. Have a look. He's talking to Sam, his brother, a lawyer in Seattle."

Seth Levine was a brilliant postdoc MD, exceptionally popular among the residents of Arcadia. He specialized in a process called homology directed repair, a critical component of the treatment plan for Sarah Moore. Leo opened the folder and read.

Sam, not sure where you are, but I need your help. I've got a problem here. You know my work has focused on therapeutic uses of gene editing, but it's research, Sam, none of it's ready even for human trials. Suddenly this very sick little girl—brittle bone disease, totally genetic—shows up and it's now become clear to me that Leo means to treat her. Where do I begin? We're supposed to have clearance from the RAC (the NIH's Recombinant DNA Advisory Committee), and we don't and wouldn't get it if we asked. If I don't do something, if I don't somehow blow the whistle on the thing, I would feel completely complicit and might even lose my medical license. If I do blow the whistle, I'll probably never get another job. And there's something else. I don't think this is the first time SBD's gone way over the line. There's a boy here, I wasn't around when he was born, but I strongly suspect that he's an edited clone—that's at least two big no-nos: cloning and editing of human embryonic cells. Leo treats him as a son, so threatening to blow the whistle on him could give me lots of leverage. What should I do, Sam? We need to talk ASAP.

Leo looked up. "Bastard. After all I've given him."

"So what's the plan, Leo? Just say the word and I'll revoke all his clearances and have him out of here in an hour."

Leo thought for a few moments. "The Sarah thing is not a big deal. If that leaks then we get a big PR win—bending the rules to save a little girl's life—and legally we get a slap on the wrist. But on no account can he be allowed to say another word about Ned. Not another word to anyone." The chief of security nodded. "And, Calvin, as much as I'd love to crush the fucker, we need him to stay mum forever. That means the carrot not the stick. Got it?"

* * *

A month later, when Leo entered the main room of Agnes's house, he found Agnes and Ned sitting on the floor. Ned was crying and Agnes sat quietly with her arm around the boy. When Ned saw his father, he tried to stifle his tears and sit up straight. It was only two days after Sarah Moore's death.

"We're sad about Sarah," Agnes said to break the silence. "It's the first time Ned has known someone who passed away."

Leo stood in front of his son.

"Ned, when I was your age, I had a sister."

Ned looked up at Leo with curiosity.

"She died, and I thought no one ever had been sadder than I was. So I know . . ."

"Then why couldn't you save her, Dad? Sarah didn't want to die."

Leo stared silently at the child on the floor and dropped wearily to the sofa.

"It's OK to feel sad, Ned," Agnes said. "But that feeling will pass, and before too long you'll have happy memories of your friend."

Agnes stood up and changed the subject.

"Leo, someone told me that nice Dr. Seth left. Rather suddenly. Everyone liked him so much."

"What?" Leo said, his thoughts elsewhere.

"Dr. Seth."

"Oh," Leo said. "Yes, he was a good man. Great researcher. But he wanted to do a type of research that SBD has decided not to pursue, and he got a great offer from Stanford, which needed him to start right away."

"Too bad." Agnes gave Leo a look that few others dared. "And too bad that he didn't have a chance to say goodbye, even to his friends."

Leo left the room and hopped aboard his cart for the short drive back to the genetics lab. He heard a beep on the path behind him and slowed as Calvin Wei pulled up alongside. Leaning over, Calvin wordlessly handed him another manila folder. Leo opened it and read the single sheet inside.

Hey, Sam, thanks so much for all your advice. It really helped. So here's what's happened. Turns out I completely misunderstood the nature of the procedure they proposed for the little girl, which was all by the book. And the boy too. I went and looked at his files and found it was a natural pregnancy with unusual mutations. Leo decided to keep the kid when the mother put him up for adoption. I don't know why I overreacted, working too hard, I guess. And, Sam, you've got to promise me not to mention this to anyone. I've signed all sorts of NDAs, and besides, it's hugely embarrassing. If it came out that I was thinking of making false accusations, I'd never get another job. Speaking of which, I got the most amazing opportunity—to run the sickle cell program at Stanford. I would have loved to stay at SBD, but they don't have a sickle cell program, which, as you know, is my real passion. Thanks, Bro, for being there.

When Leo finished reading, Calvin said, "It was a close call, Leo. Very close."

17

Ned's Journal, April 1

I DON'T LIKE APRIL FOOLS' Day. I don't think the kids mean to be cruel. They think it's funny. Olaf Johnson gave me a piece of candy. It was chocolate on the outside, so I ate it, but inside it was cheese. I can't eat cheese, it makes me fart. A lot. All day. It was really really embarrassing. At least, when the teacher wasn't looking, Lilith kicked Olaf Johnson in the shins, hard, and told him it wasn't funny.

I had another argument with Dad about outside. He doesn't care how I feel. I can't talk to him about stuff. About Lilith, for example. When Dad was yelling at me this morning, I felt that he was afraid. He seemed angry, but I knew that he was really afraid. Of what, I don't know. Sometimes I wish that Muir were my father. Muir calls me "buddy"—Dad never does. Muir treats me like a person, not a child. Dad takes me fishing, which I really don't like. I'd rather go hunting with Muir. If you ever read this, Dad, I'm sorry if it hurts your feelings, but it's the truth.

You know, there are things about me that no one knows. OK, here it is. I hear voices. I mean, not like thinking in words. Real voices. It happened a lot when I was a kid. I asked Lilith once, when we were young, what her voices said. She said she didn't have them, so I figured it was just me. Since then, I've kept it to myself. Sometimes the voices are me, or a part of me, and sometimes they're other people. Sometimes they mumble and I can't understand what they're saying, and it's kind of like a low hum, like the sound in a room when everyone is talking at once. But most of the time I can hear pretty clearly what they're saying. They tell me when I'm about to do something wrong. I'm not scared of them. When I was younger, I used to think of them as my "helpers." So there it is.

And something else. I don't like music. OK, to be entirely truthful, I really can't hear it at all—it sounds like noise. Everyone knows that when I go to a birthday party, I can't sing Happy Birthday. Lots of people can't sing. What they don't know is that I can't hear what they hear. I didn't lie about it. They just didn't ask.

I decided I'm going to ask Lilith out on a date. A real date. Dad and Muir won't like it, but I don't care.

All for now.

18
Paradise
(Ned, Age 10)

NED COCKED HIS LARGE head to the left, turning his right ear up and forward. Muir heard nothing. The ten-year-old gestured with his nose to the far side of a large scrubby meadow, at the opposite edge of which Muir and the boy were crouched in the cover of low-growing shrubs. After about half a minute, Muir heard it too—the distinctive crack of branches broken by the footfall of a large animal. They had come to this place by navigating a trail of spoor, each a heap of grassy tan lumps the size of bowling balls, and following the occasional footprint, where the distinctively smooth impression of the rear heel allowed them to determine the animal's direction of travel.

Lacking permafrost, it wasn't the type of tundra early humans found after crossing into North America through Alaska, but the grasslands of the high-elevation shrub-steppe were close enough, and the animals introduced to this part of Arcadia appeared to be thriving. Muir nodded and led the way around the perimeter of the meadow toward the sound. The boy who followed him was short for his age, only a couple inches over four feet, but otherwise had the build and appearance of a child at least three years older. His thick neck supported a skull that—although no longer freakishly large for his body—remained unusual enough to merit a second glance. The elongated skull bulged strangely to the rear, as if the occipital lobes were too large to be contained. Ned's chin remained weak, and distinct ridges of bone had now emerged to create prominent arches over each eye. Despite his low center of gravity and slightly bowed legs, Ned moved fluidly in a low crouch following Muir along the forest edge.

Muir, whose rifle still hung on a strap across his shoulder, stopped, uncertain about where the animals were likely to enter the meadow. Ned silently touched his nose and held up two fingers. Two animals probably meant mother and calf, always a dangerous combination. Muir finally spotted the pair through a break in the trees, a female Asian elephant and her calf. Muir and Ned exchanged excited glances.

Unlike the mother, the calf was completely covered in a thick coat of reddish-brown fur. The visible hairs on the outside layer of fur, about a foot long, gave the smaller animal an extraordinarily shaggy appearance. Shorter fur grew in circular rings down its trunk. At four years old, the calf already sported a large shoulder hump, upward-curving tusks, and short stubby ears, far different from her mother's great floppy tags of flesh. This was a sight that hadn't been seen in North America for ten millennia: a wooly mammoth calf foraging in the wild.

Muir, knowing that the elephant was likely to be protective of her offspring, wondered whether perhaps they should retreat when, with a gut-rattling bellow, the pachyderm mother flared her ears and turned toward the crouching man and boy. Muir knew how to deal with charging elk and moose but had no experience with elephants. Deciding it would be best to remain in a crouch, he reached out to draw Ned close to him, only to find that Ned had stood up and walked into the clearing. The elephant started her charge. Muir was about to leap forward to grab Ned when the elephant stopped short and locked eyes with the boy, who stood calmly facing the massive animal. The mammoth calf stood awkwardly behind her, swinging its foreleg back and forth. Muir reached Ned and stood behind him, his hands on Ned's shoulders. Both of them watched as the elephant's ears drooped into the forward relaxed position and her tail uncurled from between her hind legs. She looked over her shoulder at the mammoth calf, and then lumbered off to the break in the woods from which the two animals had emerged.

Muir's heart raced. He was stunned by both the suddenness of the charge and its termination. "Ned, what were you thinking? You could have been killed."

The boy turned. "I don't know. I wasn't . . . really thinking." Ned's preadolescent soprano voice, normally slightly singsong in its intonation, was steady.

"OK, buddy. Sorry. I'm not really angry at you. Just scared. Weren't you?"

Muir put his arm around the boy, and they walked together back in the direction of the ATV.

Muir had spent many happy days with Ned exploring the far corners of Arcadia. By this time, Muir was used to surprises. When Ned was only seven, Muir had knelt with the boy at the edge of a large stand of *Dryopteris* and explained how to differentiate the species from other types of ferns by separately examining the axis, pinna, and pinnules. When they returned home, Ned picked up a crayon and drew from memory a botanically accurate picture of *Dryopteris*. By age nine, he could identify hundreds of plants on sight.

Shortly after becoming fascinated by plants, Ned developed an enthusiasm for birds. Muir taught him many of their names and habits, but the boy's knowledge soon eclipsed his own. When they were together, Ned was always the first to hear birdsong. Once he asked Muir whether something was wrong with Muir's ears. "No, Ned," Muir had replied, "nothing is wrong with my ears. It's the other way around; your ears are very special, very strong. You're lucky." Muir was relieved that the boy didn't follow up with more questions. He had never lied to Ned and had no intention of starting now. The question of what to tell Ned about himself, and when, was one on which he imagined he and Leo were likely to disagree. He hoped it was a discussion they would not need to have for many more years.

When Ned was nine, Muir had decided it was time to take him on his first hunt. Muir discovered that Ned was nearly as terrified of the sound of guns as he was of dogs. So Muir gave him a small bow and set up a target near the house. Ned spent every spare hour practicing. Being strong for his age, he progressed quickly through a series of larger and more tightly strung bows. From the first day, Muir noticed that, without instruction, during the aiming part of the shot, the child suspended breathing, achieving the stillness of an experienced archer. For a couple of years now, Ned and Muir had bow hunted together almost weekly, traveling all over Arcadia and taking mostly jackrabbits and smaller mammals. Ned never hesitated to take a shot, but afterward, Muir noticed that the child treated the dead prey with respect, even tenderness.

* * *

Leo could not remember exactly when Ned had started calling him "Dad." He knew that Agnes had always referred to Leo as "your father." When the child started greeting him as "Dad," Leo instructed Agnes to put a stop to it. But Agnes was stubborn. When the child persisted, Leo concluded that telling the boy to stop could create more problems than it solved. Leo, however, remained steadfast in his determination not to call the child "Son."

"Ned, how about fishing today?" Leo asked.

Leo knew that Ned feared the water but had nonetheless decided that fishing would be his thing with Ned, in part because he had no wish to be the child's second-favorite hunting companion. Besides, if Ned feared and disliked the water, then this was something he just had to get over. Fishing would be good for him.

"We'll take the chopper. Ever been out to Quadrant 23?" This was a remote part of Arcadia near the southeast corner of the property. "There's a new lake there, and we managed to reestablish the redband trout. Great sport fish. I'm anxious to see it. Sound good?"

"Can Lilith come?" Ned asked.

"Sure, why not?"

"OK. Sounds great, Dad." He then squinted briefly in concentration. "And, Dad, remember, 'If wishes were fishes then no man would starve.'"

Leo smiled. "I like that one."

"And, 'There are plenty of fish in the sea.' And," warming to his subject, "'It's time to fish or cut bait.' And of course, the old favorite, 'Give a man a fish and he eats for one night. Teach him how to fish and he eats for life.'"

Ned's hobby of the moment was aphorisms. He loved old sayings, maxims, and adages of all sorts. No matter the topic, he delighted in plucking them from his memory and dropping them into the conversation. The fact that he didn't always understand their meanings didn't faze him.

"That's enough," Leo said, laughing. "Proves my point that fishing is not only fun, but the source of much wisdom."

The newly created lake did not yet have a name. The Arcadia scientists had taken a severely degraded Harney Basin wetland and restored it to the sort of small glacial lake that was its original form. Using a genetic modification that eliminated a hormone necessary for the female carp to produce eggs, together with a gene drive to push the modification quickly through the population, Arcadia's scientists eliminated the invasive carp within three seasons. The other impediment to restoration of the native redband trout was low pH, which resulted from groundwater draining through the tailings of an abandoned mine. This they corrected by removing the tailings and treating the water with lime.

The team monitoring the project had acquired a small wooden boat. The narrow planks were painted white, the top rail a faded blue. The squat tug-like shape made Leo think of his father.

Lilith and Ned knelt at the pond's edge trying to catch frogs with their hands as the helicopter pilot helped Leo pull the small boat into the water.

"OK, kids, let's go."

Lilith ran over and jumped into the boat. Ned stopped short at the water's edge.

"I can't," Ned said.

"Sure you can. It's easy."

Ned put out a trembling hand, which Leo stared at for a moment before extending his own to hold the boy as he stepped cautiously into the gently rocking boat.

Ned sat next to Lilith. He steadied his nerves by reciting, "A rising tide lifts all boats," and, "Blood is thicker than water," and then, after a pause, "You can lead a horse to water, but you can't make it drink."

Lilith laughed. "Good ones, Ned."

Satisfied, the boy busied himself with his rod as Leo slowly rowed toward the deepest part of the lake, where the trout were most likely to be found.

"Lure or night crawlers?" Leo asked. "Which do you want to try first?"

The boy opened the lid of the worm jar, in which dozens of night crawlers squirmed.

"Worms, Dad. Definitely."

"Ich," said Lilith. "A lure for me."

Ned caught the first fish. When he saw a slight vibration in the line, he jerked his rod up as Leo had taught him, and then resisted the urge to reel it in fast. "Slow and steady," Leo reminded him.

When Ned pulled the agitated fish from the water, Leo was thrilled to see that it was a healthy redband trout. Just over a foot long, the fish sported a luminescent red-orange stripe along each side, set in a field of tiny black dots. Yet another species, Leo thought, that was previously close to extinction and now would live on, thanks to him. The boy carefully removed the hook, looked closely at the fish, showed it to Lilith, and then placed it gently back into the lake.

"You know," Leo said, speaking as much to himself as to Ned, "this might just be the moment when the Anthropocene turned beneficial."

"That's great, Dad," Ned said. "But, uh, what does that mean?"

Lilith did not appear to be listening, intent on catching up to Ned by catching her own fish.

"Well, 'Anthropocene' means the current geological era—you know, like the Jurassic era with the dinosaurs."

"Uh huh."

"We call it that because something happened that had never happened before. One animal, man," Leo hesitated, "uh, *Homo sapiens* actually, became so numerous and invented such powerful technologies that they changed every corner of the planet."

"Changed how?"

"Well, for example, we split the atom and left traces of radiation all over the place. We dug up carbon and injected it into the atmosphere, changing the climate. We dumped things into the ocean, changing its chemistry. We caused thousands of species of plants and animals to disappear. So what Anthropocene means is an era when the planet took a form mostly created by us—and this is the most important thing—created carelessly, without thinking about what we were doing. In other words, our influence on nature and the planet was bad, not good. You understand?"

Ned could not think of an old saying appropriate for such a calamity, so he simply nodded.

"So when I say this is the moment when the Anthropocene turned beneficial, what I mean is that we're still the main influence on the planet, but instead of being a bad influence, we're now starting to use our technology to make things better, like this lake and the trout. And it's starting here, at Arcadia."

"I got it." He paused to think. "Here's one, Dad: 'The road to Hell is paved with good intentions.'"

Leo, startled, stared at the boy.

"I got one," Lilith screamed. "And he's bigger than yours, Ned!" Ned helped her pull a fourteen-incher into the boat.

Lilith's was the last catch of the day. Despite trying different bait and different parts of the lake, the trout refused to bite. After a while, Lilith and Ned put down their rods and lay on their stomachs, their chins propped on the rail of the boat.

"Hey, Dad, what's that?" Ned asked, pointing at a stretch of fencing visible through a clearing on the far side of the lake.

"That's the boundary fence."

"What's that for?"

"It marks the edge of Arcadia. It's how we can be sure that people from outside don't come in without permission."

"Why not? Why not let them come?" Ned asked.

Leo, wishing to avoid the subject of security, paused to formulate an answer. But Ned seemed to forget his question and went on, adding, "What's it like outside? Is it nice?"

"It can be," Leo said, "but not as nice as here in Arcadia."

"I'd like to see it."

"Outside is only for grown-ups."

"When will I be grown up?"

"Oh, a long time from now. Not something to think about yet. You know, Ned, what's important is that I created Arcadia as the place where you belong. We all belong someplace, Ned. And you belong here in Arcadia, with me, and Muir, and Agnes, and Lilith. You understand?"

Ned continued to stare at the boundary fence. "I guess so."

19

Ned's Journal, July 22

MUIR AND I WENT out early this morning to bag a deer for my party tomorrow. We didn't have to go far. I got a doe with my longbow about thirty minutes after beginning the stalk. At the usual place above the north meadow. She was a beauty, with a huge white patch under her chin—never seen one so big. Wish I had a crossbow but Dad says it's too dangerous. Muir made a sled and I dragged it back to the kitchen. Can't wait until tomorrow.

Can't believe I'm fifteen. I always thought I'd become more like the other kids when I got older. Well, I haven't. No one really knows what I think and feel, and I'm pretty good at hiding it. But some stuff I can't hide, like being scared of dogs. And water. They think I'm a wimp, but it's something I just can't control.

If they knew how really different I am, then—well, I don't know, but I don't think it would be good. I even smell different from the other kids.

Maybe there are more people like me outside. I spend a lot of time thinking about what it must be like in Burns, in Portland, in all the places I've never been. It must be awesome. I thought about running away. I don't care if someone reads this. It's true. It's not fair to be stuck here forever.

Lilith's been really nice to me lately. I want to kiss her. There, I said it. Maybe there's something to this journal business after all.

All for now.

20

The Birthday Party

(Ned, Age 15)

LITTLE TEPEES OF DRY tinder spouted flames that licked persistently at the elaborate cross-hatching of wood forming the base of the tower. Above, a geometric arrangement of branches, like a tree that imploded from its fractal irregularity into a stack of perfect triangles and pyramids, awaited the arrival of the conflagration. Thick smoke poured from wood fiber heated nearly to the point of combustion. Then, with a sudden roar, a bright orange ball of flame exploded from the base and rose up through the stack, leaving the whole tower burning brightly.

The bonfire was a birthday tradition. Today, Ned's fifteenth, the guests circled the inferno, cheering when the flames reached the top of the piled wood. Ned, with Lilith at his side as usual, stood between Muir and Leo. Nearby, Agnes chatted with Clip and his wife. The party also included a half dozen other friends of Ned and Lilith, together with their parents, all residents of Arcadia. As the bonfire settled down into a pleasing mass of dancing yellow flame, each eye in the circle appeared the same, its black pupil reflecting a little triangle of flickering light.

Ned had continued to develop faster than his *sapiens* peers. At fifteen, although still short, strangers would have guessed he was eighteen. As he grew, the proportions of his body looked less odd, and from the neck down he appeared to be a solidly built normal young man. Above the neck, his shaggy red hair, left long in accordance with current teenage fashion, largely hid both his sloping forehead and pronounced occipital bun. Yes, the face was broad—the nose, mouth, and teeth on the large side, and the chin recessive. But none of these would cause a stranger to think that something was seriously awry. The facial feature that did turn heads—or would have done had a stranger ever seen Ned—was the prominent boney ridge above each eye. Brow ridges are extremely rare in *Homo sapiens*. When they appear, as they do in a few of the aboriginal people of Australia, they are almost never as pronounced as Ned's. There was no disguising that Ned was different.

Other than Leo and the rogue geneticist Dr. Shen, only Muir, Polly, and Agnes knew the truth about Ned's origins. The simple cover story promulgated when Ned first emerged from A Wing had been largely accepted by the residents of Arcadia: Ned's physiognomy was the result of a rare genetic variation revealed by prenatal testing. The pregnant mother had been brought to SBD for possible treatment. When born, the strange-looking infant was rejected by his mother, who returned to Spain. Leo became personally interested and, in an act of compassion, decided to adopt and raise him as his own child. That was the story. Like Seth Levine, Arcadia's sophisticated geneticists knew it didn't quite hang together, but with the passage of time they had ceased to speculate about what sort of procedure could have resulted in the strange-looking child. Seth Levine remained at Stanford and had kept his side of the bargain. So the outside world, at least for now, remained unaware that there was anything unusual about Leo's "adopted child."

Ned himself was aware of this account of his origins and had not inquired about his biological parents. Instead, his curiosity focused mainly on the world outside the bounds of Arcadia.

"You know what this is?" Ned had said in the course of a huge argument with Leo. "It's a prison. I'm the prisoner and you're the warden."

"Don't be ridiculous. This is a paradise, and you're damn lucky to be here. You have no idea what you're talking about."

"Yeah, well, if it's so great, why are you so afraid of letting me leave? You afraid that if I leave and see the real world, that I won't come back?"

Leo didn't answer.

"You go outside. Muir goes outside. Muir takes Lilith outside. I'm the only one. It's just not fair."

"It's too dangerous. Trust me. Not yet."

Ned's birthday dinner had been the same for years: spit-roasted venison from a deer bow hunted by Ned and Muir, sweet potatoes, and mint chocolate chip ice cream, his favorite. The adults drank Leo's beer of choice, a microbrew IPA the helicopter crew fetched periodically from the northern Oregon town of Hermiston. Earlier in the evening, everyone had been concerned that the celebration might be rained out. The weather radar showed a serious cluster of storms sitting just behind the Cascades, struggling to move east into the Harney Basin, but seemingly stalled by the mountain peaks. In the end, the weather held, and the party relaxed at the long picnic table enjoying the periodic collapse of the upper part of the bonfire, watching as a burst of sparks floated skyward on a plume of superheated air.

At the far end of the table, one of the guests asked Leo if he had heard from Polly.

"Not directly, but I get reports. She's living in Cambridge with some sort of sociologist. Good luck with that," Leo said, drinking a swig of beer. Two years before, Polly failed to return from England at the end of term. A month later she sent for her dogs.

The woman who asked the question, Clip's new wife, Anne, had come to Arcadia to study weasels. An expert in the family *Mustelidae,* she focused her work on the world's smallest carnivore, using advanced genetic techniques to understand its evolution, taxonomy, and habitat. Everyone who knew him had been surprised when Clip became interested in the young woman and asked her on a date. They were even more surprised when the neatly dressed and highly disciplined young woman said yes. Soon thereafter, Clip's ragged T-shirts disappeared like the molting of a bird's juvenile plumage, and a new, age-appropriate Clip emerged.

One of Ned's friends called across the table, "Hey, Ned, what do you think of this year's bonfire?" His friends delighted in challenging him to come up with aphorisms on difficult or unlikely topics.

"Well," he said after a moment's thought, "'where there's smoke there's fire.'"

"You can do better than that," Anne called out, laughing.

"OK, then. How about, 'The burnt child shuns the fire.' Or, along a different line, 'A picture is worth a thousand words.'"

"Speaking of which," Leo said, rising and clinking his beer bottle with a knife, "it's time for presents." He presented Ned with a next-generation drone and a hoodie with a Wi-Fi audio device built into the hood.

"I invented it," Leo said, "with a little help from R&D. Anyway, when you want to listen to music, you just pull up the hood and name the song you want. No need for earbuds, as the speakers automatically locate the ear canals and then send a highly focused cone of sound directly to your eardrums. No one else can hear, usually, that is. And the stereo effect is kind of strange. To be honest, it's not quite ready for prime time, but I still wanted you to be the first to have it. Happy birthday, Son." Without any prompting from Agnes, Leo had started using the word "son" shortly after Ned turned twelve, when the boy left Agnes's house and moved in with

Leo. The guests clapped, unaware, as was Leo, that Ned lacked the neurological capacity to detect and enjoy melody.

"You mean," Ned replied, taking the hoodie from his father, "you wanted me to be your guinea pig." Everyone laughed. "But seriously, thanks."

Agnes gave him a hand-knit sweater and a kiss. Lilith, now a young-looking seventeen, rose from the table. Standing a couple of inches taller than Ned, she handed him a framed picture of herself. In the photo she wore a low-cut dress of which Muir did not approve. Ned kissed her cheek in thanks for the gift.

Muir, the only one who had thought to ask Ned what he wanted, stood to present him with an antique Kyrgyz crossbow. The nomadic Kyrgyz, who ranged across the Central Asian steppe hunting on horseback, were reputed to have made the best crossbows in the world. For a brief moment, Leo appeared to be annoyed, but he smiled broadly when he saw Ned's delight in Muir's gift.

After presenting the weapon to Ned, Muir offered a toast. It was typically succinct.

"Ned, we all love you. We love your compassion, your integrity, your gentleness, your courage. Friends, please join me in a toast to Ned, the finest young man I know."

Ned, his ears blushed pink, received many hugs, including from Leo. Muir thought it a shame that Polly was not here to see the change in her husband.

As the last cinders faded, sending a lazy plume of gray smoke toward the moonlit sky, the long, jagged ridge of the Cascade Mountains lost its grip on the roiling storm front. Dark clouds tumbled down the eastern slope of the range. A groundskeeper, dousing the remains of the bonfire with a hose, looked up as the first band of dark cloud passed over the moon.

PART III
SIEGE

21
First Date

DAD," NED SAID, DIRECTING a conspiratorial grin to Lilith across the table, "Lilith's going out on Wednesday."

"With her cousin," he added.

"Uh huh," Leo said.

"And Lilith," Ned said, "asked if I would like to go with her."

Leo looked up from the hydrological report he was reading over Saturday lunch. It was a gray late-winter day, seven months after the convivial celebration of Ned's birthday.

"Where?"

"Burns," said Lilith. "We're going bowling."

"Out of the question."

"Dad, please. You can't . . ."

Lilith interrupted and put her hand on Ned's forearm.

"Leo, I know you only want what's best for Ned. But he can't stay here forever. He needs to understand how to navigate the outside world, and the longer you wait, the harder it'll be."

"Lilith's right, Dad. 'A man shall leave his mother and a woman shall leave her home.'"

Leo smiled. "I'm not sure the person who wrote that had in mind a date at a bowling alley in Burns."

"It's not really a date," Lilith said. "Just my cousin and one other guy from here. Just bowling."

Leo took off his reading glasses and looked at the two teenagers.

"Well, I suppose we have to start somewhere." Lilith reached for Ned's hand under the table. "And Burns seems as good a place to start as any. I'll organize it."

"Thanks, Dad," Ned said. "You're the best."

* * *

"Here's what we're going to do," Leo said to Calvin Wei, Arcadia's chief of security. "Let's have the chopper land out of town, maybe somewhere along Route 20 where no one will see it. Let's send them in a pickup, which no one will notice, but of course with a vehicle full of your guys right behind. All the staff at the bowling alley sign an NDA and we pay them enough that they keep their mouths shut."

"I'm not sure that's such a good idea, boss." Calvin's Chinese features radiated professional competence and confidence. "Signing an NDA in advance will tip off everyone that something's up. Better to just buy out the place for the night—we'll say it's a birthday party that's being catered. We replace the staff with our own people."

"You're right. But make it all invisible, or else Ned will have a fit."

"Sure, boss. No problem."

"And one more thing: profile Lilith's cousin and her family. We're taking no chances."

* * *

Lilith did not know her cousin well. Brandi-Lynn was the daughter of Lilith's late mother's brother, whom she and Muir had met only a few times when visiting Meredith's parents in Boise. The girl sat alone on the other side of an orange Formica table, dressed all in black: platform boots, a leather skirt, and a low-cut top with straps and buckles, covered by a black fishnet shawl. Brad, a classmate of Lilith's at the school in Arcadia, wearing round Harry Potter spectacles, sat next to Lilith and Ned. He stared nervously into his tall glass of Mountain Dew, trying hard to disguise his fascination with Brandi-Lynn.

"Well, it's just like the bowling alley in the Village," Ned said, his voice tinged with disappointment. "I don't know, I thought it would be bigger, somehow better. And where is everybody? I thought there'd be more people."

"Wha'd you expect?" Brandi-Lynn asked. "Wednesday night in Burns. And bowling alleys, they're all the same, you know."

Ned decided not to mention that he did not, in fact, know this.

"Seen the new *Star Wars* yet?" he asked the group.

At this Brad looked up. "Kind of lame, right? But still, pretty fun. I mean, not as good as *Jedi Resurrected*. That was way cool. But still, the new android dog ..."

Ned had never seen anything like the heavy black makeup around Brandi-Lynn's eyes. Her jet-black hair hung in straight bangs across a pale forehead. He'd always suspected that life on the outside was different and was delighted that Brandi-Lynn turned out to be so exotic. Breaking the awkward silence, Ned asked, "How's the school in Burns? Must be great."

"Are you kidding?" Brandi-Lynn answered. "It's *Mean Girls* Central. They're only sixteen and they're already the Stepford Wives. If you're not fucking popular, forget it. If you're just yourself, they torture you."

Ned did not understand the references to *Mean Girls* and *Stepford Wives* and glanced at Lilith, who mouthed "movies."

"At our school in Arcadia," Ned said, "kids who are alike tend to hang out together. Is that what you mean?"

"Not really. This is way worse. It's like there's only one way to be. You've got to go to the big church just outside of town. You've got to wear the same shit. You've got to talk the same way, and like the same shows, and post all day on Instagram."

"And if you don't?" Ned asked.

"Then you're a freak. If you're lucky, they just ignore you. If you're not, well, if you're a guy you get beat up. If you're a girl, then the other girls do everything they can to make your life miserable."

"Like what?" Lilith asked.

"Let me tell you, cuz, it's not pretty. They spread rumors, mostly that you're a slut. One girl told everyone that she saw me behind the Walmart giving a blowjob to the ugliest guy in our class. They tell you about everything you're not invited to, just so you know you've been left out. If you want to get in with the most popular girls, you've got to make up nasty things to say about the weird kids' clothes, hair, whatever. You get texts all day saying you're going to burn in hell because you don't go to their church."

Ned's eyes widened. He felt terrible for Brandi-Lynn and didn't know what to say.

"I'm really sorry, Brandi-Lynn," Lilith said. "That sounds terrible. What can you do?"

Her laugh had a bitter edge. "What can I do? Well, you're looking at it. I went Goth. If I was going to be treated like a freak, then I thought, why not be a real freak and really stick it to them?"

Lilith sat back and took a long look at her cousin. "Well, Brandi-Lynn, I think you look great. I really do."

"Uh huh. You know, looking great is not the point. I started out just to shock, but now it's kind of who I am. And it's taught me something—that my being in Burns is just a big cosmic joke. I don't belong here. Like I'm really supposed to be someplace else."

Ned turned abruptly to look straight at Brandi-Lynn. "I know what you mean. I do."

"I'm counting the days," she continued. "I'm gonna move to LA, where I can be whoever I want to be. I'll blow this place as soon as I can ditch the 'rents."

This got Ned's attention. "You mean leave your parents? You can do that?"

"Uh, yeah. You know, when you're eighteen," Brandi-Lynn said. "As soon as I hit eighteen, they can go fuck themselves. They don't help at all. They wish I were just like all the other girls. The first thing I'm doing after eighteen is to leave Burns."

Ned immediately thought that Lilith would turn eighteen next year and that he was almost two years behind. In the past few years, the voices in Ned's head had made only rare appearances. But now a small chorus distracted him with a running commentary. *What a nightmare, you'd never make it on the outside . . . No, Ned. That's what you've been missing and what you need . . . Another freak, just like you. And she's cute . . . Remember, Lilith is the only one for you . . . Yup, a big cosmic joke. That's you, Ned . . . Ugliest guy in class, d'you hear that? . . . You don't belong here.*

The group bowled ten frames without keeping score. Ned, who practiced diligently at the lanes in the Village, bowled three strikes and four spares. Lilith tried hard to match or beat him. Brad, who was totally tongue-tied in the presence of Brandi-Lynn, tried too hard to impress her and thus bowled terribly. Brandi-Lynn seemed bored with bowling and didn't really make an effort.

When the group sat down again, Lilith asked her cousin, "Brandi-Lynn, you have a boyfriend?"

"Nah. There's no one for me here. If a guy asked me out I'd figure it was a trick, you know, to humiliate me."

A wave of empathetic hurt passed over Ned's face.

* * *

Agnes had explained to Ned that, on a real date, it was his job to walk the girl home. And so, when the chopper landed at Arcadia, the two friends walked slowly from the pad back toward Muir's house.

"I'm sorry that was a little weird," Lilith said.

Ned, brooding, walked for a few moments in silence. Then he asked, "Lil, you go out all the time. Is that . . . is that what it's really like on the outside? I mean, what Brandi-Lynn said about school in Burns, about fitting in?"

"Well, it's not like here, that's for sure."

Before rounding the final bend where Muir's house would come into view, Lilith stopped walking, still holding Ned's hand.

"I've known you forever, and now, we just went on a date. A real date," she said.

"We did," he answered.

Lilith leaned forward, placed her hand on the back of Ned's neck, and kissed him. On the lips. Twice.

22
Man or Beast

CLIP," LEO SAID. "WHAT part of 'no calls' do you fail to understand?"

"Sorry, boss, but I really think you'd better take this one."

Leo sat in front of Muir's desk in the corner of the main tissue lab. He twisted around to look at the phone in Clip's extended hand.

"Why?"

"It's the *New York Times*."

"So what? Transfer them to PR."

"They say they're calling about Ned."

Leo stood. "About Ned?"

"Well, he didn't exactly say 'Ned,' but that's what he meant." Leo and Muir exchanged a look. Leo took the phone.

"Mr. Bonelli, this is Joe Krueger from the *Times*. Are you watching Pastor Joe on the House floor?"

"Should I be?"

"He's speaking at this moment on the floor of the House. He says that you've created a monster and is calling for Congressional hearings."

"A monster?"

"He says you're harboring this creature. Calls it a stealth attack on humanity. He says your wife has fled to England in horror. Is it true? Have you brought back the Neanderthals?"

"Now, wait just a minute. Did you say 'harboring'?"

"Mr. Bonelli, I need to know. Is this true? In your view, is whatever you've done legal and ethical? And why did you do it? Mr. Bonelli, I need a comment."

Leo regained his composure sufficiently to say, "I have no comment at this time." He cut off the call and slammed the phone down on Muir's desk.

"What was that about?" Muir asked.

"They know about Ned."

"Oh my God," Muir said. "How?"

"Pastor Joe. Just broke the story on the floor of Congress, of all places. How the hell could he have found out?"

"Polly?" Clip said.

"She wouldn't," Muir said.

"Possible," said Leo.

"It doesn't matter," Muir said. "You've got to tell Ned what . . . who he is. Now, Leo. He has to hear it from you, not from some lunatic congressman on TV."

"He's not ready."

"You mean you're not ready. Doesn't matter, Leo. You have no choice."

* * *

Congressman Joseph O'Malley returned from the floor of the House to his office, where his staff clustered around a wall of screens, each tuned to a different network. The cleric's face appeared on every one. His social media director looked up from her laptop. "Twitter is exploding. There's no other news. You'd think aliens had landed." She chuckled. "I guess they kinda have."

His political director was ecstatic. "This is the one we'll ride to the White House, Joe. It's got everything we need: jealousy, fear, even the beast of the apocalypse rising up live in prime time. Science run amok, exactly as we've predicted. This time they really did go too far. It's a gift, and now you own the issue. I've already made it clear that we'll cut the balls off anyone who tries to get out in front of you here."

"Polls?" Pastor Joe asked.

A junior aide answered. "We're out with a flash poll, but nothing back yet. We should know by the time you're done with the press."

The political director could not contain himself. "Joe, the hearings will be bigger than McCarthy. Bigger than Watergate. PJ in charge. All Joe, all the time, for at least three news cycles. The champion of the people. The defender of the faith. Taking on the richest man in the world. Slaying the monster. And then we announce for president a week later. It'll be the strongest start to any campaign in the modern era."

Pastor Joe had the look of a man whose ambitions were endorsed by an omnipotent deity. "How's my hair?" he asked, leaving to address the assembled press on the Capitol steps.

The man who spoke for God wore a $5,000 Ermenegildo Zegna suit. He approached the microphone with faux reluctance, wearing a face perfectly composed to reflect a combination of worry and determination.

"It was with a heavy heart that I had the duty this afternoon to share with the American people the horrifying news that we have been attacked from within. One man—drunk on power and wealth, a man who schemes in the shadows, a man infatuated with technology who has lost sight of morals, of decency, of common sense—because of this one man, humanity itself is now in mortal peril. Using powers properly reserved to the creator, this reckless man has upended the natural order of things and brought back to life creatures whose extinction cleared the way for the Almighty's most perfect creation, man. Leo Bonelli has given us an evil, Godless beast, half man, half animal. A monster driven by the urge to breed with humans, to dilute the purity of our stock, and reestablish its own dark hegemony over the planet. The unnatural creation of this beast was a sin, an act of betrayal of our shared humanity, an act of treason. It cannot stand, because our shared humanity is the touchstone for all things. God and humanity are absolutes, the yardsticks we use to measure right and wrong. Without them, we are lost. So today I called on the floor of the House for immediate hearings, for commonsense steps to hunt down these creatures and protect the American people from their menace. I also have called for an immediate halt to all genetic editing. This tampering with God's recipe for life must stop. God wants it to stop. The American people demand that it be stopped. I have called on the speaker to convene hearings within a month. You now know all that I do, ladies and gentlemen, so there is no need for questions."

Pastor Joe remained behind the podium for a few moments, enjoying the sound of the cameras clicking like a chorus of cicadas.

* * *

Leo walked through the Village to the house he now shared with Ned. He always knew this day would come. He reminded himself that countless parents had delivered similarly hard news to their children. Creating Ned had been the right thing to do. He was not about to second-guess that decision, made years ago on the long plane trip back from Singapore. And yet he was feeling something unfamiliar. It was fear.

Leo found Ned sitting outside on the front terrace.

"Hey, Dad. You're back early."

"I was over at botany. With Muir."

Ned looked up, sensing something was wrong.

"Son, we have to have a talk."

Ned pushed back the hood of his hoodie and Leo heard that he had been listening to a podcast, not music.

"OK."

"I want you to know that you are every bit as much my son as Lilith is Muir's daughter. In every way that counts, you are no different from any of the other children."

"I know. Being adopted is no big deal."

"Well, you're not exactly adopted. Let me put it this way, Son. There are lots of different ways children are brought into this world. Back in 1978 people were shocked when the first so-called 'test-tube baby' was born—where scientists brought the sperm and egg together in the laboratory, and then implanted the embryo in a woman. And there have been many variations since."

"So you're saying I was a test-tube baby?"

"Well, sort of. And the reason you don't have a mother is that we no longer need genetic material from both a man and woman. Almost all your genetic material came from me."

"Almost?"

Two security guys passed the house in an electric ATV and waved at Leo and Ned.

"There is something else. We made some modifications to my DNA. We introduced some traits from another type of human that is now extinct. They were called Neanderthals."

"Cavemen?" Ned asked, his voice tinged with alarm.

"So, Ned, as the result of these genetic modifications, there are some ways in which you could be considered a kind of Neanderthal."

"Wait a second. Are you saying I'm not a human being? Are you saying I'm a Neanderthal?" Ned felt his identity slipping away, like a boat disappearing over the edge of the horizon.

"No. You are human. But there once were many different types of humans, and one of those types of human is what we now call Neanderthal."

Ned stood up. "That explains some things. Why I'm short and funny-looking, for example."

"You are not funny-looking. You're different. Everybody is different to some extent."

Ned started pacing. "Bullshit. That's bullshit, Dad. You made me, and could have made me any way you wanted, but you chose to make me a freak?"

"You're not . . ."

"And then for almost sixteen years you let me think I'm just like everyone else, while all the other kids—everyone in Arcadia—has been looking at me thinking I'm some kind of monster?"

"There's nothing wrong with Neanderthals."

"Nothing wrong? Can you hear yourself? Do you think that ever, in the history of the world, when someone called someone else a Neanderthal, they meant it as a compliment?"

At this thought, Ned dropped back in his chair, staring at the ground. Tears started to flow. "It's not fair," Ned sobbed. "I'm a joke. And everything's been a lie." His sobs came from deep in his gut, convulsing his body.

Leo stood and looked on helplessly.

"There's no one else like me in the world. And I'll never be normal like . . ."

Leo moved to put his arm around the young man. "Son . . ."

Ned looked up.

"Don't you dare call me 'Son.' I'm nothing to you but another lab experiment."

Leo put his hand on Ned's shoulder. Ned stood up, pushing him away, hard. Leo stumbled, almost falling backward.

"Don't you touch me. Don't you fucking touch me again. Ever."

* * *

Leo declined to speak to the press. Later that night he released a short statement:

Human beings have been shaping life to our purposes for all of history. The rise of civilization depended on our creation of domesticated animals and food crops. Genetic modification of plants has saved millions from starvation. Reproductive technologies have made it possible for thousands of couples to have children, and the genetic therapies developed by SBD have saved countless lives. An attack on genetics is an attack on civilization itself, and on the health and potential longevity of every one of us. It is true that I had a child using an unconventional reproductive technology. The work was done in a jurisdiction in which it was fully lawful. It is true that my genome was modified to give the child certain traits that we discovered through the sequencing of the genome of a type of extinct human we call the Neanderthal. The achievement was a major breakthrough in genetic engineering and represents a landmark in the long history of science. All of us will benefit. I am happy to report that my child is now a healthy fifteen-year-old. Although a different type of human, he is owed the same respect and dignity that we extend to all humans. Most importantly, he is still a child with the same right to privacy as any other child. He will not be made available to the media. I will have no further statement on this subject. This matter is closed.

23
Hate

LEO WAS WRONG. THE matter was by no means closed. The public furor over Pastor Joe's revelations escalated exactly as the ambitious congressman hoped. The National Academy of Sciences issued a statement confirming that de-extinction of a member of the genus *Homo* was contrary to prevailing ethical guidance. The Justice Department announced that the FBI would investigate whether any laws had been broken. Politicians of both parties condemned Leo and SBD. And Pastor Joe rode this wave from the fringes of the far right to establish himself as a populist hero.

Arcadia itself morphed from a quiet refuge to a fortress under siege. Leo's security forces apprehended scores of reporters attempting to penetrate the boundaries of Arcadia and shot down a dozen video-equipped drones. *OK! Magazine* estimated that the first photograph of Ned would fetch far more than the record $7.5 million previously paid for the picture of a famous child. Ned was the number-one celebrity on the planet, but the public had never seen him.

For a week following the difficult conversation about his origins, Ned refused to speak to Leo. He relented only after Lilith told him he was being juvenile. Ned again became infuriated with his father after he realized that Leo had installed an internet firewall that filtered out not only the death threats and hate speech, but all Ned-related items.

"We haven't changed," Muir argued, "it's just the digital-age equivalent of Victor Frankenstein's pitchfork-wielding villagers seeking to kill the thing they fear."

"It's worse," Leo replied. "Our brain usually filters out the vile stuff that pops into our heads before it comes out as speech. But the path between the brain and the fingers seems to bypass that filter. What comes out online is raw vitriol. If it's about you, Muir, you never completely recover from reading that kind of shit. I don't care how mad at me it makes him; he can't be allowed to see it."

* * *

On a July afternoon Leo flew back from SBD's Washington offices and walked directly to Muir's lab. He paced back and forth in front of Muir's desk.

"Bad news," Leo said. "We couldn't stop them. The hearings are going ahead, within a month, Pastor Joe as co-chair. It couldn't be worse. Live national TV, three days. A total circus. And I have to testify."

"Why?"

"I've been subpoenaed. No way out."

"And Ned?"

"That's a bit of good news. They got all tripped up by their insistence that he's not a person. Only a person can take the oath, so he can't be called to testify. At least Ned will be spared."

"Is that really a good thing?" Muir asked.

"What? Why?"

"I think you've got to consider letting the world meet Ned. When he's just an abstraction, it's easy to believe he's a monster. But when you see him, meet him, talk to him—well, then that becomes ridiculous. We've got to let people see with their own eyes that he's a bright, charming, curious teenage boy."

Leo stopped pacing and turned toward Muir.

"You've got to be kidding me. I will not allow the world to turn Ned into a sideshow freak. To gawk and laugh. To scream their hate. No. That's all we can expect from a public life for Ned. It's hard enough turning sixteen under normal circumstances, Muir. He's got to be protected from the press and the public. It's my highest priority."

Muir's face was set in a look, familiar to Leo, which meant he disagreed but did not intend to continue the argument.

"Well," Muir said, "at least the Polly thing was good." Polly had finally spoken to a reporter in the UK and flatly denied that her separation from her husband had anything to do with Ned. She had also emailed Leo an assurance that she was not the one who had tipped off Pastor Joe.

"Yes, I'm grateful."

"Did you thank her?" Muir asked.

"Not yet."

"So, if not Polly, who did leak Ned's existence to Pastor Joe?"

"No idea," said Leo, who slumped into one of the chairs next to Muir's desk.

"Do you know, Muir, that I'm no longer the richest person in the world?"

"How's that possible?"

"After the SEC announced charges against the company for failing to disclose its role in de-extincting Ned, the stock fell out of bed. And so, on paper at least, I have less than a hundred billion. Less than Gates. And I could lose the company, Muir. The board could fire me as CEO, even though I still own more of it than anyone else."

Muir remained silent.

"It's all falling apart, Muir. I bet everything on Arcadia and Ned. Bets even I could not afford to lose. And . . ." After a moment, Leo stared straight at Muir. "And you warned me, Muir. You did. So did Polly. Don't think I don't remember."

* * *

That night Ned, wide-awake, sat in front of his Mac. Leo's engineers had succeeded in firewalling Ned's access to all Ned-related content, but they had neglected to firewall the sites that contained the instructions on how to hack the firewall. These Ned had found and—following the broken-English instructions from some disaffected teenager from Novosibirsk—had hacked his way through the defenses built around his devices. And now, in every spare moment, he clicked from place to place, weaving together the picture of a world fixated on him.

He read it all. The debates about whether he was a monster or a savior, and whether he belonged in a zoo or in prison. The world's most eminent scientists asserting that Leo had crossed a line. *Saturday Night Live* spoofs in which panicked clergymen prayed for protection from an oafish caveman. Hard-to-follow theological debates regarding whether he was the Antichrist. Philosophers reminding the world that Neanderthals were a type of human and should be accorded all the same moral and legal entitlements of other people. Accusations from Chinese bloggers that the US was building a Neanderthal army and China needed to catch up. Posts and comments speculating about his genitals, and even a dozen sites claiming to offer Neanderthal-on-human porn. As one anthropologist wrote, it was as if the resurrection of the enemy from some ancient war had triggered an alarm implanted by humanity's ancestors deep in our DNA.

And then there were the threats. Ned read countless posts, pregnant with fear and hate, calling for his execution. One comment replayed itself in his mind over and over:

> *God said, "And I will put enmity between your seed and her seed." He knew the devil's spawn would try to destroy humanity by raping our daughters, by infecting the purity of the human race with his evil seed. Only one way to kill the demon: nail the fucking monster to the cross and burn him alive. Do it, dude, and you'll spend eternity at the right hand of a grateful God.*

Ned's voices reemerged with vigor. Some told him that the internet haters had a point. They reminded him it was true that he had feelings for Lilith, feelings that may well be what his enemies meant by "impure." One voice told him to run. Another replied, *Run where?* A persistent voice asked, *If you really were the devil's spawn, would you know it?* He did not tell Leo, Agnes, or even Lilith about the lively debate occurring inside his head.

* * *

Two weeks later, Pastor Joe introduced a bill in the US House of Representatives titled "The Protection of Humanity Act." The proposed law imposed a five-year moratorium on the editing of any animal genome and a permanent ban on the editing of human germ line DNA for any purpose. The bill required that any creature created through synthetic biology or genetic editing without the prior approval of the FDA must be remanded immediately to the custody of the federal government. The bill was referred by the speaker to the House Committee on Science, Space, and Technology, whose chairman immediately scheduled three days of hearings.

24
The House of the People

THESE HEARINGS WILL COME to order."

The chairman of the House Committee on Science, Space, and Technology spoke these words with an exaggerated Texas drawl, as if to assure the nation that, despite the assemblage of intellect seated before him at the witness table, the common sense of the American people would prevail. Common sense, pundits noted, is what seemed to be lacking when the House leadership chose to put hearings about genetic therapy into the hands of a follower of Christian Science, a religion the core belief of which is that sickness is an illusion that can be cured by prayer alone.

Leo, dubbed "NeanderDad" by the tabloids, had entered the chamber moments before with a small entourage of lawyers and advisors, setting off a frenzy in the media scrum at the back of the room. Walking down the center aisle, Leo blinked against the staccato flashes from the photographers clustered in front of the witness table. People fanned themselves to alleviate the heat of the packed room. Leo and his advisors sat in the row behind the witness table and the excitement subsided.

The chairman deferred to Pastor Joe for the opening statement. The congressman rose, energized by the television lights and looking cool and confident. He paused, looking down, as at the beginning of a sermon, and then looked up, fixing his eyes squarely on the lens of the active TV camera, knowing that millions of voters would feel that he was speaking directly to them.

"God made man flawed and gave him free will," he said. "So it was inevitable that the day would come when a man would seek to usurp the Lord our Father. Leo Bonelli made the mistake of thinking that wealth, power, and knowledge made him a god. He was blinded by the illusion that he could control nature and remake man as he wished. I think every one of us, believer or not, knows someplace deep in our soul that this sort of arrogance was bound to end in disaster. For only God is perfect; all humans struggle against vanity, greed, and a long catalog of sins and weaknesses. So when a mortal and imperfect man attempts to step into the shoes of the immortal and perfect God, nothing good can come of it."

Pastor Joe continued to ignore the audience in the hearing room and address himself solely to the camera. "And so, my friends, this leaves us now with the question of the creature, an unholy creation whose very existence perverts the plans of God and threatens the purity of humanity. It's no accident that the creature was brought forth in America, a Christian nation. So now it's up to us, to America, to decide its fate. I have convened the top theologians and scientists to help us make the momentous decision of how best to protect humanity from this peril. I was delighted that Chairman Pollack invited me to co-chair these hearings, and I invite all Americans to join us in this crucial debate and decision."

The committee's majority and minority staffs had fought for days over the witness list, and the minority's one small victory was to schedule the president of one of the country's most respected bioethics think tanks as the lead witness. Leo listened closely as she gave a long and balanced account of man's involvement with genetics, from animal husbandry and plant breeding through direct modification of DNA in the 1970s, and of the corresponding development of the ethical frameworks in which those technologies were researched and then applied. *Perhaps*, Leo thought, *this won't be so bad.*

The majority's senior counsel, a close ally of Pastor Joe, began the questioning.

"Madam, in your opinion, when Mr. Bonelli edited his own DNA to approximate the genome of an extinct species, *Homo neanderthalensis,* and then inserted the edited chromosomes into a human egg, which was subsequently brought to term in a surrogate human mother, did he comply with the prevailing research and ethical guidelines at the time, or for that matter, now?"

"No, he did not."

A low murmur rippled through the audience.

"How so? What parts of the ethical guidelines did he violate?"

"That sort of modification of human germ line cells—that is, cells that get passed down from generation to generation—is exactly what the guidelines were intended to prevent. We had then, and still have now, a moratorium on that sort of work."

"Why? What's wrong with it? Didn't we just hear in your testimony that we've been modifying DNA, through breeding, and then subsequently through direct intervention, for a very long time?"

"Basically, because of concerns about safety and ethics. Editing, although it's advanced enormously, still doesn't have the kind of accuracy we'd want for other types of clinical interventions. Bottom line, it's too risky, especially when you're talking about human beings."

"And the ethical issues?"

"It's complicated, and there are many different views, all of which I think deserve to be heard. But basically, most of us in the field think that it's manifestly wrong to create a human being merely to satisfy scientific curiosity."

"That's all?"

"No. There's also a strong feeling on the part of many of us that humanity itself is not really ready to take charge of its own genetic destiny. Once we start to modify our own germ line, we're basically taking on the decision of what humanity should be."

"In other words, editing the germ line is playing God?"

"No, I'm not saying that. It's substituting human judgment for the process of evolution."

Later, when the minority counsel's turn came, she went back to this point.

"Ma'am, if your child were born with a fatal disease caused by a single gene, would you allow the modification of that gene?"

"Of course."

"And if you were pregnant and your fetus had a germ line mutation, hemophilia, say, that could be safely eliminated, freeing both your child and her offspring from the disease, would you do it?"

"Yes."

"What if we had no way of knowing whether your child would develop pancreatic cancer, but you were offered a germ line modification that in effect immunized the child against any of the genetic or epigenetic causes of that terrible disease. Would you allow it?"

"Probably, provided at the time the accuracy and safety issues had been addressed."

"So the point is that not all germ line modifications are unethical."

"Perhaps. But really, the line between ethical and unethical is not so clear. It's a tough call, very fact specific, and the consensus evolves as the technologies change."

"Exactly. Thank you. Let the record show that the witness has testified that Mr. Bonelli faced guidelines that were unclear and that were constantly evolving to accommodate a rapidly advancing technology. No further questions."

Leo smiled for the first time that day. The second time was when one of the revered pioneers of genetics, now in his late nineties, refused to be baited into condemning germ line modification. Instead, with a good deal of humor and modesty, he became one of the few to support it outright: "A lot of people say they're worried about changing our genetic instructions. But those are just a product of evolution designed to adapt us for certain conditions that may not exist today. We all know how imperfect we are. Why not make ourselves a little better suited to survival?" Rather than permit the elderly icon to be attacked, the chairman quickly dismissed him from the witness table.

The next few witnesses were doctors and geneticists. All were quick to condemn the decision made by Leo to create Ned, but then offered vigorous defenses of genetic science generally. They argued that genetics was a world-changing technology, probably the most important ever. They warned that the science was global and mobile, and that if the United States imposed constraints not embraced by other countries, the science would simply get done elsewhere, as it had during the previous ban on federally funded embryonic research. These witnesses agreed that the only effect of the moratorium proposed by Pastor Joe would be to put the United States at an enormous economic and competitive disadvantage, particularly in comparison with China, which planned to eliminate genetic disease, and perhaps make other upgrades to its population, by sequencing the genomes of half of all embryos in that country.

José Vargas, the Cornell geneticist who had undertaken the de-extinction of ice-age megafauna for Arcadia, testified next. When he completed his statement, the chairman recognized Pastor Joe to ask the first question.

"Sir, you have testified that we are quite far down this road of allowing science to interfere with the propagation of the human race."

"The human *species*, yes, sir. In vitro fertilization was followed by preimplantation genetic diagnosis, where we select embryos preferentially based on the absence of disease-causing mutation."

"And what about selection on other grounds?"

"Yes, sir, that is happening too. To the extent that genetic sequencing of an embryo tells us other things—gender, hair or eye color, for example—parents can take these into account as they wish."

"And so my question, Doctor, is where will it end? Where is this road you say we are following going to lead us?"

"I'm not sure I understand, Congressman. We don't know. It will take us where the science permits, and where we decide we want to go."

"Tell me, Doctor, how many men, women, and children were killed during the Nazi experiments with eugenics?"

The room erupted noisily, and the ranking minority member called out over the din, "Mr. Chairman, the gentleman goes too far. He cannot compare the witness to a Nazi. Withdraw the question, sir."

"I am not comparing the witness to a Nazi," Pastor Joe said. "I simply asked a question about history."

"You may continue, Congressman," the chairman said.

"So, Doctor. I simply asked how many were killed during the Nazi experiments with eugenics?"

"How many? I'm not certain. That's not exactly my field."

"Not your field? A quarter million human beings slaughtered in the last century in the name of using genetics to improve humanity, and it's not your field?"

"I just meant I didn't know the exact . . ."

"And how many sterilized?"

"Exactly, I don't . . ."

"Four hundred thousand by 1941. Four hundred thousand people whom the elites of the day deemed unfit to pass their genes on to the next generation. Four hundred thousand souls whose only sin was to be poor or disabled. So do you want to reconsider your answer, Doctor, as to where this road of yours is leading us?"

"Sir . . ."

"No need to answer, Doctor. It was, as I believe you academics put it, a rhetorical question."

Leo overheard a reporter sitting in the row behind him whisper to her companion, "Shit, he's good. Insert knife without warning, then twist slowly." Leo agreed. *But*, he thought, *unlike these hapless academics, I know how to handle a man like Pastor Joe.*

The afternoon session included a group of historians and philosophers, one of whom caused a ruckus by advocating aggressive use of genetic editing to "break the mold of history." This debate, he argued, was a battle between science, which has the future "in its bones," and a political culture that is inevitably rooted in a sugar-coated past. What is civilization other than an effort to seize control of history and point ourselves in a better direction? What was the American Revolution? The hacking of history. "So," the telegenic young scholar asserted to the committee, many of whom looked shocked, "imagine that we could edit the genome to remove one of our worst characteristics—say, intolerance or hate or the propensity for violence—why wouldn't we? It's what we do. I say point ourselves in a better direction if we can."

The majority counsel, noting many nodding heads in the audience, decided to be elaborately polite in her approach to this witness.

"Professor, I wonder if you could tell us whether you think there is any difference between information and knowledge?"

"Not really. I think knowledge has to be based on information, on fact, on truth."

"That, sir, contradicts thousands of years of human experience. Just as there are many different types of intelligence, including emotional intelligence and moral intelligence, there are many different types of truth. You live in a world of information, of facts that can be digitized, shared, and analyzed, mainly by machines. But knowledge and wisdom are something else altogether. They can't be captured in a spreadsheet. Knowledge and wisdom answer the very different questions of what the facts mean, what truths are embedded in those spreadsheets, and, most importantly, what we ought to do about them."

"Of course that's right, I didn't mean . . ."

"And doesn't wisdom, as it has grown, slowly, organically, naturally over thousands of years, doesn't wisdom counsel us that stepping into the shoes of God, taking over the power to create and shape life to our will, is both unnatural and dangerous? That man is both too ignorant and too flawed to wield such powers?"

"Ma'am, I don't think so. Wisdom has taught us that we—and the other genus *Homo* species that preceded us—were lucky enough to acquire intelligence and reason through evolution. Wisdom teaches us to use the skills we have, which is exactly what we've done over the past ten millennia as we created agriculture and cities and cultures. We didn't say that sickness was God's will and turn our back on medicine. Saying we shouldn't pursue genetics is like saying we shouldn't use our opposable thumb. It's like saying we should never have gone down the road of experimental physics, because it could lead to the atomic bomb. Here's the thing: We're on the verge of making the shift from evolution by natural selection to the intelligent design of organisms of all sorts. It's probably the most important thing that's happened since life emerged on Earth four billion years ago. You'd better get used to it, and turn to the real question, which is, 'What do we want to become?' That's . . ."

"Professor," she interrupted, "you're a philosopher, a student of literature and civilizations. Tell us what our forebearers intended us to learn from the myths of Prometheus and Icarus? What truth is embedded in those stories?"

"You know, I'm glad you asked that. People generally think Icarus is a warning against hubris, but if you read it, his father also warns him not to fly too low, a warning about complacency. And most importantly, father and son were trapped on Crete, and nothing in the myth suggests they should have just stayed put and not tried to fly. The lesson of the myth is to go for it, but be aware of the dangers of hubris. Fly, but not too high. An apt metaphor for genetics, I think. Don't be paralyzed by caution, but proceed cautiously."

"And did Mr. Bonelli? Did he proceed cautiously?"

"Well . . ."

The lawyer's voice acquired an edge.

"So, in your view, Professor, editing mistakes, unintended mutations, monsters like the Neanderthal created by Mr. Bonelli—all these are acceptable risks? Giving tyrants and dictators the power to change humanity for their evil purposes—an acceptable risk? Unleashing of the dark instinct that led to eugenics and the murder and forced sterilization of countless innocents—also an acceptable risk? Is that your testimony?"

"You know, ma'am, the day that one man invented fire, another guy became an arsonist. The prospect of both benefit and abuse is embedded in every technology, every advance. Where would we be if we had succumbed to our fear of arson and banned fire?"

The chairman signaled to his counsel that the time was up and that he wished to bring the day's session to a close. The lawyer smoothed her skirt, brushed back her hair, and adjusted her posture.

"One final question, Professor. You just spoke of benefit and abuse. Please tell me if the following is true, yes or no. The technology that Mr. Bonelli is promoting, genetic editing, could be abused by a terrorist to introduce to American mosquitos a gene that turns their saliva into a deadly toxin, so that each person bitten by a mosquito would die a horrible death. Yes or no?"

"Well, yes, in theory. But . . ."

"No buts, sir. You have testified that Mr. Bonelli is enabling the creation of a weapon of mass destruction more insidious and terrifying than the atomic bomb."

"I am not, I don't think . . ."

"Time has expired," the chairman said, bringing down his gavel with a satisfied grin.

25
Betrayal

But a human being regarded as a person, that is, as the subject of a morally practical reason, is exalted above any price; for as a person . . . he is not to be valued merely as a means to the ends of others or even to his own ends, but as an end in himself, that is, he possesses a dignity *(an absolute inner worth) by which he exacts* respect *for himself from all other rational beings in the world. He can measure himself with every other being of this kind and value himself on a footing of equality with them.*

Immanuel Kant, *The Metaphysics of Morals (1785)*

CHAIRMAN POLLACK OPENED THE next day of hearings with a bang of his gavel.

"Today's hearing," he said, "will focus on three things: Is the creature human? What is the nature of its threat to humanity? And finally, what should be done to protect America and the whole human race?"

Day two's first witness, an eminent paleoanthropologist, approached the witness table with slow and uncertain steps. He had mistakenly worn a heavy tweed jacket and wiped the sweat from his forehead with a woolen sleeve.

Pastor Joe led off the questioning.

"Professor, in your opinion, are Neanderthals human?"

"No. I mean, it's a semantic question, but from a scientific point of view, the question might be seen to come down to whether *Homo neanderthalensis* is a species separate from *Homo sapiens*, or perhaps a subspecies. Recent genetic investigation points to a separate species. But really, in either case, most of us would not consider the Neanderthals human. A member of the genus *Homo*, sure. And . . ."

Pastor Joe knew that the scholar's rambling did not make for compelling television and tried to interrupt. But the professor was determined.

"And . . . and this is important, I have to say that we don't even know whether the creature, the boy called Ned, is even a Neanderthal."

"What do you mean? He has the DNA of a Neanderthal; doesn't that make him a Neanderthal?"

"No, he has the genome of a *Homo sapiens*, modified to substitute a number of key Neanderthal traits for human traits. And not only could there still be many genetic differences from historical Neanderthals, but I remind you that he wasn't raised by Neanderthals or influenced by Neanderthal culture. So really, nothing in science tells us what exactly to call him."

"I see. As a human creation and not a creation of God or evolution, he is a kind of hybrid. Neither here nor there. As I've said, a kind of monster." An aid pushed a piece of paper in front of the congressman, who continued smoothly, "I'm sure you know, Professor, that the word 'monster' derives from the Latin *monstrum*, meaning an aberrant occurrence, usually biological, that is outside the natural order. Would you call the creature an aberrant biological occurrence, outside of the natural order?"

"Well, yes, I suppose I would."

"So the monster . . ."

"I didn't say . . ."

The congressman carried on, "The monster, the monster that approximates a Neanderthal, is that fair?"

"Yes, approximates . . ."

"So this approximate Neanderthal monster, can we expect him to be a cannibal, an eater of his own kind, and of humans?"

A wave of gasps and exclamations swept through the audience.

"I beg your pardon?" said the professor.

"The great science writer H. G. Wells, speaking of Neanderthals, wrote, 'when his sons grew big enough to annoy him, the grisly man'—that's what Wells called Neanderthals—'the grisly man killed them or drove them off. If he killed them he may have eaten them.' Is that a correct description of typical Neanderthal behavior?"

"Well, we really have no idea. He wrote that in a novel, I think. Yes, there is some evidence that Neanderthals engaged in cannibalism, but so did lots of early hominins. So did *sapiens*. Some still do."

"And these cannibalistic monsters, did they mate with humans? I read that their males routinely raped human women."

"No, you can't say . . ."

"They didn't mate?"

"Yes, they mated, but we have no idea if it was rape."

"Really? Are you asking the American people to believe that human women willingly had sex with these grisly cannibalistic monsters?"

"Sir . . ."

"Let's go on to another topic. Wells also says the two races were 'intolerable to each other.' Would you say that Neanderthals were enemies of humanity, with whom we engaged in an epic battle, the outcome of which established which species would rule the world?"

"Sir, the work you are quoting from is just a novel. It's fiction."

"Perhaps, but I'm told that even you scientists call it 'invasion biology.' When resources are limited, and a new species comes into the territory of another and competes for those same limited resources, then there is conflict, is there not?"

"Well, yes, of course."

"Right. So we and these cannibalistic monsters were mortal enemies and engaged in an epic battle that endured for millennia. When we won, they became extinct and we survived. It seems to be a pretty risky bet to bring them back. In fact," Pastor Joe paused dramatically here and leaned in toward the cameras, "what appears to me to be at stake is the risk of our own extinction."

The ill-prepared paleoanthropologist was tortured in this manner for another half hour until, appearing shell-shocked, he was dismissed from the witness table.

A law professor then testified that in America and every country around the world, the word "person" meant an individual of the species *Homo sapiens*. He reminded the lawmakers of the 1997 Universal Declaration on the Human Genome and Human Rights, which made clear that it was the "human genome" that entitled a person to "inherent dignity" and human rights under the law.

Leo and his lawyers sat in the front row behind the witness table. The photographers clustered on the floor in front of the table were able to catch Leo's incredulous reactions to much of the testimony, and one of them snapped a photo just as Leo's expression transitioned to one of surprise when the majority counsel announced, "Mr. Chairman, our next witness is an employee of Mr. Bonelli, Mr. Muir O'Brien."

Leo believed that Muir was back in Arcadia watching the proceedings on television with Ned. No one had told Leo or his lawyers that Muir would testify. Leo turned his head and watched Muir walk slowly from the door in the rear of the hearing room to the witness table. Muir stared straight ahead and did not acknowledge Leo.

After taking the oath, Muir sat clutching both chair arms tightly. Leo saw the whiteness of his knuckles, and a drop of perspiration rolled down the back of his neck, leaving a small dark stain on his blue collar.

The majority counsel started the questioning.

"Mr. O'Brien, can you please tell us what you do for Mr. Bonelli?"

"I run the botany and horticulture operations for an SBD re-wilding project known as Arcadia."

"Having known him for a long time, would you say he is a man of good character?"

"Yes, ma'am. He's been a generous mentor and friend to me and to my daughter." Muir paused. "He's a good man."

"And would you say he was a good husband?"

"What does that have to do . . ."

"Please answer the question, sir."

"It's not easy to know what goes on inside other people's marriages."

"For example," she persisted, "did you ever observe Mr. Bonelli and his wife having arguments, fights?"

"Yes, of course, every couple . . ."

"And did Mrs. Bonelli ever complain about how she was treated by her husband?"

"Yes, but . . ."

"Did she say he was abusive?"

"Not in that way."

"Well, then, in what way?"

Muir looked down and did not speak.

"You're under oath, Mr. O'Brien. What did she say?"

"That . . . that he had changed. That he was no longer kind and affectionate to her."

"Cold, manipulative? Did she use words like that?"

"Yes, but . . ."

"Would you say that Mr. Bonelli is a moral person?"

"I don't know what that means," Muir answered.

"You know, a person who tries to do the right thing, as opposed to being arrogant, or selfish, or dishonest."

"I . . . I mean, who am I to judge?"

"You are a witness under oath, and you're required to tell us what you observed and what you experienced. Is Mr. Bonelli someone who always tries to do the right thing? Who refrains from doing things that would advance his interests because they would be wrong? Are these attitudes that characterize Mr. Bonelli?"

"Not exactly . . ."

"So we've established that Mr. Bonelli was cruel to his wife . . ."

"I did not say that."

"So what about the creature whom he calls his son."

"Ned is a wonderful young man."

"I'm not asking about the creature. I'm asking about Mr. Bonelli. He calls the creature his son. Did he always treat him like his son?"

"I don't know what you mean."

"Did they always live together? Did he always call him 'Son' and treat him with affection, or is that something new, perhaps since the congressman first shone a light on what he had done?"

"No."

"No, what?"

"No, they did not always live together, and he did not always call him 'Son.' But today he calls him 'Son' and is a most affectionate and responsible father. He loves Ned and Ned loves him."

"That's strange. Did you always call your daughter Lilith 'Daughter'? Did you always live with her?"

"Of course."

The lawyer, previously all efficiency, relaxed her pose and gave Muir a warm look.

"I'm sure you did, Mr. O'Brien. You're a good man. Let's turn to something else. Would you say you know the creature well?"

"Yes. I've known Ned all his life. I know him very well."

"Mr. Bonelli tells us it's just like a normal human teenager. Do you agree?"

"Yes."

"It looks like a human teenager?"

"More or less."

"Really? Doesn't it have prominent brow ridges, you know, those prominent ridges above the eyes that we see on chimps and gorillas?"

"Yes."

"That's not normal, is it?"

"No."

"Does it have other traits that humans don't have? Other abnormalities?"

"Not really." Again Muir hesitated. "Well, he has a strong sense of smell, and also rather extensive peripheral vision, if that's what you mean."

"Ah, really? More like the smelling ability of animals?" She didn't wait for an answer and moved on. "Have you hunted with the creature?"

"I wish you would stop calling him that," Muir said, suddenly angry. "He has a name. His name is Ned. And he's a teenage boy, not an 'it.'"

"Answer the question, please."

"Yes, Ned and I have hunted together. Frequently."

"And how did it do? Is it a good hunter?"

"Yes. Excellent, really. A natural."

"It's a natural predator, then. Would you say it was dangerous?"

"What? Well, maybe to rabbits."

"And if it hunted humans? Would it be dangerous then?"

"What? That's absurd. No one would hunt a human."

"A Neanderthal would. We've heard testimony that Neanderthals and humans engaged in a bloody battle for survival. A battle to the death, in fact."

"That doesn't mean . . ."

"So," she interrupted, turning to another subject. "Does the creature think of itself as a Neanderthal?"

"Yes, at least since he was told about his . . . origins."

"Naturally. And would you say it would like there to be more Neanderthals?"

"I suppose."

"Does it want to see a Neanderthal population reestablished somewhere? This park or zoo place where you work, for example?"

"No, he's never said that. And it's not a zoo."

"Mr. Bonelli testified yesterday that he had the ability to make the creature sterile, but chose not to. Why do you think that was? Because he intended it to reproduce, perhaps?"

"I don't know."

"Mr. O'Brien, I understand you have a daughter, almost eighteen years old now. Lilith. Is that right?"

"Yes. She just turned eighteen."

"She has interacted with the creature, yes?"

"They were raised together. They are very close friends, like brother and sister."

"Really? Brother and sister? Isn't it true that your daughter and the creature went on a date?"

"I wouldn't call it that."

"What would they call it?"

"Well, I suppose . . ."

"Yes, a date. And have they kissed?"

Muir, whose hands were already sweaty and cold, started to feel numb. He wanted to disappear. To be anywhere other than where he was.

"Yes."

"Mr. O'Brien, how would you feel if your daughter were to have sexual relations with the Neanderthal creature?"

"My daughter is a good girl, she wouldn't . . ."

"Mr. O'Brien, answer the question. The Neanderthal is a very mature sixteen and your daughter is eighteen, and they are dating and kissing. Do you or do you not want your daughter having sexual relations with the creature?"

"I'm her father . . ."

"The Neanderthal creature could be father of your grandchild. Do you want that?"

"I don't want any grandchild yet, and no one . . ."

"Mr. O'Brien, answer the question. Do you want the creature to father your grandchild?"

Muir slumped in his seat, deflated and seemingly confused. He appeared ten years older than when he entered the room.

"No. I don't."

* * *

When the chairman gaveled the session to a close, SBD security surrounded Leo and escorted him through the crowd out to the wide hallway of the Rayburn House Office Building. Leo ducked into a men's room and stopped short when he saw Muir bent over a sink, covering his face with a wad of paper towels.

Sensing someone standing behind him, Muir uncovered his face and stood upright. His eyes met Leo's in the mirror.

Leo felt a warm flush and sensed his accelerating heart rate.

"You fucking bastard. How could you?"

Muir's eyes were bloodshot.

"Leo, I had no choice. They subpoenaed me. They told me I wasn't allowed to tell you or your lawyers. Believe me, I didn't want . . ."

"But what you said. After all that I've done. Do you really hate me that much?"

"I don't. You know I don't."

"Did you think about what might happen to Ned if they get their hands on him? What they could do to him?"

Muir stared at the tile floor as Leo stormed out of the restroom.

26
Purity

THE FINAL DAY OF the hearings proceeded largely along the lines of the prior sessions, with Pastor Joe promoting the message that modern genetics provides a "back door" to a new type of eugenics. A philosopher testified that at its core eugenics was the practice of "people selection" and that genetic editing simply takes eugenics to the next level through the practice of "gene selection." An historian of the eugenics movement suggested that this new type of eugenics would focus on eliminating the people contemporary elites found distasteful, such as people who were overweight or religious. The entertainment value of the hearings remained high, in part because Pastor Joe's staff fed him the streaming video ratings in real time, in response to which he was able to ramp up the salaciousness of the content whenever eyes started to leave the screen.

Leo was the final witness of the day. In his opening statement he asked the committee to think back to 1978, when Louise Brown was born having been conceived in a test tube. Many condemned the process as a "moral abomination" and sought to stop it. But it was not stopped, and now we had five million people who would not have existed without this technology, ten million parents who would have been denied the blessing of children. In light of this experience, Leo asked, who should have been regarded as being on the side of life, those who promoted the technology or those who condemned it? Leo humbly admitted that he had jumped the gun in proceeding to de-extinct a Neanderthal when he did, but he reminded everyone that it was his own DNA that he put at risk, and that countless impatient visionaries, including five Nobel laureates, had engaged in self-experimentation. This use by scientists of their own bodies had been the catalyst behind many great scientific breakthroughs, including game-changing advances such as vaccination. And finally, he spoke of Ned the person, his gentle charm, generosity, and intelligence. He painted a picture of a teenager who memorized old sayings as a hobby and loved *Star Wars* and the outdoors. Leo spoke of his love for this son. It was as good a performance as his coaches and handlers could have hoped for.

The majority counsel then questioned him for two hours about every detail of Ned's creation. Leo, as instructed, gave the shortest and simplest answers possible, trying not to appear defensive. The lawyer then turned brusquely to a list of quick-fire questions.

"You say, sir, that you love the creature. Did you consider the very considerable risk of horrific birth defects resulting from the known inaccuracy of genetic editing?"

"We knew exactly what the accuracy was and were able to calculate and mitigate the risk through working with strands more than fifty thousand base pairs long."

"Did you consider the risk of changing the coding sequences only, leaving the noncoding DNA from your own genome? The possibility that the edited genes simply wouldn't function as they did in the original Neanderthal?"

"Of course, we knew this was a risk."

"This creature you call your son, did you consider when creating it that its immune system might not be able to cope with modern pathogens? That the creature might have to spend its life living as the boy in the bubble?"

"We knew it was a risk."

"Did you create a companion for the poor creature?"

"No."

"Did you create a female of the same species so it would have a mate?"

"No."

Whatever sympathy Leo had earned through his statement was evaporating fast.

"I gather a poor Spanish farmer's wife was subjected to the risk of giving birth to the creature. Did you advise her of the enormous size of the Neanderthal head, and the mismatch between it and the human birth canal?"

"No, but we were careful to choose a woman who could handle it . . ."

"But you didn't tell her so she could make up her own mind? And did you tell her we currently think that only 2 percent of the pregnancies that resulted from a mix between humans and Neanderthals resulted in successful live births?"

"No."

"And how much did you pay her?"

"I can't remember."

"Let me refresh your memory. You were worth hundreds of billions at the time, you put this woman's life in jeopardy without disclosing to her the relevant risks, and paid her only $40,000."

"I believe we paid off her debts as well. And her life was not in any . . ."

"Do you agree that eugenics are a great evil that should remain prohibited?"

"Yes, of course."

"Really, sir? In eugenics, they tried to shape the race by selective breeding, and also of course by keeping some people's genes from being passed on at all. But at least people kept reproducing naturally and the children that resulted were receiving genetic material from their parents in the normal way. But what you are doing is far worse and far more dangerous. It's something the Nazis could only dream of, and yet you want it made legal?"

"You are wrong," Leo answered. "It's still entirely possible for us to use breeding techniques to make the human race smarter or stronger or whatever, but we've wisely decided not to do that. Equally, genetic editing is just a tool. How we decide to use it is a separate question. My goal is human health and longevity. You can't seriously compare this with the horrific motivations of the Nazis."

"Why, Mr. Bonelli, did you not create the creature to be sterile? It's easily done, right? Just give him an uneven number of chromosomes, like a mule, am I right? And is it true that responsible geneticists routinely ensure that their creations cannot freely reproduce until they're proved safe?"

"Yes, it's a common precaution. And yes, it would have been possible. But I wanted him to have all the dignity and autonomy of a human, including the ability to love and be loved, and to reproduce."

"Thus you consciously and deliberately ensured he was able to mate with human females."

"Sure. Why not?"

A moderate congressman from Pennsylvania took up the questioning.

"Mr. Bonelli, you have to admit that there are some real issues here. We really have no idea what could happen if the creature were allowed to procreate with a human female."

Leo interrupted. "I remind you, sir, that in my view Ned is human."

"OK, then with a *Homo sapiens* female. I mean, we have no idea what might happen."

"Excuse me again, sir. We know exactly what would result. You and I have somewhere between 1 and 2.5 percent, perhaps even 4 percent, Neanderthal DNA, as a result of your and my ancestors having done exactly what you seem to find so problematic. Ned's child would inherit half of his genome from Ned and the other half from his mate. And, by the way, it could be a very good thing for the genetic diversity of humanity. Did you know that we have lower genetic diversity than either chimps or penguins? Anything that increases genetic diversity of humanity makes our survival more likely in the long run."

"But isn't it, well, just unnatural? I thought that science and morality were on the same page on this one; that is, that the whole definition of a species is a group of animals that mate with each other, and whose offspring are fertile. I mean, having sex and trying to reproduce with another species has been taboo for all, I think, of human history."

"Congressman," Leo explained, "interspecies breeding takes place all the time, both in nature and as the result of hybridization by humans. Some of the greatest treasures of the plant kingdom—wheat, grapefruit, peppermint, the London plane tree—have resulted from interspecies breeding, and there are many animals of different species who do the same, but mostly within the same genus—like *Homo sapiens* and *Homo neanderthalensis*. Think of cattle and bison, or African bees and honeybees, there are probably hundreds of others. Now you're right, of course, that humans cannot successfully breed with other types of animals—but remember, *Homo neanderthalensis* is a fellow member of the genus *Homo*, a fellow human."

The chairman called on Pastor Joe to resume his questioning. The audience stirred in anticipation, and the photographers hoisted their cameras while Leo sought to maintain a calm and respectful mien.

"We heard this morning that the Neanderthals were our species' number-one competitor, a fierce and bitter enemy—we fought a war for survival and won. Now we bring them back and let them take over?"

"Take over?" Leo replied. "One sixteen-year-old Neanderthal boy against seven billion *Homo sapiens*? Congressman, the only way Ned could change humanity would be if the uniquely Neanderthal traits that are passed on to his children and their progeny provide an evolutionary advantage and natural selection works its magic over, I don't know, maybe ninety generations, or a few thousand years. And why, exactly, would that be a bad thing?"

Pastor Joe sensed his opening and took it, slamming his fist on the desk and causing his water glass to bounce perilously.

"Yes. Exactly. That is what this is all about. The corruption of the human line, the extinction of humanity by stealth. It's the final fight between God and Satan, exactly as the Bible predicts. We cannot stand by and risk our own extinction. That creature cannot be permitted to spread his poison. We are called by God, by humanity, and by common sense to stop this by any means necessary."

Pastor Joe pushed back his chair, as if intending to stand up. But then, appearing to collect himself, he clasped his hands together in silent prayer. The click of camera shutters was the only sound in the room. The congressman then looked up and proceeded as if his outburst had not occurred.

"Sir, can you tell us the meaning of 'watermarking,' when used in the context of synthetic biology?"

"Yes." *My God*, Leo thought, *they know. Only Shen could have told them. Shen. It must have been Shen who tipped off Pastor Joe about Ned*. Leo, his heart now pounding loudly, struggled to keep a neutral face.

"Sir," Pastor Joe prompted.

"Watermarking," Leo said, his voice wavering almost imperceptibly, "is the practice of writing a mark into modified or synthetic DNA, a basic precaution to ensure that it can easily be distinguished from the original."

"Mr. Bonelli, yes or no. Did you have Ned's DNA watermarked?"

"Yes."

"And so what did you write into the creature's DNA? What message did you choose to be passed down forever to all of its descendants?"

"I don't remember. It's a technical detail."

The only sound in the hearing room was the dull hum of the inadequate air conditioning.

"Let me prompt your memory, sir. Did you sign your creation with your own name?"

Pastor Joe paused to underscore Leo's failure to reply.

"Is it true," the congressman asked again, "that within the creature's genome is the coded statement, 'Leo Bonelli *fecit*'?"

Leo glared at his interlocutor and remained silent.

"And what is the meaning of that, sir, for those of our fellow citizens who do not understand Latin? Does it mean, 'Leo Bonelli made it'?"

"It means nothing," Leo snarled. "It's like choosing a password for a website. You just need to choose something you can remember."

"My apologies, sir, but it means everything. It tells us most eloquently about the depth of your arrogance and presumption. Leo Bonelli made it. Leo Bonelli has replaced God. Leo Bonelli and not Jesus Christ is the redeemer of mankind. I think the American people will understand exactly what you meant."

Pastor Joe turned to the TV cameras and raised his hands, as if in benediction.

"Do you now see, friends, what I've been talking about? Man's greed and vanity are nearly insatiable. Scientists talk of modesty and caution, but they act with reckless arrogance. What could be more arrogant than writing your own name in the very fabric of creation?"

"That is totally misleading," Leo interrupted. "You've twisted a routine laboratory procedure into something it's not. It's typical of your . . ."

Leo's lawyer touched him on the shoulder from his seat behind the table.

"Be careful what you say, Mr. Bonelli," Pastor Joe replied. "Your billions, or trillions, or whatever they are, do not make you immune from contempt of Congress any more than they make you immune from the laws of God."

"And," Leo shot back, "your fundamentalist obsession with the idea that *Homo sapiens* was created by an imaginary supernatural being does not make *you* immune from the Constitution, the laws of this country, or from basic decency."

Members of the audience gasped, the cameras clicked, and reporters smiled, knowing they had the lead quotes for their stories. In the commotion, Leo could think about only two things: how to protect his son and how he would destroy Shen.

The chairman intervened. "That's enough, gentlemen," he said, bringing down a large gavel. "This hearing is adjourned."

* * *

As Leo entered the back seat of the limo that would take him back to the K Street office of his lawyers, he signaled his desire to be alone with a wave of his hand.

Clip, who had remained back at Arcadia, answered the phone.

"Sorry, boss, rough day."

"Clip, pull up everything on Shen. Can you believe the bastard double-crossed me? How many millions have we paid him over the years? And he screwed me."

"I don't get it," Clip said. "What did Pastor Joe have to offer him that he wasn't already getting from us?"

"No idea. Here's the plan. Cut him off. Not another penny to him or his lab or any project that he's involved with. Tell the university in Singapore that if he isn't fired tomorrow they'll never get another penny. Put the word out that if you do business with him, you'll never do business with SBD."

"Right, boss."

"And, find the dossier. I put all the dirt on Shen in one place, as an insurance policy. Copy it and send it anonymously to the Singapore police. And send it to the Chinese authorities as well. Maybe we'll get lucky and they'll extradite him to rot in a Chinese prison for the rest of his life."

* * *

That evening Pastor Joe returned to his district in Ohio for a raucous rally in support of the new legislation. At the end of his speech, covered live by most of the national media, he announced that he was a candidate for president of the United States.

The next day, when reporters asked the chairman whether or not he would support Pastor Joe's bill, he responded, "No comment."

27
Power

A BIBLE SAT ALONE ON the reception area coffee table, still covered by an almost invisible plastic shrink-wrap. A framed flag of Texas occupied pride of place on the opposite wall. Photographs of Chairman Pollack with various world leaders and other dignitaries surrounded the large flag. Kurt Walsh sat on the couch silently noting the names of the people in the photographs and filing them in his memory. Such details could be useful.

"The chairman will see you now," said the bubbly intern sitting behind the reception desk. In another era Kurt would have been called a power broker. For thirty years he had shuttled between K Street and the Hill on behalf of those who could afford him. His public profile was nonexistent, and yet he could count on one hand the number of politicians who made the error of not taking his call. Leo and SBD had been his clients for two decades.

"Kurt, my friend," Chairman Pollack said when Walsh entered his office. "Welcome. Thanks so much for coming over." Both men knew, of course, that it was the lobbyist—and not the chairman—who had requested the meeting.

"You doubtless have heard, Mr. Chairman, that Senator Dorsey has decided to endorse your opponent in the primary. Tough break. But it's early days." The only thing Kurt was sure of was that the chairman had not heard this news. It was his signature opening gambit in every meeting—remind them that he knew more, and knew it sooner, than they did. He watched with pleasure as the congressman's political director squirmed in his seat.

"Yes, of course," the chairman said smoothly. "Too bad. A decision he'll come to regret."

"I know you have a packed day, Congressman, so shall we get right to business?" Kurt looked at the chairman's chief of staff and political director with a warm smile. "I'm sorry, gentlemen, but I think the congressman will want to hear what I have to say on his own. Your call, of course."

The chairman nodded at his two staffers, who left the room.

Kurt Walsh once described his job as connecting people who need or want things with the people who have the things that they need or want.

"You're here for Leo, I assume," the chairman said.

A half hour later, when the two staffers reentered the room, Kurt and the chairman stood in a corner of the office, away from the window, speaking.

"Irritating blowhard," the chairman was saying.

"True," Kurt replied. "Anyway, I know that Leo will be very pleased he can be of help."

* * *

At that moment, twenty-five hundred miles to the west, Muir and Ned stalked a doe in the wooded slopes north of the Village.

Muir, having no idea how events had changed Ned's feelings about him, was reluctant to be the one to reach out. Ned, sensing this, asked if Muir would take him hunting.

"Ned, we've got to talk about it. I'm not like your dad. I can't just sweep things under the rug and pretend they didn't happen. OK?"

"Sure."

"I was subpoenaed. That meant I had no choice. If I hadn't gone to Washington I would have been thrown in jail. I had no idea what they were going to ask. I didn't have any preparation. They told me I was not allowed to talk to your dad or his lawyers. I just took the oath and sat down at the table."

Muir fidgeted with a twig and then continued. "What I wanted most was to protect you. You know that, I hope?"

"Yeah. I know that."

"But sometimes our deepest values conflict. Sometimes we have to choose between loyalty, even love, and other things we believe in, like truth. I've always told the truth, Ned. I'm not sure why, but probably because of my dad, who believed in the truth more than anything."

Ned nodded.

"So when they asked me questions, I told the truth. Some were trick questions, and I was too dumb to see them coming, and they took what I said and twisted it horribly, and I didn't know what to do. But some of the questions were perfectly clear. I mean, it was clear to me that if I answered truthfully it would be bad for you. In the moment, I had to choose between telling the truth and protecting you. I chose to tell the truth. I hope you can forgive me."

"I get it. I think when you tell the truth, there's nothing to forgive."

The two sat silently for a while. Comfort with silence was one of the many things they had in common.

"Actually, Muir. I do have a question. They asked you if you wanted me to be the father of your grandchild. You said no. Was that the truth?"

Muir turned and looked at Ned. "I really wish it weren't. I love you like a son. But I'm Lilith's father, and I just can't . . . I wouldn't want my grandchild to have to go through what you've gone through. And so, yes, that was the truth. And I know it must hurt you terribly. I'm sorry."

Ned held his gaze. "I could never be without Lilith, you know. You can't stop us from being together."

Muir gazed at the horizon over Ned's shoulder. "I know."

* * *

Two weeks later the House Committee on Science, Space, and Technology held a regularly scheduled meeting on Capitol Hill, one of the scores of standing committees and subcommittees that convened each day. Because there was nothing of interest on the agenda, few of the members attended. A single reporter, who had received an anonymous tip, sat in the audience. Moments after the chairman gaveled the short session to a close, the reporter's scoop appeared on the website of the *Washington Post:* "Congressman Pollack, chairman of the House Committee on Science, Space, and Technology, announced today that his committee would take no action on H.R. 342, the so-called Defense of Humanity Act, effectively killing the legislation introduced by Congressman 'Pastor Joe' O'Malley." Two hours later a furious Pastor Joe appeared on the Capitol steps before a noisy scrum of reporters.

"What happened here today, folks, is an outrage. We're supposed to be the people's house doing the people's will. But today was one of those days, of which there are far too many, when the power of money defeated the will of the people. I am filled, my friends, with a righteous anger—an anger that is a gift from God. Do you feel it too? Let it rise up in your heart. Feel its power. Heed its call. Know that God's will and God's law will prevail. He always finds a way. I know the American people are not willing to give up on humanity. I give you my word, you've not heard the end of this."

28

Righteous Anger

NED'S LARGE NOSE WAS pressed like a puppy's against the helicopter window. He had flown in the chopper many times to destinations around Arcadia, but now, as the aircraft passed over Arcadia's western boundary, the land below was, for Ned, terra incognita. He watched the eastern slope of the Cascades rise quickly, the open forests of ponderosa pine giving way to the richer greens of Douglas fir. Lilith sat next to him. Agnes sat across the aisle reading her magazines.

After Lilith's grandfather had died, her grandmother moved from Boise to Portland. As Lilith entered her teenage years, she grew closer to her late mother's mother, visiting her frequently, usually without Muir. She had asked Ned to come with her many times, but Leo always rejected the trip as too risky. This time, with the hearings over, the defeat of Pastor Joe's legislation, and Muir arguing that Ned needed a distraction, Leo had agreed.

Calvin Wei told Leo that Ned's second trip outside of Arcadia would be a low-risk operation, provided the travelers remained inconspicuous. Leo, whose face was known to most Americans, could not go. Agnes insisted that she be the one to accompany Lilith and Ned.

The helicopter headed toward the Northwest Industrial area of Portland, the closest landing spot to the University Park/Portsmouth neighborhood across the river, where Lilith's grandmother lived in a tiny Queen Anne cottage. Ned was transfixed by what he saw from the air as they approached the helipad: a great expanse of treeless black macadam occupied mainly by enormous warehouse buildings and long freight trains. An elevated roadway, packed with dense traffic, bisected the complex. Ned couldn't believe that so many people would have someplace to go, and all at the same time.

Alighting from the chopper, Ned was struck first by the novelty of the smell. The usual notes of forest and field were missing, replaced by the harsh scents of a city. The area around the helipad appeared abandoned. Pigeons perched on the shattered windows of the nearest building, on which a sign, reading, "Riverside Electric & Supply Co.," hung crookedly from the façade. The absence of trees and green disoriented him. He experienced a kind of low-grade stress that felt like incipient illness.

Two SUVs, one a blue Land Cruiser and the other a black Suburban, stood by. In accordance with Leo's longstanding conviction that black Suburbans with tinted windows virtually screamed VIP, Ned, Lilith, and Agnes climbed into the back seat of the blue vehicle, driven by a single plainclothes guard. The two other heavily armed Arcadia security men entered the black Suburban that followed behind.

After turning the corner at the far end of the abandoned building, Ned could see a squat block-long structure with tractor-trailer rigs backed up against a row of loading docks like piglets lined up to feed from a sow resting on her side. He thought it strange that he saw no people. Then, as the lead vehicle entered the next block, Ned spotted a cluster of strange-looking men with beards and straggly hair. Their clothes were ragged and they seemed to wear too many of them, coats on top of coats, and scarves around their necks although the day was mild. The group stood around a battered oil drum that emitted smudgy gray smoke.

"Who are those people, Aggie?"

"Homeless people, dear. It's a disgrace. These are people who don't have jobs or a place to live. And for various reasons they've left their families. And even worse, the government does nothing for them—or if it does, the men don't want the help. Sometimes they're sick. It's complicated."

Ned stared, unable to take his eyes off the unsettling image. Lilith, who had seen it all before, said to Ned, "Well, actually, I don't think it's that complicated. Those people should be helped."

After a few more blocks, the industrial buildings became more modern and the potholes less numerous. A few stores appeared and Ned saw the occasional person walking along the sidewalk. Still, it was a strange environment, too bright, too hard. The place seemed somewhat unreal, like the image on a screen, which was his only other experience of sight not given depth and context by smell.

Ned was pulled from this reverie when a car that had been stuck behind the slow-moving convoy passed them at high speed, sounding its horn. Ned looked up to see the driver of the other car, his face twisted in anger, stick his hand out the window, middle finger up. He shouted, "Fucking idiot. Fuck you. Fuck *you*," and drove off.

Ned was confused. "Aggie, I don't understand. Why was he angry at us?"

"People, sweetheart. People. What can I say?"

The two SUVs turned onto St. Johns Bridge and crossed the Willamette River. Ned remained glued to the window. Like one of SBD's big computers, he absorbed the stream of passing images for later consideration and analysis. He saw his first billboard, which said "Gentleman's Club" in large letters. Curiously, the picture was not of a gentleman but a pretty woman with large breasts packed into a small blouse. Another one showed an enormous cell phone, and it read, "I want it all. I want it now." Ned did not understand these messages. His scan of the streets had registered small bits of paper, plastic bottles, and aluminum cans stacked in corners and occasionally blowing down the sidewalk. Is this what people did with their trash in cities? An aphorism popped into his mind: "It's an ill bird that fouls its own nest." He stared at the purple hair of a teenage girl. He was pleased to see a man, a bit older than Ned, but even shorter. He turned his head to follow a woman speeding down the sidewalk on Rollerblades, her rear swaying rhythmically from side to side.

No one noticed anything unusual about the oncoming car until it swerved sharply out of its lane and struck the driver's door of the blue Land Cruiser at high speed. The Land Cruiser spun clockwise and came to a jolting stop against the curb. When the airbag deflated, the three stunned passengers saw their driver's head flop to the right at a strange angle. He did not move. A moment later, gunfire erupted. Agnes, Ned, and Lilith slid off the rear seat and crouched on the floor. Agnes peered between the two front seats to see their two guards, sheltered behind the open doors of the black Suburban, exchanging fire with three men in black ski masks. The attackers' assault rifles spat a steady stream of fire at the Suburban, shattering its glass and puncturing its black skin with scores of bullet holes. Ned, unable to bear the noise, covered his ears with his hands.

"Ned. Lilith," Agnes said. "You need to leave. Now, while they're still shooting at the other car."

Ned looked up. "No, Aggie. No. I won't leave you. I don't care what they do to me."

"Sweetheart, you have to. You have to do this for me. Please."

"No. I won't leave you."

The shooting stopped. Peering up at the mirror, Agnes saw both of their guards lying dead or wounded on the street, and one of the attackers slumped over the curb, bleeding heavily. The other two attackers pulled open the rear doors of the black Suburban. "Fuck," one shouted. "He's not here." The attackers turned to stare at the Land Cruiser.

Agnes swept open her raincoat and lay down on top of Lilith and Ned, pulling the coat tightly around them all. The first attacker to reach their car put his arm through the driver-side front window and fired a single shot into the driver's skull. The second attacker, rifle drawn, approached from the other side and peered cautiously through the window. He yanked open the rear door, shot a round into Agnes's back, and shifted his stance, preparing to fire a second round. At that moment, one of the guards lying by the side of the Suburban, mortally injured but not yet dead, managed to prop his rifle on the ground and fire a single shot. The man who had just shot at Agnes looked down and touched the exit wound on his chest. He dropped his rifle and fell over backward.

The sole surviving attacker, still standing at the driver-side front door, moved to open the rear door, but stopped short at the sound of an approaching siren. After a moment of hesitation, he turned and ran. Only one minute after the attack began, the street was once again quiet.

Ned was as stunned by the silence as he had been by the cacophony of the attack. He pushed himself up. Agnes rolled to the side and fell heavily, face up, on the back seat. When the police arrived, they found Lilith still curled tightly on the floor and Ned kneeling over Agnes, rocking back and forth, weeping quietly, and calling her name over and over.

29
Dead End?

Somehow, against all logic, another kind of human had come in and stolen posterity from the Neandertals. How that theft was accomplished is the oldest question in human evolutionary science.*

JAMES SCHREEVE, *THE NEANDERTAL ENIGMA* (1995)

NED AND LILITH STOOD at Agnes's grave, holding hands. It had never occurred to Leo that death might come to Arcadia, so the Village had no cemetery. Ned begged Leo to bury Agnes at home, and Agnes's closest relatives had no objection. So Agnes was interred on a small hillside just outside the Village. For the past month, the two teenagers had visited the grave every day after school, mainly in silence.

"Lil, do you forgive me?" Ned finally asked one afternoon.

"What do you mean?"

"It was my fault."

Lilith took hold of his other hand and drew him close. "Ned. Don't ever think that." She squeezed his hand until he nodded.

* Schreeve and some others prefer to use the original German spelling, "Neandertal," rather than the more common anglicized "Neanderthal."

The surviving attacker had been apprehended within days of the attempt on Ned's life that cost Agnes hers. The double-wide mobile home where he lived with his brothers in a rural area outside of Portland was stocked with assault weapons and survival rations. When arrested, the surviving attacker told police, "My brothers and I, we were only trying to kill the beast, you know, like Pastor Joe said." The brothers' sister worked for the fuel supplier at the heliport. The day before, she had received an anonymous call warning her that the infamous Neanderthal would be aboard the chopper scheduled in for the next morning. She mentioned the strange call to her brothers. Arcadia security, using SBD's big hardware, had worked furiously for days to determine the source of the leak, without success.

Pastor Joe, while careful not to endorse the assassination attempt, called the brothers "good people," and in answer to a reporter's question, described their outrage as "natural" and "understandable." He called the deaths of Agnes and the three SBD guards "highly regrettable," while pointing out that, as far as Ned was concerned, it was not attempted murder because the intended target was not a person.

"Do you still cry, Lil, when you think about her?"

"Not so much. Well, sometimes."

Ned stared down at the small boulder that marked her grave. Since the terrible day in Portland, the voices in Ned's head had gone completely silent. "For me," he said, both to himself and to Lilith, "it's the little things. Like when I saw one of the new lab techs wearing a blue dress just like the one Aggie wore. It made me so sad, like she died all over again."

A small doe poked her head through the brush at the edge of the meadow. Ned and Lilith looked her in the eye and did not speak. After a few moments, the deer traversed the open field just uphill of the grave and disappeared into the woods at the other side.

"You know, Lil, I've been thinking," Ned continued. "Maybe I just wasn't meant to be. I mean, when a species becomes extinct, there's a reason, right? Evolution throws up something better. That means Neanderthals deserved to die out. Why should the result be any different this time around? I'm here, but I'm still nothing more than a dead end. When I die, Neanderthals will be extinct again. So my life really doesn't matter."

Lilith hugged Ned around the neck and kissed his cheek. "You're not a species, Ned. You're you. And you matter. At least you matter to me."

* * *

At Muir's suggestion, Ned began working part-time in the botany lab. He was assigned to the team that monitored and nurtured the tiny shoots that sprouted from genetically modified seeds and spores. Those with obvious editing errors and unexpected mutations were carefully analyzed and then culled. The tiny plants were subjected to various combinations of light, moisture, and atmospheric gases to determine what was required for optimal growth. And in a long-running project lead by Muir personally, the growing medium was inoculated with different mixes of mycorrhizal fungi and bacteria to determine whether the soil required adjustment to more closely match ice-age conditions.

Although Lilith was not forthcoming with her father about the evolving nature of her relationship with Ned, she was sufficiently worried to tell him about Ned's uncharacteristically gloomy comment about being the meaningless dead end of a dead-end species. Muir, also alarmed, tried to think of things that might lift Ned's spirits. The next day, he had an idea. He ordered a selection of books on Neanderthals and gave them to Ned. It was an inspired move. From then on, Ned spent every spare hour sitting on the floor in a corner of his room devouring these texts.

One afternoon Muir found Ned in the lab bent over a large tray of seedlings. The younger ones consisted of pure-white leafless shoots, fragile, tender, and improbable starts for what would become sturdy trees. On the slightly older batch the white shoot had morphed into a narrow brown stem supporting a single green maplelike leaf, rather like the oversize head on an infant. These plants had resulted from the genetic modification of the surviving maple *Acer parviflora* to match the genome of the extinct maple subspecies *Acer browni*, once native to much of Oregon. Each tray had been exposed to a different set of environmental conditions, and Ned's task was to make close observations of the results and enter the information on an iPad.

"Anything interesting?" Muir asked.

"Not really," Ned answered. "But that's a good thing, right? Means it's another one just fine with modern soils."

The two walked slowly up the aisle scanning the hundreds of trays of identical seedlings.

"Hey, Muir," Ned asked.

"Uh huh."

"Those books you gave me. Did you read them yourself?"

"No."

"They're incredibly interesting. I learned a lot. I may look like a stupid caveman, but you know, 'Never judge a book by its cover.'"

"You don't look like . . ."

For the first time since the attack, Ned grinned. "Relax, Muir. It was a joke."

Muir smiled and put his arm across Ned's broad shoulders.

"But I really did learn all sorts of neat stuff," Ned continued. "For instance, did you know that almost all species in the genus *Homo* had brow ridges like mine? Turns out you guys are the funny-looking ones with your smooth foreheads."

Muir laughed.

"And I thought that *Homo sapiens* evolved out of Neanderthals, you know, that we were more primitive, and that modern humans were the new and improved version. But it's not true. We both evolved from the same ancestor, *Homo erectus*—you and we were sort of like two alternative versions for the next step in evolution. And what's more, initially we were more successful. We had all of Europe to ourselves for a very long time. So it's not that we were the stupid cavemen and humans the more advanced ones."

"Kind of like cousins," Muir said. "Each descended from the same grandfather."

"Exactly. Neanderthals were up, mainly in cold Europe and the Middle East, and *sapiens* were down in Africa. Then the first time, maybe around one hundred thousand years ago, you guys came out of Africa and met the Neanderthals in the Middle East. No one knows what happened, but *sapiens* retreated and once again Neanderthals had the place to ourselves. And then, twenty or forty thousand years later, you again wandered up from Africa, but this time the result was different."

Two members of the hort staff approached Muir, agitated because the air-filtration system in an adjoining greenhouse was down and they couldn't get it going again. After figuring out that they had changed the filter but failed to press the reset button, Muir turned back to Ned.

"Ned, so tell me. I had no idea. You say the second time they met the result was different. Different how?"

"This time, the *sapiens* arrive again from Africa, and just like that, the Neanderthals go extinct. And no one really knows why."

"But why's that such a mystery?" Muir asked. "It happens all the time. One species arrives, stronger, smarter, or better adapted, they compete for resources and prevail. The other disappears. We're seeing that here in Arcadia."

"Right. But all the books say that wasn't the case, Muir. We, the Neanderthals, were stronger, much more powerful. I mean, look at me. Neanderthals had bigger brains, and not just bigger brains, but more brain per pound of body mass. Better eyesight. A sense of smell that *sapiens* had lost. We had speech and language, just like *sapiens.* We matured more quickly and lived longer. We had fire. We had tools. We wore clothes. We were adapted to the cold, and you guys had been running around in sunny Africa. So it makes no sense. We were the ones who should have prevailed."

"Interesting. But surely someone has a theory?"

"I've read lots of different explanations, but I don't really buy any of them. Some say it was disease, or too much inbreeding, though most think that you guys won because you had developed more intellectually, with things like symbolism and better imaginations. Others say that *sapiens* bred with us until the Neanderthals were just sort of diluted out of existence. The one I like is simpler than all that."

"How's that?"

"You killed us because that's what humans do. You form groups, and then kill the people not in your group. One book calls it a genocide, the 'Pleistocene holocaust.' You were tall and dark with small heads. We were short and white with big heads. So you did what *sapiens* do and killed off the people who were different. Simple."

Muir appeared confused. "I don't get it, Ned. Even if *sapiens* did try to kill them off, how could they win if the Neanderthals were stronger and better adapted?"

"Exactly. That's the thing, there must have been something else. Something that allowed you guys to defeat us."

"I'll see if I can find more books for you, Ned. But I wish you would stop saying 'you.' I really don't want to be responsible for my entire species." Muir smiled, but Ned did not.

"Yeah, well, that's fine for you to say. But I have no choice. There's no one else around to represent my species."

* * *

The next day, Ned and Lilith sat together under a ponderosa pine about a quarter mile outside the western edge of the Village. It was a private spot and Ned lay on the ground, his back against the tree, reading.

"Lil, listen to this."

"What?"

"It's an amazing detective novel where Neanderthals are alive all over the place. One of them is named Stefan. One character asks, 'What did you learn from Stefan?' And the other says, 'His people'—meaning people like me, the Neanderthals—'were smarter than all of us . . . They had bigger brains, more room to store wisdom about nature. And our ancestors . . . killed them . . . because we envied their wisdom . . . not because they were ugly, but because their minds were beautiful.' I love that—'their minds were beautiful.' And you know what? It might not be total fiction."

"You said it was a novel."

"Lil, you promise not to tell your dad?"

"Not to tell him what?"

"OK. I think I'm not the only one."

"Ned . . ."

"Wait a sec. Hear me out. Some Neanderthals survived. I'm sure of it. And so are many other people, Lil. Really smart people. One of the books your dad gave me is called *Neanderthals Are Still Living*, by a Russian professor. It makes perfect sense that there should be pockets of surviving Neanderthals in all sorts of remote places. He talks about southern Russia, the eastern Himalayas, Mongolia. The local people have all sorts of different names for these surviving tribes."

"You mean like the Yeti or the Abominable Snowman? Come on, Ned, you're smarter than that. Don't get me wrong, I mean, it would be super exciting if there were some left, but . . ."

"No, Lil, think about it. They say we became extinct only thirty thousand years ago. That's nothing. When the British came to India they discovered a tribe, called the Bo people, who had lived on one of the Andaman Islands for sixty-five thousand years—that means they coexisted with the Neanderthals, and the Bo were still around. If the Bo could survive unnoticed on a small island, then why couldn't small groups of Neanderthals do the same?"

"Ned, I get that in principle it may be possible, but really, does any serious scientist think it's true? You have to be careful not to . . ."

Ned interrupted. "Yes. Absolutely. A bunch of them. And they've got all sorts of evidence: footprints, pictures. One scientist, a Dr. Kofman, has been up in the Caucus Mountains. She believes that the Almas, a kind of wild man that the local people have seen for years, are surviving Neanderthals. These scientists have organized big expeditions to search for Neanderthals; one of them came very close to finding some. That's what I'm meant to do, Lil. I'm gonna go find them."

Lilith smiled.

"You're right. You should try."

"Thanks, Lil," Ned said, pulling her in for a kiss.

30
Roots

LEO'S GULFSTREAM G650 TAXIED to a remote corner of Düsseldorf International Airport and came to a stop next to an armored Mercedes-Maybach with blacked-out windows. An identical decoy vehicle and three armored SUVs with guards waited a discrete distance to the rear. Since the attempt on Ned's life in Portland, Leo was taking no chances.

Ned bounded down the steps of the plane, his hands pressed against his ears to muffle the roar of the jets. He stood on the tarmac, transfixed by the close-up view of takeoffs and landings on the adjacent runway. An orange VW pulled alongside the gleaming Gulfstream and a German immigration official stepped out. Leo approached the official and walked with him a few yards farther away from the distracted teenager.

"*Guten morgen*, Mr. Bonelli, welcome to Germany."

"*Guten morgen*," Leo replied, delivering an obsequious smile. He handed over his passport, to which the official gave a cursory glance before returning it.

"You understand that my son does not have a passport."

"*Ja*. We are prepared for this. The Federal Foreign Office has determined that your son is not a 'person' for purposes of our Immigration Act, and thus he does not require a passport to enter the Federal Republic. As we informed your attorney, because he is being admitted under the rules that apply to," he glanced at the paper he was holding, "'pets and livestock,' a medical certification is required." The officer looked relieved to have gotten through this part of his speech.

Leo glanced to be sure that Ned was still distracted, and then handed over a document that addressed the boy's immunization history and certified him free from a number of diseases relevant only to pets and farm animals.

"This is satisfactory," the official said, holding the document against his clipboard and applying a round stamp with an efficient thwack. "Have a nice stay in Germany."

Leo admired the pragmatism of the Germans. He walked back to where Ned was standing.

"That was an A380, Dad. Did you see it? Pretty awesome."

Leo put his arm around Ned. "A great feat of engineering. Let's go, Son."

* * *

When Ned had shared with his father his wish to travel in search of surviving Neanderthals, Leo had responded harshly, admonishing Ned for failing to distinguish between serious science and the unsubstantiated drivel of a few crackpots. But Ned's dream by that time was too strong to be so easily dislodged, and father and son skirmished over the issue for weeks.

Muir, still estranged from Leo following his damaging testimony at the congressional hearings, felt reluctant to intervene. But for Ned's sake, he argued to Leo that a trip—any trip—would distract Ned from the public furor over his existence and his grief over Agnes's death. Muir encouraged Leo, one way or another, to allow the boy to pursue his growing interest in Neanderthals. Muir also thought it would be good for Lilith and Ned to have some time apart. Although Leo resisted at first, he acquiesced when Muir came up with the idea of a different type of trip, focused not on the search for living Neanderthals, but an exploration of Ned's Neanderthal roots, including visits to scientists working on the mystery of Neanderthal extinction.

Ned, while not surrendering his goal of searching for surviving Neanderthals, embraced Muir's compromise and, after some additional research, proposed three destinations: the Neander Valley outside of Düsseldorf, where bones were first identified as belonging to another type of human and which now hosted the world's only museum dedicated to *Homo neanderthalensis*; the enclave of Gibraltar at the tip of the Iberian Peninsula, where some paleoanthropologists believed the Neanderthals made their last stand; and Africa, in order to visit the homeland of the San people in Botswana and the Mbuti pygmies deep in the Ituri Rainforest of the Congo, both thought to be among the genetically oldest humans and thus perhaps Ned's nearest living relatives. Ned had read that these so-called primitive peoples required young men to learn the names of their ancestors for the forty prior generations. "No one," Ned told Lilith, "knows the name of a single Neanderthal who ever lived, even though they survived far longer than *Homo sapiens* have so far. It seems so unfair; without names, they're just an abstraction, hardly real." The first two destinations proved feasible, and Ned agreed to put off the visit to Africa to a subsequent trip.

Two days before their planned departure, Leo poked his head into Ned's room.

"Think you can get it together to leave a day early?" Leo asked.

"Sure," Ned said. "What's up?"

"Flight ops just called. There's some kind of big storm, they called it a 'super-El Niño,' coming right at the coast. Unless we can get away tomorrow, we'll probably be delayed a couple of days."

"Sure thing, Dad. I'll be ready."

* * *

Ned and Leo stood on a flat grassy field tucked into the narrow valley of the Düssel River, a short walk from the undulating walls of the Neanderthal Museum.

"It was early August 1856, this valley was being excavated for its limestone and two Italian workmen were shoveling mud from the floor of a small cave, the Feldhof Cave, which was located right here, only about twenty meters higher than where we're standing now."

The director of the museum gestured upward toward a platform that marked the elevation and location of the former cave.

"The two workmen were startled to find a cache of unusual bones. Initially people thought they were bear bones, but the mine's owners sent them to a teacher and fossil enthusiast named Johann Carl Fuhlrott. It was Fuhlrott who eventually advanced the theory that the bones were evidence of another species of human."

"Lucky timing," Leo said, "I mean, with Darwin right around the corner."

"*Ja*. It was only three years later that Darwin would publish *On the Origin of Species*, and the discoveries made here were vital in helping prove that Darwin was right: modern man evolved in the same way as other animals and was not created in his present form. The ripples from the discovery made here that summer are still reverberating around the world."

As they arrived back at the museum, Ned asked, "What was it like? I mean for the Neanderthals? What were they doing in that cave? Was it where they lived, or . . ."

"We're almost sure it was a burial site. Neanderthals cared for their sick and elderly and disposed of their dead to protect them from scavengers. We used to think that only *Homo sapiens* had developed symbolic thought and what we would recognize as a culture, but that's almost certainly not right."

The director put on a pair of white cotton gloves, unlocked a glass case, and withdrew a large honey-brown bone fragment with two evenly spaced, perfectly round holes.

"The Divje Babe Flute," he said, grinning broadly, "better known as the Neanderthal Flute, on loan from Ljubljana. It's the femur of a bear, about forty-three thousand years old. Isn't it splendid?"

He quickly replaced the priceless artifact in its case. "I wasn't supposed to do that," he said, "please don't tell."

Ned laughed.

"And, Ned," the director continued, "it's not only the flute. Now there's evidence that they used pigments to decorate themselves and also wore jewelry made from feathers and shells. So don't let anyone tell you Neanderthals didn't have a culture."

A few minutes later, Ned for the first time stood face-to-face with another Neanderthal. The mannequin, incredibly lifelike, was almost exactly Ned's height. His broad mouth, uncannily like Ned's, was set in an infectious grin. The curators had dressed him in a blue business suit in order to demonstrate that a Neanderthal would pass the so-called "subway test": Take a Neanderthal man, give him a shave and a haircut, dress him in a suit, and put him on the subway. Are his fellow passengers likely to notice something amiss? If not, he's passed the "subway test."

As Ned gazed at the mannequin, the staff clustered around him, taking photos and videos with their phones. By this time photos of Ned had already leaked, so Leo didn't object.

"Totally awesome," was all Ned could say. The museum's staff broke into spontaneous applause. They had spent their careers trying to educate the public about *Homo sapiens'* place in the broader family of the genus *Homo*, and to dispel the arrogant notion of Neanderthals as lumbering cavemen. None of them ever imagined that they would see a Neanderthal in the flesh, and each was thrilled to find Ned so bright, charming, and curious.

"But how did it happen?" Ned asked. "I mean, here you have all the evidence you could want showing that Neanderthals were smarter and stronger than *sapiens*. So how come the whole world thinks we were knuckle-dragging oafs?"

The director walked the group to a large poster showing a hairy ape-man. "Here's your answer, Ned. Marcellin Boule, a Frenchman, was a leading paleontologist of his day, and he attempted to reconstruct the appearance of the Neanderthal from the best skeleton then available. He got it all wrong. He showed a beast that was more simian than human, with sloping shoulders, a huge head jutting forward, a kind of ferocious gorilla."

Ned stared at the framed poster of a fierce creature, who gripped an oversize club and glared menacingly at an out-of-frame victim.

"And at the time people tended to think that intellectual or moral worth could be detected from appearance, so people viewing this image assumed that Neanderthals were stupid and vicious."

"Well, we all know, 'Appearances can be deceiving,'" Ned said with a grin.

"Quite so. When they were debating what to call the new species, one of the names proposed was *Homo stupidus*. Can you imagine? Once this idea took hold in the nineteenth century, it's been very hard to dislodge. And you have to understand, Ned, that all this fed into a key meme in *sapiens* culture, the idea of the 'wild man' or the ogre."

"I don't understand," Ned said.

"Every human culture has some kind of legend of a wild man or monster, because somewhere deep down—or maybe even in *sapiens* DNA—lurks a remembered fear, perhaps of Neanderthals, and perhaps of the long struggle for dominance between the two species."

Ned turned away from Boule's imagined monster.

"But," the director continued, "once people get to know you . . ."

Leo put his hand on Ned's shoulder. "Let's not get ahead of ourselves, shall we? I don't think we can put the reputation of an entire species on the shoulders of a single teenage boy."

The director responded quickly. "*Ja*. Quite so. You are, of course, right."

Ned spoke to the director as the group walked down a ramp toward the next exhibit. "You said 'long struggle for dominance between the two species.' Tell me, is that your opinion of Neanderthal extinction, that it resulted from a long struggle with humans?"

"Not exactly. First of all, here at the museum we're careful to tell our visitors that we really don't know why Neanderthals disappeared. On the other hand, we've got lots and lots of evidence, and every year come closer to the truth."

"Yes, I understand that, but I'm asking your personal view. You said 'long struggle for dominance . . .'"

Ned detected a stir of unease among the museum staffers listening to this conversation, as if he had unwittingly asked an awkward question. The director answered.

"Ned, I've spent a good deal of my life thinking about this. First of all, most species that have ever existed have gone extinct, so in that sense there's nothing unusual about it. Also, there's no doubt that when two similar species occupy the same territory—especially when resources are scarce—they compete."

"I get that," Ned said. "But isn't it true that in a head-to-head competition we should have won?"

"Think of it this way. After all the Heinrich events—those were repeated periods of terrible cold—Neanderthals may have been living on the edge, weakened a little more by each cycle of cold. During this period their habitat changed from rich woodland with lots of plants to eat and easy-to-hunt game, to what we call 'steppe tundra,' with fewer plants to eat and only difficult and dangerous animals to hunt. Toward the end, Neanderthals were probably living in scattered small communities. Their genetic diversity would have suffered. In my view, Ned, there was no one reason for the extinction. When a population is small and scattered, then disease, inbreeding, and even just random fluctuations in population size could have proven to be the last straw."

Ned did not look satisfied with this answer. "But that doesn't sound to me like a 'struggle for dominance.'"

"Again, we really don't know. But we do now know that the two species interbred—I'm sure you're aware that non-African humans typically have roughly 2 to 2.5 percent Neanderthal DNA in their genomes. But I have to say, interbreeding actually was relatively rare, and I personally don't think the genetic evidence points to Neanderthals simply being overwhelmed and replaced due to interbreeding."

The director paused. His staff glanced at each other in anticipation of what was to follow.

"We scientists are supposed to avoid speculation, especially when the question is so fraught with wider implications. So let's start with the one thing we know for sure: The anthropological evidence shows that whenever and wherever modern humans showed up, Neanderthals and other hominins disappeared soon thereafter. Maybe it was bad luck, but Svante Pääbo—you know of him?"

Both Ned and Leo nodded.

"Svante said if Neanderthal extinction was caused by bad luck, then the bad luck was us. I think he probably is right. I'm not sure I would go so far as Harari, who called it a 'genocide.'"

"Why not?" Ned asked. "What about the ninth rib?"

The director smiled. "I see, Ned, that you've really been doing your homework. Yes, I accept that interpretation of Shanidar 3. I agree that a thrown spear and not a thrusting spear probably caused the wound, meaning that a *sapiens* probably killed that particular Neanderthal in a violent attack. But that doesn't necessarily mean that violent conflict with modern humans was the cause of Neanderthal extinction."

"No, but it could have been, right?" Ned asked.

"I think, young man, that's been enough speculation for one day. Besides, there are other theories. For instance, the division of labor hypothesis? You know that one?"

Ned frowned.

"This is the idea that in Neanderthal culture both males and females hunted, whereas the humans coming up from Africa had the men doing the hunting and the women doing everything else. This kind of specialization was efficient. Or," the director continued, "if you don't like that one, what about the dog theory? That *sapiens* succeeded in partially domesticating the wolf, creating wolf dogs to help them in hunting. This not only gave them an advantage in hunting for big game, but the wolves were intensely territorial, so these proto-dogs would have been extremely aggressive toward Neanderthals competing for food in the same places. One biologist says that we should look at this as an alliance between two apex species, against which the Neanderthals didn't have a chance."

"I've always been afraid of dogs," Ned said. "Really terrified."

"Now that's interesting," the director said. "Would you be willing . . ."

Leo interrupted. "Professor, I'm so sorry, but we're expected in Gibraltar and need to go. This has been a most interesting visit, for both of us."

31
Gorham's Cave

NED SAT TWISTED TO the right, his face pressed to the window, as Leo's plane approached Gibraltar. He saw a narrow hyphen of flat land that connected the mainland to "the rock," a knife-edged ridge that dropped steeply to the water on one side and more gradually to a narrow ledge on the other. A runway, extending far into the sea on both sides, completely bisected the hyphen. The busy main road that linked the British territory with Spain crossed the runway. As the plane circled, Ned watched gates descend across the road. Within seconds of touchdown, the gates reopened and the backlog of cars poured across the runway.

A half hour later, Ned and Leo stood at the side of the narrow road notched into the base of Gibraltar's steep eastern coast. Above them, a sheer rock face rose to the spine of the peninsula; below, waves crashed into a boulder-strewn coast.

"Africa," said Ned, pointing across the nine-mile strait of churning water to a landmass floating on the horizon.

Professor Colin Ruskin opened a locked gate and led Ned and Leo down a narrow concrete path.

"You see, to the left?" Ruskin said, pointing. "That's it. Gorham's Cave."

Ned and Leo stopped to stare at the jagged teardrop-shaped opening only meters above the ocean spray.

"And the others?" he added. "You see? That's Vanguard, and then Hyaena, and over there, that's Bennett's Cave."

The affable and slightly rumpled Gibraltarian paleoanthropologist could not have been more different from the meticulous German who had hosted them in the Neander Valley. The group of three stepped over the threshold to the sandy floor of Gorham's Cave.

"Can you believe our luck?" Ruskin said. "Easy digging through meters and meters of sand that blew in over the millennia. Top layer was Phoenician, then below that, Neolithic, then Upper Paleo, and then," he gestured with a grand sweep of his arm, "all this. An incredible treasure trove of Neanderthal culture."

Ruskin guided them to a spot on the cave floor protected by a low wooden barrier.

"Where you're standing, Ned, this hearth—this is where the last known Neanderthals on the planet lived and died. Last *known*. Of course, there could be other places where they survived even later, but for now, it's here. Where they made their last stand."

Ned stared, awestruck.

"When was that?" Leo asked.

Ruskin frowned. "Well, there's a bit of a debate about that. Leo, you've been around scientists all your life. Too many of them are inclined to resist change and defend the orthodoxy they were taught."

Ned looked up from the hearth and stared at Ruskin, who continued.

"Anyway, when the original radiocarbon dating of objects found in this cave proved that the Neanderthals hung on much longer than anyone previously thought, all my colleagues said, 'Impossible!' It's true that now we've adjusted the dates back a bit due to technical issues, but the fact remains that Neanderthals survived to live on here, at the very tip of Europe, maybe as late as thirty to thirty-two thousand years ago. They were tough old birds, not so easy to snuff out."

"And . . ." Ned hesitated, looking at Leo, and then decided to go on. "What about even later? What do you think about Professor Porshnew, or Dr. Kofman. Or Myra Shackley?"

The professor tugged at the strap of his yellow hard hat. "I hope you're not putting me in with that crowd?"

"No, sir, I didn't mean . . ."

"It's OK, Ned. But really, no one takes them seriously."

"Why not?" Ned persisted. "Myra Shackley came really close to finding Neanderthals during her expedition. Why couldn't they be right?"

"Ned . . ." Leo started to intervene.

Ruskin ignored Leo and put his hand on Ned's shoulder. "I'm sorry, young man. I can see why the idea would be incredibly alluring to you. And I'm terribly sorry to disappoint. But don't go there." He hesitated for only a moment, thinking. "You know what? Here's something much more interesting."

Ned listened skeptically.

"My colleagues spend a lot of time trying to figure out the details of Mousterian culture. I mean, that's what we're doing here—trying to understand how these last Neanderthals lived. They had retreated across the face of Europe to Gibraltar and now stared out at the shore of Africa, only fourteen klicks across the water. What did they eat? What did they wear? What did they do for fun? Did they have art? Music? That's what paleoanthropologists do."

"Uh huh."

"But I'll tell you what interests me even more than all that. If Neanderthals had not gone extinct, and if they—or should I say you—had gone on to live and develop side by side with *sapiens,* perhaps segregated in different parts of the planet, but both surviving to develop their own cultures and technologies, what would they be today? Do you follow me, Ned? The measure of what we've lost as a result of Neanderthal extinction is not the Neanderthals as they were thirty thousand years ago here in this cave; the measure of what we've lost is what the Neanderthals would have been today if they had survived."

Ned's eyes slowly lit up. "You're right. You're saying that it's apples and oranges to compare Neanderthals as they were to modern humans as they are. The more interesting thing is what we would be like if we'd survived . . . what the world would be like if we'd survived."

"Right. Here's how I see it," Ruskin said. "The Neanderthals almost certainly had a different cognitive landscape. They had different skills and traits. Those differences between Neanderthals and humans, projected forward over thirty millennia, would almost certainly have led to some major changes in culture and civilization. A world peopled by Neanderthals—by modern Neanderthals—would almost certainly be a very different place. It's really interesting to think how."

"Give me an example," Leo asked. "And I know it's just speculation, but still . . ."

"OK. Take one thing, for sure. If two species of hominins had advanced, then it's pretty clear that *sapiens* culture would not be anthropocentric, with a worldview that puts us at the center of all things. The Bible wouldn't say, 'so God created man in his own image.' No one would think that *sapiens*, uniquely, had dominion over the earth if *sapiens* existed side by side with another intelligent species. Just that alone would mean a very different history and a very different present."

"I never thought . . ." said Ned, thinking out loud. He was interrupted by a loud thud. The three turned to see a cloud of dust rising from where a large stone had detached from the roof of the cave and crashed to the sandy floor.

"That," Ruskin said, laughing nervously, "is why we wear hard hats." After glancing at the cave ceiling above the spot where the three were standing, he continued. "Anyway, I think if Neanderthals had survived there might also be significant cultural differences. The evidence suggests that Neanderthals were highly egalitarian; for example, it appears that both the men and the women hunted. Combined with what some think was a highly empathic cognitive model . . . well, isn't it possible that a culture not built on hierarchy and patriarchy could look pretty different?"

Leo suggested that he and the professor step outside the cave to discuss the ways in which Leo might support his work.

Ned sat on a rock and stared out through the jagged black frame of the cave's enormous opening to the east. The distinctive mouth of Gorham's Cave, almost two hundred feet across at the base, rose asymmetrically to a misshapen peak. It seemed to Ned that he could feel the entire continent of Europe pressing at his back. In front, through the aperture of stone, the morning sun illuminated the gently rolling surface of the Mediterranean Sea, turning the easterly side of each swell a deep blue. "'Be it ever so humble . . .'" he muttered to himself. He could imagine calling such a place home.

When Leo returned to the cave, Ned, lost in thought, did not notice. Leo stood still for a minute, watching his son sitting at the edge of the excavated hearth and staring out at the sea.

"Son, time to go."

"Dad," Ned said, standing up. "I have an idea. Don't say no right away. Just think about it. It's not that Neanderthals lost the game of evolution, that we weren't fit to survive. Instead, our distant cousins came up out of Africa and wiped us out. And that was wrong. So now you have a way to right that wrong. You made me; you can make others. And with Arcadia we have a place where Neanderthals could be left alone and build a life."

"Come on, Ned, with everything that's happened, you can't be . . ."

"Wait, Dad, hear me out. Arcadia is all about taking the plants and animals that man extincted when he came to North America, and giving them a second chance, right? Why not Neanderthals? Maybe we could even build the culture we would have built had we not been exterminated. Think of it, Dad, just like Professor Ruskin said. Think of what a second type of human, a different type of human, might give to the world. Maybe that's what Arcadia's really for."

Before Leo could answer, his phone buzzed.

"We'll talk about it. Let me take this, it's Muir. Will you go tell the professor that I'll be there in just a minute."

When Leo stepped out a few minutes later to rejoin Ruskin and Ned, his olive face was noticeably pale, and for the first time ever, Ned thought he saw his father's hand, still clutching the phone, tremble slightly.

"Professor, will you forgive us? There's been an . . . emergency. We need to return home immediately."

32
Deluge

AFTER LANDING IN PORTLAND, Leo's plane taxied over to the waiting helicopter, in front of which stood Muir, Lilith, Clip, and two senior scientists from Arcadia.

"How bad?" Leo asked.

"As bad as it could be," Muir answered. "The devastation is . . . you'll see."

"And our people?"

Clip answered. "Three security teams, four hort staff, and Donna from the nursery, all out in the field when the dam went. We're still searching, but that's eleven missing and presumed dead."

Tears rolled freely from Ned's large eyes and Lilith rushed over to hold him.

As the chopper approached Arcadia from the west, the passengers stared silently out the windows. At first, things below appeared relatively normal. Then, when Lake Arcadia should have appeared, shimmering nearly to the eastern horizon, the passengers saw in its stead an enormous crescent-shaped smudge, the few pools of remaining water a disturbing shade of dirty clay red.

Leo turned to the project's chief hydrologist, a distinguished scientist whom he had poached from NOAA and who was supposed to be the best in the business.

"How the hell could this have happened? Before we started to fill the aquifer and reengineer the drainages, you told me that we had modeled everything: worst-case global warming scenarios, the thousand-year storm. You said the math was solid. How's it possible that a single storm could knock us out?"

"There were scores of variables in those models, Leo. All it takes is a few wrong assumptions and, well, the model becomes very wrong."

Leo's eyes flashed. "Like what?"

"Well, we assumed a storm double the size of the October '62 storm, the largest cyclonic front ever known to have passed beyond the Cascades. We didn't imagine that one could be three times wetter. *Three times* . . . We modeled a cyclonic front stalling out for a day, but not for three days. We've never seen anything like it in meteorology. The Harney Basin gets an average of six inches of rain per year. During the storm we got thirty to forty inches of rain *a day* over three days. None of this should have been possible."

"Yeah, well, it happened," Leo said. "Hydrology was the key, Sam. Exactly what I brought you on board to do. You knew we were going to take this place with no drainage to the sea—what did you keep telling me at the beginning, 'Any precipitation that falls in the Great Basin stays in the Great Basin'? We were going to take this place and spend almost twenty years raising the aquifer to levels not seen for fourteen thousand years. Then add on top of that almost nine feet of rain in three days. Doesn't seem like you needed a very complicated model to predict what would happen."

"These things always seem easy to predict after the fact, Leo. You know that. Two black swan events occurring concurrently can knock any model flat on its face."

The helicopter hovered over the collapsed dam at the east end of the former lake. The north side of the dam had sunk into the earth at a crazy angle, its raw and jagged edge all that was left to suggest the formerly concave middle section, which had fragmented catastrophically and disappeared downstream. Only the south side of the structure stood plumb and level.

Leo turned from the window, incredulous, and addressed Arcadia's chief engineer, who held his forehead in his hand. "The excuse for the dam failure?"

"Leo, I'm so sorry. We . . . I made a mistake. A fairly simple mistake. We did extensive testing of the geological conditions. We even moved the north end foundations twice when we found a risk of shear dislocation, and then a brittle sandstone layer that tilted upstream."

"I remember. It cost me a lot of money."

"The shale layers that we built on were stable and strong, and oriented optimally. There should have been no problem . . . But, well, you know these shales are hydrophilic—they attract water and could be weakened if they became too wet. But there was an impermeable layer above, so we concluded there was no risk of the reservoir water above affecting them."

"And?"

"We didn't think about the fact that you were planning to fill the aquifer below, and thus that the groundwater level would rise. We used standard geological models, and the water hadn't been that high since the end of the Pleistocene, so to the engineering team, it seemed perfectly safe. Instead, very gradually over the past two decades, the groundwater level came up from below and weakened a critical layer of calcareous shale. When the storm put the foundation under enormous pressure, the shale layer fractured, the north-side foundation shifted, and the dam suffered a catastrophic failure. Leo, it's my fault. I'm so sorry."

The chopper continued beyond the collapsed dam into the wasteland that had been Arcadia and landed on a high plateau about ten miles to the east. Muir and Ned, who knew this part of the property intimately from their many hunting trips, found themselves disoriented. Ned smelled nothing but death and decay. The plateau was now surrounded by groundwater, the high desert steppe now more like a desert island in a sea of sludge. In the distance, they spotted trees surviving above the line where the torrent unleashed by the dam collapse had swept through, the slopes below deeply scored by the rushing water and all that was borne in its wake.

Muir broke the silence. "We bought a satellite image taken yesterday, Leo, and did a quick analysis." Muir choked up and took a moment to regain his composure.

"About 70 percent of the ecological restoration was lost. And when I say lost, I mean completely gone: topsoils scoured away, trees and plants uprooted, nothing left. And we have no idea about the animals. Most must have drowned."

"The mammoths?" Ned asked.

"I'm not optimistic."

The hydrologist turned to Leo. "A lot is still underwater. We don't even know if it will drain. We have no idea how long it will take the water to dissipate. Months. Perhaps years. We're thinking about whether we can somehow relieve pressure on the south end of the aquifer."

Leo was silent, unable to take his eyes from the scene of devastation. What he saw was a foreseeable and preventable failure. A failure of analysis. A failure of engineering. It was all just a matter of calculation, and they had gotten it wrong. Ned sat on a small boulder with his knees drawn in and his stocky forearms folded across them, rocking ever so slightly back and forth.

"Muir," Ned said, looking up, "all those years. All your plants. I'm so sorry." Muir gazed out over the wreckage of his life's work with a stony stare.

* * *

The Village at Arcadia, which sat on a small rise uphill and upstream of the lake, remained largely unscathed. Ned said he was exhausted from the long flight home from Gibraltar and went to his room. Leo and Muir stood in the front room of Leo and Ned's house. Since the congressional hearings, they had mostly succeeded in avoiding being alone together. Muir turned to leave.

"Want a bourbon, Muir?" Leo asked.

Muir noticed that, for the first time since he met him, Leo was not wearing the biometric device on his wrist.

"Sure, thanks," Muir answered. Leo gestured to a chair facing away from the window.

"Let's talk about something else. How was the trip?" Muir asked. "Ned have fun?"

"You were right, Muir. It's not that he's forgotten about Agnes and the attack, but he was a different person when we were away. He finds everything outside fascinating. He watches and listens and files it all away. Much of it he doesn't understand, but he misses nothing. Much more mature than a *sapiens* his age. More thoughtful. More curious. And he's consumed by paleoanthropology. In fact, it worries me a bit. He's fixated on Neanderthal extinction."

"Not really so surprising."

"No." After a short pause, Leo continued. "And when we were away I got a report on Shen. He won't be bothering us anymore."

"How so?"

"He was fired from the university and jailed a few days later on a warrant from China. They shut down his lab and confiscated his bank accounts in Singapore and Cyprus. Last week, the Chinese finally succeeded in obtaining extradition. He was put on a plane in chains and disappeared into the Chinese penal system. He deserves whatever horror they have in store for him."

Muir wondered just how much of Shen's fate had been engineered by Leo. Probably most of it. The thought made him uncomfortable. Muir wanted to change the subject.

"Leo, what about the leak, the call to the woman at the heliport alerting her that Ned would be on the chopper and where he was headed in Portland? I haven't heard anything about progress on that." Only a small group knew about the trip, and with all of the technology at Leo's command, Muir couldn't figure out why the leaker had not been identified.

"Very odd," Leo said. "We still don't know. Calvin quickly identified everyone who knew even a piece of the big picture. Needless to say, we looked at motive and every possible means of communication for each of them."

"Not all communication involves technology, Leo. People still write letters or talk in person."

"True, but the sister got a phone call, and Calvin worked back from that."

"And who looked at Calvin Wei?"

Leo gave Muir a strange look. "Why? You know something?"

"Not at all," Muir said quickly. "Just asking."

"I trust Calvin." This time it was Leo who changed the subject. "When we were in Gibraltar, Ned asked me to create more Neanderthal individuals." Leo paused, as if hearing it himself for the first time. "And he wants Arcadia to become a kind of refuge for the reestablishment of Neanderthal culture."

"This was his idea?" Muir asked.

"Yes. He said we have a chance to right a monumental wrong. That having a second species from the genus *Homo*, with a different cognitive tool kit, could be just what the world needs."

"And?"

"Could be it's what I owe him. And really, it's not crazy. Not crazy at all . . ."

* * *

Two days later, no one noticed when three out-of town lawyers entered the squat redbrick Harney County Courthouse in Burns.

They entered the chambers of a cranky state judge who posted the Ten Commandments in his courtroom and instructed juries to consult "our Lord Jesus" in reaching their verdicts. Thrilled to have received a call from Pastor Joe himself, the judge agreed to issue the order drafted for him by Pastor Joe's legal team in DC. And he agreed to issue it ex parte—without notice to or participation by Ned or Leo or their counsel—and to stall the filing of the order until Pastor Joe had a chance to break the story.

Later that day, Pastor Joe summoned the press. Standing before reporters in the Capitol Rotunda, he read a statement.

"As all of you know, following the illuminating hearings held earlier this year, I tabled legislation intended to address the threat to the American people posed by the monster created by Leo Bonelli, and the terrifying risks posed by so-called 'synthetic biology.' The American people cried out for action. But Chairman Pollack, without explanation, killed my bill. To this day he has declined to explain his decision. But do any of us doubt that Mr. Bonelli's billions were somehow at work here? At the time, I vowed that this shameful betrayal would not go unanswered and promised America that God would find a way. Last week, a just God once again called forth a cleansing flood and utterly destroyed Leo Bonelli's bizarre zoo and its unnatural creatures, vengeance against his arrogance and presumption. And just this morning, the Lord, acting through a pious and distinguished judge in Harney County, Oregon, struck out against the machinations of Chairman Pollack and Mr. Bonelli. I am thrilled to announce today that justice has prevailed. Yesterday, the court issued an order for the immediate detention and castration of the monster. The judge . . ."

The assembled reporters erupted. "Excuse me, Congressman, did you really say 'castration'?" the loudest asked.

"Yes, sir. Castration. The judge acted under long-standing laws in the state that permit the destruction of dangerous or vicious animals or, in some cases, their sterilization. The evidence presented at my hearings was more than sufficient for the judge to conclude that the creature is not a person, and thus is covered by our laws dealing with animals. And my hearings also established a clear and present danger to the human population. Although we could have asked for its destruction, our Lord and redeemer preaches mercy, even unto the creatures. So the judge ordered that the creature be immediately detained, and that within thirty days the sheriff certify back to the court that the creature is no longer capable of reproduction. May I say in closing that this is what the American people can expect from me when I'm their president: relentless pursuit of what's right, tenacious resistance to those with power and money who think they can run roughshod over our democracy, and pragmatic effectiveness—there's always more than one way to shoot a squirrel, folks. God bless America."

As a cacophony of shouted questions echoed under the rotunda dome, Pastor Joe left the microphone with a triumphant smile, surrounded by a half dozen aids.

*   *   *

Leo, alerted by SBD's staff in Washington that Pastor Joe was holding a press conference, had watched it live on his computer. As he clicked to close the streaming video, his phone buzzed. It was Calvin Wei.

"Leo, I just got a call from the Harney County Sheriff's Office. They say no one is to enter or leave Arcadia. The sheriff is on his way."

PART IV
LEO

33

We Are the Heroes of Our Own Story

Generation after generation, age after age, that long struggle for existence went on between those men who were not quite men and . . . our ancestors. Thousands of fights and hunts, sudden murders and headlong escapes there were amidst the caves and thickets of that chill and windy world between the last age of glaciers and our own warmer time. Until at length the last poor grisly [Neanderthal] was brought to bay and faced the spears of his pursuers in anger and despair. . . . What acts of devotion and desperate wonders of courage! And the strain of the victors was our strain.

H. G. Wells, *The Grisly Folk* (1921)

As the Harney County Sheriff's helicopter sped toward Arcadia, Ned and Lilith—unaware of Pastor Joe's announcement—lay sprawled on a patch of soft moss at the edge of the clearing where Agnes was buried.

"Do you think maybe he's right?" Ned asked Lilith.

"Who?"

"Pastor Joe. Maybe he's right. Maybe I am a danger to humanity and I just don't know it."

"That's completely ridiculous, Ned, you can't think that way. How in the world could you be dangerous?"

After a few moments of staring up into the pale maple leaves, Ned continued. "On the other hand, for most of history, there were all sorts of different kinds of people wandering around. Maybe that's how it's supposed to be."

"Right," Lilith said. "Humans lived with Neanderthals before, and now they're back. Big deal."

"But that's not what I see online, Lil. Over and over people say that man is unique, 'made in God's image.' I don't mean to be critical; actually, I think it's completely understandable. Doesn't everyone make themselves the heroes of their own story? What's the saying? 'History is written by the victors.' The winners simply assume they won because they're superior or favored by the gods, even when it's really just an accident or good luck."

"Right. Forget Pastor Joe. You aren't a danger to anybody, except," Lilith added, putting on her faux sexy voice, "perhaps to me."

Ned laughed and reached out for her hand. After being momentarily distracted by the distant sound of a helicopter approaching the Village, Ned propped himself up on one elbow and turned to face Lilith.

"You know what else? Early on, *sapiens* humans divided into tribes, each with its own creation myth. What I realized is that I stand outside all that."

"So?"

"Think of it this way, Lil. The facts of my creation are actually known. I don't need a myth or superstition or religion to explain why I exist. I'm a tribe of one. I exist because Dad and Dr. Shen chose to make me."

Lilith sat up, leaning against the smooth mottled bark of the young tree. "It's funny you say that, about not being part of a group.

I feel the same way. Even the girls' soccer team was a bit of a disaster, remember?" she said, laughing. "Somehow, I always feel, I don't know . . . out of place." Lilith squeezed Ned's hand. "Unless, of course, I'm with you."

Pulling him close, Lilith planted a kiss. He responded with an urgency she hadn't felt before. There was no yielding by one to the other, only a tide of desire that ebbed and flowed, with equal intensity, between the two.

* * *

Only a mile from the meadow where Ned and Lilith lay kissing, the Harney County Sheriff's Department chopper landed on one of the Village helipads with a rough bump and skip. The sheriff and his deputy were taken by the long route to the Village security office, were they presented the court order and demanded to take custody of Ned. Told that Ned was out hunting and that security would dispatch an ATV to bring him back to the Village, they waited patiently. The wait was not long. Within an hour, Leo appeared and presented the sheriff with a temporary restraining order from a federal judge in Portland, staying the state court order and enjoining the sheriff from detaining Ned or proceeding with his castration.

"It's temporary," Leo explained to Muir later that day, "and we have no idea whether the federal court will make it permanent. Even if it does, Pastor Joe's team is sure to appeal."

"The Feds will stop it, Leo. They have to, it's just . . . barbaric. This is the twenty-first century, how could they possibly . . ."

Leo interrupted. "You're wrong. It's almost normal. Right through the late twentieth century lots of states forcibly sterilized the mentally ill, criminals, even epileptics. Hell, all around the world they did it to people considered genetically defective, or just for population control. And that's people, Muir. If they find that Ned is not a human being, not a person, then they'll almost certainly win. State judges have all sorts of authority to have animals spayed, neutered, or destroyed."

Muir stared in stunned silence.

"There's another hearing in front of the judge in six weeks. He's going to take testimony. My lawyers say we need Polly."

"Polly? Why Polly?"

"They want her to testify that she couldn't have children, and that's in part why I created Ned. Plus, they want a mother figure to convince people that he should be treated just like any other child. And since we're not together anymore, she'll be credible. They'll know she's not just saying these things to help me."

"You think she'll do it?"

"She might . . . if *you* ask her."

"Me? No. Go yourself," Muir said. "She's still your wife. All those years you communicated with her through Clip—or not at all—that was part of the problem. If you want her to agree, you've got to ask her yourself."

"No. If she sees me she'll get emotional. It'll remind her of all the reasons she left me. She'll say no. She likes you, Muir. She knows how fond you are of Ned. If you ask, she'll say yes. I'm certain."

And so, against his better judgment, Muir flew to Cambridge and proceeded by taxi to Polly's modest row house. Bay windows overlooked a quiet street and small front garden. A larger walled yard in the rear allowed Polly's dogs to roam freely. Muir did not meet her companion, the sociologist, who she said was away at a conference. Polly suggested that she and Muir attend Evensong at King's College Chapel. As the guest of a fellow of the college, Muir donned a white surplice and sat with Polly in the choir stalls of the famous chapel, his large calloused hands caressing the dark wood of the elaborately carved seats, whose surfaces were worn and polished from five hundred years of human touch. When the choir entered from the far end of the nave, invisible behind a massive screen, their disembodied voices created an ethereal sound that descended from the fan vaulting far above his head, where impossibly thin ribs of stone branched into conical vaults that seemed to float in defiance of gravity, hovering just like the last limpid note sung by the boy sopranos. Muir was not easily impressed by things that occurred indoors. He had been moved by the sublime in nature, but never before that moment had he shed a tear of aesthetic delight in the works of man.

* * *

When the service was finished, Polly and Muir walked together to Fitzbillies, a Cambridge tea shop and bakery famous for its Chelsea buns.

"You get to do that every day?" he asked Polly.

"Could do," she said. "But I make it about once a week." He thought that Polly seemed happy.

"So he wants me to come back and testify?"

"Yes."

"What about? To what end?"

"You're enormously respected, Polly, and would make a really sympathetic witness. The lawyers want you to testify that you watched Ned grow up and that he's a normal child, not some kind of monster, and that the reason you left the marriage and the country had nothing to do with Ned."

Polly interrupted. "I've already said that, publicly."

"Yes, but they also want you to say that you couldn't have children together and this was part of Leo's motivation in creating Ned. They . . ."

"No! That's a lie."

"What? A lie? Leo said . . ."

"I don't care what Leo said. It's not true and I won't say it. We could have had children. In fact, I got pregnant soon after we were married, but he convinced me to abort, saying the time wasn't right." Polly stared at her teacup.

"I'm sorry, I didn't know," Muir said.

"No, Muir. No need to be sorry. At the end of the day it was my decision. I could have said no. I don't blame him for that. It was later, though, that he became adamant that he didn't want children. So it's ridiculous to suggest that he created Ned because he wanted a child. So, no, I won't do it."

Before Muir could reply, she added, "And he should have come to ask me himself."

"I told him that," Muir said.

Polly smiled at Muir gratefully.

"Please don't judge me, Muir. I know how fond you are of Ned, and really, he's the innocent in all this. I don't want to do anything to hurt him. But how dare that man ask me to lie? And to get you to do his dirty work . . ."

"I'm sorry, Polly. I didn't know. I always thought you just couldn't have children."

"Of course you didn't know. This is what the man does. He manipulates people to get what he wants. Do you have any idea what it was like, Muir? I loved him, but now I think he never really loved me."

Polly took a large bite of Chelsea bun.

"You know, Muir, the early years weren't so bad. When we had no money, lived in the cottage in Cupertino, and worked day and night together on SBD. I felt needed and valued and, really, I was happy for a while, at least until it slowly dawned on me that something was missing. We were two geeks, alike in so many ways. But I see now that I mistook compatibility for love. We had a kind of ease and comfort with one another, and I stupidly convinced myself that it was love. And then, of course, with the money and success . . . well, his shell hardened, plus he didn't really need me anymore. I started as a partner and ended up as an obsolete accessory."

They sat silently for a few moments.

"Much later, you know what he said, Muir? Years later, when I asked why he married me, he said I was appropriate, that I fit the parameters he had identified for a mate. Can you imagine what it was like to hear that?"

"I'm so sorry."

A waitress refilled Polly's tea. Muir thought of his own marriage and of all those years where Meredith's happiness was the thing he cared about most.

"You know," Muir said, "if it's any consolation, now he really does seem to care about Ned."

Polly wiped a tear with the sleeve of her blouse, and then jutted out her chin in exactly the way Muir had seen so many times before.

"I wonder. You know, Muir, he didn't even tell me that he was creating Ned. I learned about it after Ned was born."

"I had no idea. I always assumed . . ." Polly stood up, indicating the conversation was finished. Muir gave her a warm hug. "I'm so glad, Pol, that at least you've found some happiness now."

On the plane home, Muir couldn't help thinking about his own relationship with Leo through the lens of what he had heard from Polly. He understood that he was Leo's employee and served his ends. But from the beginning there had been something more in their relationship; at times he thought it was close to authentic friendship. At moments he had convinced himself that Leo was lonely, even vulnerable. But perhaps this too was a delusion. Leo had shown him many apparent kindnesses over the years. Was it possible that each was simply a manipulation, a means to fulfill one of Leo's desires, and nothing more? Did it matter?

Getting up to pace the narrow aisle of Leo's jet, Muir thought about his daughter. He worried that she no longer confided in him. But then again, had she ever? Most of all, he worried that the life he had given her, so deeply entangled with Leo's and Ned's, would bring his daughter only danger and grief.

* * *

After Muir landed back at Arcadia, he walked straight to Leo's house and found him sitting in front of his computer.

"I had no idea you were such a shit," Muir said.

"Yes, well it's nice to see you too."

"You could have children but didn't want them, and you didn't even tell her you were making Ned? And then you send me to ask her to lie about it?"

Leo didn't answer.

"And," Muir continued, "you were a total shit to marry her without loving her."

"You weren't there. You know nothing about it."

"I know you and I know her. What Polly told me absolutely made sense."

"Polly is a complicated person. I gather she said no?"

"Correct." Muir paused. "So it's true?"

"You said you know me."

"I've always tried to put things about you in the best light, Leo, because you're brilliant, and what you're doing is so important, and the opportunities you've given Lilith and me have been amazing. But I had no idea you could be that cruel."

"I . . . regret what happened to Polly," Leo replied. "I'm not the same person who did those things. I now . . . I now really do care about Ned."

"Do you? Do you care about Ned because he is you? Which is the same as caring about yourself. Even if you see him as his own person, do you care for him for his own sake, or simply for how it affects and reflects on you? Which is it?"

"It's not an unreasonable question," Leo said softly.

"Do you love him?"

"I think I might."

"Then you don't. If you did, you'd know it."

Leo considered this for a moment before continuing.

"I loved my sister, Muir. That I know. And I lost her. And I loved my mother, and she walked out."

"And that's an excuse?"

"No. It's . . . "

"Leo, bad stuff happens. My wife died in my arms and left me with a newborn. Ned came out of a genetics lab in Singapore and the womb of an Andalucían surrogate and grew up without conventional parents. In his short life he's been the target of an assassination attempt and seen the woman who raised him murdered. And he's still a sweet compassionate kid who cares deeply about others."

Leo smiled weakly. "That he is." Turning to leave the room, he added, "Thanks for going to England, Muir. I appreciate your at least trying with Polly. I really do."

34
Arcadia 2.0

THE THREAT OF NED'S detention and emasculation hung over Arcadia like the sword of Damocles. If a federal judge were to lift the stay, within hours the sheriff's helicopter would again descend from the sky and—this time—take Ned away. Despite this, and despite the devastation wrought by the flood, Leo remained determined that life at Arcadia should keep, as much as possible, to its ordinary routine. On his instructions, the lab teams continued their daily schedules as if two decades of their work did not lie in ruins just over the horizon. Leo insisted that Ned attend classes in the Village's small secondary school as if everything were normal.

And yet nothing was normal. The swampy stench of post-flood decay was inescapable. Residents of the Village turned their heads to avoid the sight of the lake bottom, mostly grayish mud drying into the characteristic fracture pattern, relieved only by the oily sheen of the few remaining pools and puddles. And the young man at the center of the crisis was so transparently distraught that most of the residents of Arcadia avoided him too. Those who didn't attempted a façade of cheerful normality. But Ned, watching them watch him, saw the pity in their eyes. Their pity, which he felt by empathic reflection, served only to amplify his own sense of dread. Those around him, even Lilith, chose their words with care.

Clip, however, continued to treat Ned with the same ironic jocularity as before. Clip now lived in a small Village cottage with his wife, Anne, and their infant daughter, Crystal. The couple invited Ned to watch the latest *Star Wars* movie over a large platter of nachos and guacamole. Ned asked if he could bring Lilith, but Clip suggested that it might be best if he came alone.

Ned sat slumped on a sofa. With his head tilted down and his forehead wrinkled in a frown, the effect was to exaggerate the size of the bony ridges above his large eyes and age him far beyond his sixteen years. Anne was startled to realize that she had seen, for just a moment, the face of a stereotypical "caveman." She decided to try to puncture his melancholy with an aphorism. "Come on, Ned, cheer up. You know that 'It never rains but it pours,' and, 'What can't be cured must be endured.'"

Ned's frown faded. "And, 'It's not over till it's over.'"

"No," said Clip, "'It's not over till the fat lady sings.'"

"I've always wondered," Ned asked, grinning now, "who is the fat lady?"

"You don't know?" Anne answered. "It's Brünnhilde, the Valkyrie. The end of Wagner's Ring Cycle, fifteen interminable hours of opera. And it doesn't end until the chubby Brünnhilde sings one last aria while throwing herself into the flames at the end of the world. So it really is all over when the fat lady sings."

"How do you know these things?" Clip asked.

Ned's face again darkened. "You know, I really wasn't afraid during the hearings, or even after they killed Aggie. But now . . . I know they could come get me anytime. They . . ." He stopped, unable to finish expressing the thought.

Anne moved to the sofa and took his hand. Having her soft hand in his made Ned think of Agnes and Lilith, which only made him sadder.

"How about your Neanderthal research, Ned?" Clip asked. "Still think there might be survivors?"

"Nah. I wanted so much for it to be true. But it's just not. I'm focusing on extinction now. The more I learn, the less sense it makes. There's something missing."

"Ned," Clip said, "Does it really matter that much? And do you really want to define yourself as Neanderthal? I mean, look at me," Clip added, laughing. "I was a clueless hacker dude living in my parents' basement, and now I'm a model husband and father. Seriously, Ned, you can be whatever you want to be."

Ned found this interesting. The bad guys, he thought, were the ones who kept saying he wasn't human. Was he giving in to them by thinking of himself as a Neanderthal? Was he wrong to identify with that part of himself?

He looked up at Clip. "OK, Clip. I'll think about it."

* * *

In the house that Leo and Ned now shared, a floor-to-ceiling convex glass wall faced the lake. Leo had placed a long table in front of the window, the irregularity of its live edge contrasting pleasingly with the strict radius of the curving glass. Made from salvaged Western walnut, it served as dining table, desk, and conference table. Before the flood, chairs were positioned only at the ends of the table and along the side where they faced the water. After the storm, Leo had the chairs turned inward. When Ned returned from Clip and Anne's, he was surprised to see that the chairs once again had been rearranged, this time returning to their places facing the muddy stain where Lake Arcadia used to be. Leo sat flipping through a set of large maps and looked up when Ned entered the house.

"Ned. Sit down for a second. I need your advice."

Although anxious to return to the solitude of his room, Ned sat.

"What should we do about Arcadia?" Leo asked.

"What do you mean, do?"

"I mean, do we give up or try again?"

Ned was surprised. He couldn't think of a previous instance where his father had asked for his opinion. But he was distracted by his fear. Chaotic thoughts seemed to chase their own tails and he found it difficult to focus on anything other than what Pastor Joe, and millions of other Americans, wanted to do to him.

"You know, Dad, for a long time my only dream was getting out of here. But now the thing I fear most is being forced to leave, to be separated from Lilith . . . and you, of course, and Muir."

"Ned, I told you not to worry. I won't let that happen."

"That's what you keep saying, but what if you lose in court? Anything could happen."

Leo felt the ragged edge of his son's dread.

Ned continued. "Can I ask you a question?"

"Sure."

"I mean, I know what castration is. But. Well, what happens afterward? Will I turn into a girl? Will I stop loving Lilith?"

"No, son. You would not turn into a girl. You've already been through puberty, and we would replace the lost hormones, so you would stay exactly the same. The only thing that would change is your ability to have children. You understand?"

"I think so."

"But it's not going to come to that, so stop thinking about it. OK?"

"OK."

"Let me tell you what I'm thinking. I want to rebuild. We're going to start over, and be even more ambitious. We're going to take everything we learned the first time and then do it again, but smarter and better."

"Uh huh."

"And there's something else I want to change. This time everything in Arcadia is going to be engineered to help the people who are here stay healthy and live longer—the water, the micronutrients in the soil, the biotic background, everything. Humans will live longer here because they fit in better."

"And Neanderthals? What about them? Will they fit in better? Will I?"

"Neanderthals especially. We'll bring back more people with Neanderthal traits. More importantly, we'll see what kind of culture people with those traits create, just as you suggested."

"Really, Dad?"

"You deserve others like you. I should have seen that from the beginning. And Neanderthals deserve another shot, this time with *sapiens* doing everything we can to help them. You were right, Ned. We killed off the Neanderthals and now have the power to bring them back. So I've concluded we really don't have a choice. And who knows, maybe some of the things we lost when Neanderthals went extinct will end up saving humanity."

Ned threw his arms around his father and gave him a tight hug.

"I can't believe it. When do we start?"

"First we need to solve . . . to get your situation sorted out. This is not the right moment for word to get out that we're thinking of having additional Neanderthals."

"OK." Ned sounded disappointed.

"'Rome wasn't built in a day,'" Leo said. "So Arcadia 2.0 is going to take a little while. You need to be patient."

After Ned went to bed, Leo got up from the table spread with maps of Arcadia and moved to a smaller desk along the sidewall. Sitting, he stared at the computer screen for many minutes before starting to type. Twice he deleted what he had written and stepped away from the computer. An hour later, he clicked "send" and his email appeared in Polly's inbox.

Pol. Muir reported that you're doing well. I'm glad. Really. The events of the past few weeks have got me thinking. I want to say I'm sorry. I shouldn't have married you. I treated you badly. I now understand this. You once said I was incapable of love. You may have been right. But now I know that I love Ned. And it's changed me. Too late for us, but it has changed me. I'm sorry. That's it. L.

35
Deception

And [Zeus] bade famous Hephaestus make haste and mix earth with water and to put in it the voice and strength of human kind, and . . . to put in her a shameless mind and a deceitful nature. So he ordered. And they obeyed the lord Zeus . . . contriv[ing] within her lies and crafty words and a deceitful nature. . . . And he called this woman Pandora.

Hesiod, *Works and Days* (c. 700 BCE)

LIL," NED SAID, "I figured it out. I know why the Neanderthals went extinct."

Ned and Lilith sat in a diner that Leo had purchased in Portland, restored, transported by heavy-lift helicopter, and set down in the middle of the Village—a brightly incongruous stainless-steel note among its earthen-roofed chameleon neighbors. The diner didn't officially open until 5:00 p.m., but the husband-and-wife team that ran it welcomed Ned, Lilith, and the other high school–age students to linger in the booths on their way back from school.

"Tell me," Lilith said.

Ned leaned forward and spoke in a quiet voice.

"Here's what I found out. Really young kids can't tell lies. It takes a while for their brains to develop the necessary skills, usually somewhere around eighteen to twenty-four months. To lie, you need first to be able to create a mental picture of something that isn't there or that doesn't exist—and young children can't do it. Turns out gorillas can't deceive either, but chimps can. The point is that it's a skill some species have, and some don't. You follow?"

"Sure. So . . ."

"So, the ability to deceive—to lie as a tactic to get what you want, and do it well—is a distinctive trait that *sapiens* clearly has. And here's the thing: it seems they were the only type of human who had it."

"You mean . . ."

"Yeah. It seems that the others—including the Neanderthals—either couldn't lie at all or weren't very good at it. And so you can see where this is going, Lil. Neanderthals may have been stronger, smarter, and better adapted, but they couldn't cope with being lied to. Deception was humanity's secret weapon. Not dogs, not projectile spears. You guys rose to the top because of your extraordinary skill in lying."

"But I don't understand," Lilith said. "How exactly did that help them if the Neanderthals were physically stronger?"

"There's a saying, Lil, 'All warfare is based on deception.' Think of the feigned attack or retreat, the smokescreen, the Trojan horse. If you know only honesty and trust, you don't have a chance against an enemy skilled at deception."

Lilith gazed out the window, thinking. "I guess that's right. But is this just your idea, or do other people think this?"

Ned pointed to a stack of books on the Formica table between them. Many pages were turned down at the corners, and little yellow sticky notes stuck out from the tops.

"Not just me. Lots. Anthropologists say that *sapiens* won because they had imagination and the other things it allows, like religion and myth. But it's not just religion and myth that result from that kind of imagination, it's also fraud, trickery, cunning, and treachery."

"It's a pretty dark view of humanity, Ned. You sure about this?"

"Look at it another way. What has humanity said about itself from the beginning? You remember Pandora from our myths class? Zeus commanded that the Gods create Pandora and give her and all her progeny 'a deceitful nature.'"

"I suppose," Lilith answered. She paused for a moment. "Wait a minute. You lumping me in with them, Ned? You think I'm like that?"

"Maybe." Ned laughed and Lil grabbed one of the books piled on the table and used it to swat him in the chest. "Or," Ned continued, "maybe, if I'm not descended from Adam, then you're not descended from Eve . . . or Pandora. Seriously, Lil. You're different. You know it, and I've always known it too."

"And you? Which genes do you think Shen gave you? The *sapiens* lying genes from your dad, or the innocent Neanderthal ones?"

"What do you think?"

Lilith leaned across the table to stroke his cheek. "I think you're the most compassionate person I know. You can tell what others are feeling and you care. I think if someone is that type of person, it would be hard to be a liar. After all, does anyone want to be lied to? Knowing that lying to people hurts them, I think it'd be hard for you to do."

"There are lots of different types of lies, Lil. Some hurt, some protect."

Two raucous ninth graders entered the diner and headed toward the booth next to Ned and Lilith. Lilith gave them a sharp look, and they quieted down and headed to a booth at the opposite end of the diner.

"Here's the bottom line. When *sapiens* came out of Africa the second time, wherever they went, the other people died out in short order. The only explanation is that *sapiens* had some trait that the others didn't and that gave the newcomers some advantage. *Sapiens* have seventy-three genes not found in Neanderthals—I think that somewhere in those seventy-three genes, or somehow in the way those genes are expressed, is the source of humanity's enormous talent for deception."

Ned sat back in the red vinyl banquette, rested his arm along the top, and watched Lilith think. After a moment, she responded.

"What I still don't understand is how we can know that the Neanderthals couldn't lie, or at least weren't very good at it."

"Neanderthals and the other types of early humans lived in very small groups, so intimate with each other that they didn't need to lie, and couldn't get away with it if they did."

"Didn't *Homo sapiens* do the same?"

"Maybe. But at some point, *sapiens* developed something that the Neanderthals probably never did—anthropologists call it 'group competition.' Once *sapiens* could make things up, they developed stories—fictional stories—that created separate origin myths and identities for various groups within the species. And before long, Lil, you had Christians and Muslims, Hutu and Tutsi, Sunni and Shia, Greek and Turk, and so on. This ability to spin elaborate stories, it not only let them kill off the Neanderthals, it drove them to spend the next thirty thousand years killing each other."

Ned and Lilith sat quietly in the booth, Lilith staring out the window and Ned searching for something in Lilith's face. The wife of the couple that operated the diner turned on the grill behind the long counter and the noisy exhaust fan above it. "Hey, kids. We're opening soon. Time to clear out."

Lilith, her reverie broken, turned back to Ned. "So what now? What do you do with this? What do we do with this?"

"It's ironic, Lil. There's a saying, 'For one species to mourn the death of another is a new thing under the sun.'"

"I remember," Lilith interrupted. "Aldo Leopold; I read him sophomore year. He said that about humans regretting that they had killed off the passenger pigeon."

"Yeah. Ironic, right? I mean, too bad about the passenger pigeon, but what about their closest human cousins, the Neanderthals? No one seems to regret that. Anyway, now there's something else new under the sun. I'm the first example of a species contemplating the cause of its own extinction."

"But does it change anything?"

"For humanity, maybe not. But for me, it changes everything."

36
Choices

LEO SAT ALONE ACROSS from the lawyers at a large conference table, ignoring the panoramic views across downtown Los Angeles and out to the Pacific. He spoke first.

"I hope you understand that it's highly unlikely that Ned would survive being taken into custody. Think of the first assassination attempt; the minute he was out in the world, they took a shot. There are people everywhere who want him dead. Millions of people think they would be doing God's will if they killed him. Let's be clear, this is not just about castration. If he's taken out of Arcadia, if he's taken away from me, he's as good as dead. Whatever it takes, that can't be allowed to happen. Whatever it takes."

"Understood." The senior partner of the LA firm sat at the center of the table opposite Leo.

"Realistically, what are our options?" Leo asked.

"Leo, I'm not going to sugarcoat this. We have lots of alternative theories under which the state court order is invalid, but none of them will prevail unless the federal court can be convinced that Ned should be considered a 'person' under the law. The Fifth Amendment, the Fourteenth Amendment—they only protect persons."

"I get that. But it's not a bright line, right? I thought you said the legal standard of who's considered a person has evolved. What about women and slaves, for example? Wasn't there a point before which they weren't treated as persons, and then the law changed?"

"Not exactly. But it's irrelevant. What will determine the outcome here is a factual determination of what exactly Ned is, and then the legal determination of whether that's a 'person' for purposes of the Constitution."

"OK. So what's the prognosis on that?" Leo asked.

A younger woman, a partner of the smaller Portland firm that had obtained the emergency stay, answered.

"We've got one thing going for us. Any serious geneticist will testify that he's not really a Neanderthal. He has a human genome that was modified to introduce Neanderthal traits, but even that's not a bright line given that so many modern humans also have some Neanderthal genes. So our best shot is to put on scientists to testify that he isn't a Neanderthal, and then argue that if he isn't another species, he should be treated as human."

"Aren't you asking the court," Leo said, "to decide where to draw the line—how many nonhuman genes you can have and still be considered a person?"

"Exactly. And the court should be very uncomfortable having to decide at what percentage of Neanderthal DNA someone ceases to be a person. Every time in history we've denied people legal personhood based on ancestry, race, or ethnicity, it's ultimately been revealed to be morally indefensible, often a prelude to genocide."

The senior partner from LA jumped in. "Karen may be right, Leo, but don't get your hopes up. Because it's not just a question of the Neanderthal genes that Ned has and we don't, it's also a question of the seventy-three genes that ordinary humans have but Neanderthals lack, all of which were deleted in the case of Ned."

"Right," one of his colleagues added. "So all they have to do is to ask a simple question: Does this creature have a genome that is within the traditional range of variability to be considered part of the species *Homo sapiens*? It's pretty clear the answer will be no. The other side doesn't have to show that he is a Neanderthal, all they have to show is that he's not a *Homo sapiens*."

Leo thought for a few moments. "Aren't we on the wrong track here? We're focusing on genotype. How about phenotype—the real-world result that his genes, whatever their mix, produces. Shouldn't our argument be completely different: that Ned has consciousness, intelligence, speech, and all the rest of the things that we've long thought of as uniquely human. That these are the things that entitle him to be treated—both morally, and by the law—the way we treat human beings."

"Two problems with that," the senior partner answered. "First, it's a slippery slope. Doesn't your dog have consciousness? Some chimps are more intelligent than some humans. Many animals communicate. There are lots of cases about this, Leo. And most judges see nothing but chaos if we start extending legal rights to animals based on their degree of intelligence, skills, or feelings."

"He's right," Karen said.

"And the second problem is that this thing is likely to go all the way up to the Supreme Court. Given the present composition of the court, they'll consider the original intent behind the Constitution, and there is nothing, absolutely nothing, to suggest that in the eighteenth century 'person' was meant to encompass extinct hominins or other types of sentient intelligent creatures. Quite the contrary, everything the framers knew and believed involved a clear bright line between man and animal. They believed that man was separate and unique in every way that mattered—theologically, morally, legally."

"The rest of you agree?" Leo asked.

Heads nodded all around the table.

"And if we lose on the constitutional challenge, then what choices do we have?"

"Then the stay is lifted, and the sheriff will need to enforce the order. You'll be required to release Ned into his custody."

"Unless," the Portland attorney added, "we can challenge enforcement on some other ground. For example, we could claim that Ned is entitled to the protection of the Endangered Species Act, but there are a ton of problems with that argument."

"You have to understand, Leo," another lawyer added, "there's no guarantee that we could get a second stay on the basis of any of these other challenges. And if we don't, then . . ."

"I get it. At that point what would our options be?"

"Legally, probably none."

The conversation stopped when a waiter entered to refill the coffee urns on the long granite counter that ran along one side of the conference room. One of the LA lawyers waved him away with his hand. When the door closed, Leo asked, "I don't mean our options legally. I mean practically."

"Well, here it gets pretty murky. It's a crime in Oregon to interfere with law enforcement. For example, if you were to hide Ned, or resist when they come to get him, this could subject you to criminal prosecution, potentially even a federal obstruction charge."

"And what if I were just to take him away to a friendly country? One with no extradition."

"Same thing. If I'm right about the federal obstruction charge, that could be a felony. And if you left, Leo, the company and all your money could be at risk. You might never be able to return to the US."

"And," one of the younger lawyers added, "anyone who helped you hide or protect Ned also would be subject to criminal prosecution. As lawyers, we can counsel you on what the law means and what is forbidden or permitted, but we can't help you evade it."

"That's true," the senior partner added, "but most likely only after the order is determined to be constitutional, that is, once the stay is lifted. For now, I think we can and should help all we can to plan for the different possible outcomes. It's a risk our firm is willing to take."

"So you're telling me that my choice might be between saving Ned and losing everything? We could get in the jet and go to a friendly country, but the price might be the forfeiture of my company, my money, my citizenship, everything?"

Again, heads nodded.

37

Spooky Action at a Distance

When two systems . . . enter into temporary physical interaction . . . and when after a time of mutual influence the systems separate again, then they can no longer be described in the same way as before. . . . By the interaction the two [systems] have become entangled.

Erwin Schrödinger (1935)

I picture two Neandertals sitting side by side, their intimacy so exact that their interior voices cross and coalesce, like two streams merging into a river, their waters indistinguishable.

James Shreeve, *The Neandertal Enigma* (1995)

ENTROPY," MUIR SAID. "YOU'RE forgetting about entropy. Everything is unraveling and you can't stop it."

A few days after Leo's return from Los Angeles, he asked if Muir might be available to take a walk and discuss his plans for Arcadia. Muir canceled his afternoon schedule and agreed to meet Leo at the animal nursery at the south edge of the Village.

"Everything unraveling?" Leo replied. "Not at the scales of time and space in which I operate."

"Leo, even if nature is like a machine that you can reengineer, which I don't think it is, you still face the limitations of all machines—the struggle to keep order from decaying into disorder. One thing I've learned is that nature runs in one direction only. Everything from DNA to galaxies wants to fly apart. The flood should have reminded you of that."

"The flood was a preventable error," Leo said.

"You know, Meredith once read the Koran front to back. It's the sort of thing she did. She was such a curious woman. Anyway, I remember one thing that really struck her. She told me the Koran describes paradise as a garden with 'rivers of water unstalling' and 'rivers of milk unchanging in flavor.' Paradise is imagined as a place where change stops, where entropy is finally defeated. It may be possible in paradise, Leo, but not here on Earth, and certainly not here in central Oregon."

"Maybe, but I can come pretty damn close." Leo stopped and pointed at a low shrub. "This plant? For the first time in human history, we know exactly how it evolved. I know the mutations that gave it an evolutionary advantage. I know the additional genetic modifications that it would need to thrive in the face of environmental change. So I can control its future."

"All I'm saying," Muir replied, "is that some humility is in order. Did you learn nothing from what happened?"

"Come on, Muir. Of course I learned a lot. But I've got to be honest with you. My ambitions this time are greater, not less. And Muir, we're having this talk because I need to know you're on board."

* * *

A couple of weeks later, after school, Ned sat at the desk in his room. He had convinced his father to open the Village's bowling alley, which was normally closed on Wednesday nights, for a date with Lilith. He was trying to read the latest issue of *Popular Science* but could not concentrate. His mind kept turning to the evening ahead. He and Lilith hung out at school and they went for walks. He saw her nearly every day. And yet tonight would be only the second time he would walk to her house, knock on her door, pick her up, and take her out during the evening for something they both understood to be a "date."

The magazine lay on his lap, opened to an article about quantum entanglement, the paradox that Einstein called "spooky action at a distance." "When two particles are entangled," he read, "one cannot be described without reference to the other, and when we cause a change in the properties of one, something seemingly impossible occurs: a correlated change happens instantly in the other, even if it's a billion light years away." Could love, he wondered, be a type of quantum entanglement? Would he and Lilith remain connected, no matter what? Ned looked up from the page, lost in thought.

Ned's bedroom door was at the end of a short hall from which a second door opened to the large lake-view room where Leo had convened a small meeting. The trio of bankers who managed his money, as well as his personal lawyers, were taking papers from their briefcases and getting settled at the table. The late-afternoon light threw long shadows from the pines, an overlay of irregular stripes on the view from the gently curving glass wall.

Leo poked his head into Ned's room. "Son, do you mind if I close the door? We're having a meeting and I don't want to disturb you."

"Sure, no problem."

On his way back, Leo also closed the second door, between the big room and the hall.

"So," Leo said when everyone was settled, "I think we're agreed. If we let Ned be detained, the odds are high that someone will get to him and finish what they tried in Portland. A week before we think the federal case may be finally decided, Ned and I will take the jet to

Dubai for a long-planned vacation. If we lose, we stay indefinitely."

"Let's hope it doesn't come to that," the senior lawyer said. "Even if the odds are against us, we still have a real chance of winning the case, and we're going to fight like hell."

"Right," Leo said, "but we've got to have a plan."

"The UAE," one of the other lawyers said, "has already issued the standard investor visa and confirmed that this will convert into passports for both you and Ned if we maintain the required level of investment for three years. Dubai was a good choice. The Emiratis are immensely practical, and almost anything is possible for a price."

"And," one of the bankers added, "the trust is now fully funded. We did a private sale of SBD shares to a Dubai trust, and the trustees then liquidated those shares in numerous market transactions. You and Ned are the trust beneficiaries. It means in the worst case you'll have at least $100 million. It was the most we could do and still be absolutely sure no one would notice."

"Leo," another of the lawyers asked, "do you really understand what gets triggered if you do this? You could lose all your wealth other than the $100 million. You almost certainly lose control of the company you spent your life building. You lose Arcadia. You might never again return to America. It may even be too dangerous to travel anywhere outside of the UAE. You could lose everything other than Ned. And there's no going back. Is this really what you want?"

"It's going to be hard on Ned," Leo said. "Leaving Arcadia, but mostly, leaving Lilith. You know she's more than just a best friend. But there's no other way. So, yes, it's what I want. Now, can we turn to the will?"

"There's even better news there. This morning the circuit court agreed to seal the record. We have our declaratory judgment in Oregon, but no one will know about it until we have to use it."

"As far as the world knows," the junior lawyer added, "Ned has no more right to inherit your estate than your dog does. What they don't know is that the circuit court granted a declaratory judgment that Ned should be treated for probate purposes, at least in Oregon, as your sole son. It's not totally ironclad, but for the moment at least, when you go, he gets whatever is left, other than the specific bequests."

"And those?"

"We did what you asked. But, Leo, I wouldn't be doing my job if I didn't ask you to reconsider about Polly. She's living with another man. If you don't divorce her, she gets to elect 25 percent of your estate. If you avoid forfeiture, it would make her one of the richest people in the world. She doesn't need it, and it then passes down to whomever she wants. Why give her that power?"

"If she wants to divorce me," Leo answered, "she can have a divorce. But I'm not divorcing her. And it doesn't matter, because either way, if I can, I want to leave her more than whatever it is she's entitled to as a spouse. It's a way of saying that I'm sorry."

"That's money that would otherwise go to Ned and his kids. Your genetic descendants. And given the circumstances, they might need it."

"I understand, but it's what I want. And Muir?"

"He's in as you asked. It's an awful lot for an employee, Leo."

"He's more than an employee."

After the meeting adjourned, Ned emerged from his room.

"Sorry, did we disturb you?" Leo asked.

"Not at all."

But Ned had been disturbed. Leo thought he knew everything about his son, but he never fully grasped the extraordinary acuity of Ned's hearing, which had improved during his adolescence to a level far beyond that revealed by the many tests conducted during his childhood. When the distant talk or other sounds he picked up were uninteresting, Ned easily could tune them out. His power of auditory focus was as sharp as *sapiens'* ability to focus within the visual field. But that afternoon, the conversation grabbed and held his attention. Now, the implications of the things he had heard tumbled in his brain. Should he tell his dad that he had heard? Is keeping a secret, he wondered, the same as lying? Can silence be deception? Rushing out the door for his date with Lilith, he decided that the fact that he had heard it all was a fact that his father just didn't need to know, at least not yet.

* * *

Ned and Lilith turned on the music system in the bowling alley, choosing a lounge music playlist that for some reason they found hilarious. Giggling like the teenagers they were, they went through all the normal rituals of trying on bowling shoes and choosing balls. Ned stood behind the small snack counter pretending to work there. Lilith ordered an extra-large Sprite and box a Jujubes, repeating the word "Jujubes" over and over, each with a different absurd pronunciation, until Ned's eyes teared up from laughter.

Ned activated two bowling lanes and the video screens that showed the score. Each of them was determined to win, and after three consecutive strikes by Ned, Lilith observed with some real resentment, "After all, it's a game all about balls and pins, and in that you have an unfair advantage." Ned blushed. When Lilith bowled, he stood behind, transfixed by the extraordinary sight of her right hip dipping, the twist of her rear, and the small wobble from her thin waist as she completed the swing. It seemed as beautiful to him as the downward sweep of a bird's wing in flight.

Between rounds they sat on wide benches covered with vintage vinyl, sipping their soft drinks and joking about the people who would be there on a normal night. Laughing, Lilith said, "If I win the next frame, you need to take your shirt off, deal?" She then stood and bowled a strike. Ned did not. He unbuttoned his polyester bowling shirt and draped it carefully over the bench. Lilith came close and ran her fingers through the fur on his chest. Ned reached out, a hand on each shoulder, and pulled her close for a kiss. But after the first kiss, he stopped, pushing her back to arm's length.

"Lil, something happened today. I can't stop thinking about it."

"What, Ned? Tell me."

"My dad had a meeting at the house. He thought I couldn't hear, but I could. And I listened even though I knew I shouldn't. And then I didn't tell him that I heard. Was that wrong?"

"What'd you hear?"

Ned hesitated.

"The lawyers think we'll probably lose the case. If we do and they come and get me, Dad thinks I'd not only be . . . that I'd be killed. So if we lose, then we might have to leave Arcadia. Move to Dubai." He paused again. "Without you. Maybe forever."

"That," said Lilith, "will never happen. You know we have to be together."

"I know."

38
Fathers and Sons

We sit in the mud, my friend, and reach for the stars.

Ivan Turgenev, *Fathers and Sons*

At first, it seemed that the great flood had transformed Leo's dream of Arcadian perfection into a killing field of fetid muck. It was a cruel irony: the Big Empty, teeming with life before Leo's interventions, appeared in the immediate aftermath of the deluge to be a kind of lifeless wet moonscape. But as the months passed and the Arcadians scanned, scoped, measured, and mapped every inch of the vast territory, a different picture emerged.

The high ground proved to be largely unaffected and appeared on their maps as a Rorschach inkblot in which they saw surviving habitat and hope. They discovered that the flooded lands in between were far from bereft of living things. Instead, under close examination, the muck was revealed to be teeming with bacteria, seeds, and spores. Arcadians learned that a flood may destroy, but it also cleanses, seeds, and nourishes.

On Ned's first trip into the part of Arcadia beyond the former lake, he had wept. But now on his daily field trips with the science teams, he knelt at the base of rocks, peered into the stumps of trees, dipped his skimmer into shallow puddles, and focused his phone's camera on the thousands of organisms that were sprouting, wriggling, and otherwise joyously erupting into life. When Leo suggested a weekend camping trip, just father and son, Ned enthusiastically agreed.

The chopper dropped them on the lower edge of a rocky plateau that rose from a sweeping arc of flooded land and sloped gradually upward toward a timbered ridgeline.

"Dad, look at that green. It's incredible how quickly the wet areas are regrowing. It's not just algae and mosses, we've found sedges, rushes, milfoils, and even a few pond lilies."

"True. But it takes a long time to get from a few wetland weeds to a complex and stable ecosystem."

"I think," Ned answered, "that Muir would say it's best to be patient."

Leo and Ned headed out along the edge of the floodplain toward a distant gap in the rocks where a walkable slope appeared to lead up the ridge. Leo set a brisk pace, with Ned following in fits and starts, kneeling to examine a plant or peer under a rock and then trotting to catch up. A half hour later, before taking the uphill turn, they stopped for water. Sitting on a slab of fractured rock, father and son scanned the flooded lowlands that stretched nearly to the horizon.

"I did this," Leo said. "My errors caused the flood, so this is something I need to fix. I'm not going to stand around and wait for nature to take care of it."

"I get that, Dad, but you're assuming the result will be the same in either case, and I don't think that's necessarily right. Muir would say that going slow, letting evolution do its thing and take its time, will get us a better result in the end."

"Is that what you think?"

"I . . . I don't know. Maybe."

Leo and Ned rose and resumed their uphill hike.

"You know, Ned, if it had been up to Muir, you wouldn't have existed."

"What do you mean?"

"I mean he believed strongly that de-extincting a Neanderthal was a terrible idea. If I had told him what I was doing beforehand, he would have tried to stop me. After you were born, he called you a mistake."

"Maybe he was right."

"Son," Leo said after a few minutes, "I had a choice. I could have waited. But if I had waited, you wouldn't have existed. Tell me, Ned, honestly. I really need to know. Do you blame me for creating you? Do you think it was a mistake?"

"No," Ned replied. "I don't blame you. I'm grateful. I don't consider myself a mistake. In fact, Dad, for reasons I can't quite explain, I've always thought of my existence as somehow . . . I guess I'd say necessary."

Leo stopped walking and looked at Ned, as if he had just heard something important. Before Leo could speak, Ned said, "Dad, can you smell it?"

"What?"

"Death."

Several minutes later they came to a slot canyon the sides of which were scoured clean to a height of about twenty feet, indicating the depth of the torrent that had swept through. Just downstream, the carcasses of animals large and small clogged a rocky choke point. A single mammoth tusk thrust at an odd angle from the putrefying tangle of flesh and bone. Ned spotted elk, wolf, and at least a dozen deer, jammed, like a multi-car smashup on the highway, against the boulders.

"I can't take the smell, Dad. It's too much. We need to get upwind."

Father and son found a suitable camping spot for the night, well away from the rotting carcasses. After dinner, as the campfire died down, Leo and Ned lay on the ground, hands behind their heads, facing the stars. It was, for each of them, one of their favorite things. As a child, long before he lived with Leo, Ned would beg Agnes to take him out to see the stars before bedtime. Leo, who rarely spoke of his own youth, told Ned during a previous camping trip that one of his few childhood pleasures had been spending the night on the deck of his father's tug as it churned its way up the Hudson, staring at the stars until he fell asleep.

"Dad, wouldn't it be great if we could think in galactic years? You know, the time it takes our solar system to orbit around the center of the Milky Way—about 250 million Earth years, I think? I figured out the other day that in galactic years, it was only about ten days ago that apes started walking on two feet. And eight hours ago that Neanderthals and *sapiens* both evolved from *Homo erectus*. Kind of makes you think."

"It's all about perspective." After a short silence, Leo continued. "In fifteen galactic years the sun will make Earth uninhabitable, and in twenty-five galactic years the sun itself will burn out."

"Dad, did you love Polly?"

"No. But marriage is not always about . . ." Leo stopped and reconsidered. "No, I didn't. And it was wrong of me to marry her."

"I love Lilith," Ned said.

"Son, you're at the age where you develop a crush on whatever girl is around."

"You know that's not true, Dad. I've always loved her, as long as I can remember. And she's always loved me. There's nothing more important to me than that."

Leo contemplated the stars in silence.

"So . . . Dad, I know about Dubai. And I won't go."

"How?"

"I overheard. I didn't mean to. But I heard it all."

Leo turned to face his son.

"For the longest time, Dad, all I wanted was to get out of Arcadia and see the world. But not anymore. All I want now is to spend my life here. I want to rebuild Arcadia with you and Muir; I want to start the Neanderthal colony. I want to give Earth all that the lost Neanderthal genome and culture may have to offer. And I need to be with Lilith."

The two watched as a single shooting star sliced through the blackness straight above them.

"Ned, do you understand that you're my clone? You know what that means? It means that you are me, or rather what I would be if I were a Neanderthal. When I look at you it's like looking in a fun house mirror—the image is distorted, but the essential features are mine."

Ned found this comment to be strange. He had never seen anything of himself in his father. Instead, almost all the things he thought of as "himself" were defined by differences or contrasts with his father. Maybe, he thought, the right analogy was a photograph and its negative. The negative gave rise to the photograph, but what was black on one came out white on the other; what read left to right on the source printed right to left on the final image. He might have been cloned, Ned thought, but he was not a clone.

"Well, I've only ever felt like me," Ned said. "But I know what you mean, kind of like identical twins meeting for the first time and find they're wearing the same shirt and have the same type of dog with the same name—you know, some kind of spooky connection. But really, I can't honestly say I've ever felt that sort of thing between us."

"Oh."

"But Dad, honest, that is how I feel with Lilith. There's so much that we just don't have to say to each other because we already know it. When she's not here, it's like a part of me is missing."

"Those are clichés, Ned, things you've read or heard, not something you really feel."

Ned flushed in anger. "You're wrong. You don't know how I feel. I'm not even sure you have feelings, so don't you dare call my feelings a cliché."

"Sorry."

Leo waited a few moments for Ned to calm down. "Look, Ned, leaving Arcadia is not what I want. But if you want to live, then we might need to leave. It's that simple."

"We won't need to leave, Dad. We'll win in court. Somehow I know that. I don't know how, but I'm sure of it."

Leo turned his head in surprise. Ned had never before expressed a view on the outcome of the case.

"You said at the hearing," Ned continued, "that you chose not to make me sterile because you wanted me to have the chance to love and be loved. If you meant it, you won't take me away from Lilith."

The two stared at the stars a few more minutes, then Leo spoke. "Let's go to sleep now."

39

Et in Arcadia Ego

Being consulted as to whether the child would live a long life, to a ripe old age, the seer with prophetic vision replied, "If he does not discover himself."

Ovid, *Metamorphoses III*: 339–358

THREE WEEKS AFTER THE father-son camping trip, Leo asked Ned to join him on a trip to the southeastern corner of Arcadia, not so far from the Idaho border, an area that had been unaffected by the flood. Leo wished to visit a lake where Muir reported catching a massive bull trout. Without Ned having to ask, Leo suggested that Lilith join them.

After the helicopter landed, the group of three ambled across a high-altitude meadow toward a small dock. The ramshackle structure, which listed alarmingly to one side, floated precariously over an expansive colony of hardy water lilies. The wooden dinghy, not much larger than a rowboat, floated placidly alongside. Only a few patches of faded red paint remained on its wide planked hull. The craft's stubby bow ended in a jaunty upward sweep, giving a somewhat comical effect. A thick wooden mast held a single lug-rigged sail the color of mustard.

Because the dinghy could take two passengers only, the chopper had brought a lightweight kayak with the rest of the fishing gear. Lilith set out in the kayak, with Leo and Ned following behind in the boat. A soft wind began to tease the surface of the water, so Leo raised the sail and headed toward the spot where Muir said he had caught the bull trout.

Leo sat on the wooden bench that ran across the stern with his arm draped casually over the long tiller. Staring at the water, Leo realized that just sitting silently in the boat with Ned gave him profound pleasure. For most of his life he was puzzled by other people wanting to be with their children. Now he understood.

At first Ned crouched just forward of the mast, holding on with one hand. But as the morning wore on, the fishing distracted Ned from his nervousness at being on the water. He studied and admired the hand-tied lures. He treated each fish extracted from the lake with reverence, studying the patterns created by skin and scale, and calming the creature with his touch as he extracted the hook.

"I'm done," Lilith called out from the kayak. "I haven't had a single bite."

"Did you change the bait?" Leo asked.

"I have an idea," Lilith answered. "Why don't I paddle across to the other side and set up the picnic. I'll read my book while I'm waiting for you. OK?"

"OK," Leo said. "But stay where we can see you. We shouldn't be too long."

Happy to be relieved of the tedium of fishing, Lilith paddled with vigor toward the opposite shore. Ned followed her with his eyes for a few minutes, until a sharp tug on his line pulled his attention back to the dinghy. Still kneeling, he carefully reeled in a medium-size rainbow trout, admiring its faded red stripe against a silvery olive field, the whole speckled with black spots.

"Good one," Leo said. "But I'm still hoping for a big bull."

Ned gently removed the hook and dipped the fish in the water before letting go.

During the next hour, Leo persisted in his hunt for a bull trout. He maneuvered the dinghy to different spots, changed his rig, tried three different lures, and then substituted bait for a lure. Ned, though looking bored, did not complain. He did finally say, "Dad, when you're ready, I'm pretty hungry."

Leo looked up at the sail hanging listlessly from the gaff. "Guess you get to row," Leo said.

As the small craft headed directly for the spot on the far shore where Lilith had spread the blanket near the water's edge, Leo had nothing to do other than watch his son pull the heavy oars in powerful, seemingly effortless, strokes. When the bow of the boat plowed into the sandy beach, Leo jumped ashore and secured the long bowline to the stump of a small tree.

Ned sat close to Lilith, who opened the picnic basket and placed its contents on the blanket.

"Oh, my favorite," Lilith said, plucking a foil-wrapped sandwich labeled "Tuna wrap." "It's got celery and grapes. What do you want to drink, Leo?"

"Iced tea, please."

"Ned?" she asked.

Ned's head was turned over his right shoulder, his chin elevated slightly. He didn't answer.

"Ned?" Then again, "Ned, what's wrong?"

"Are you hearing this?" Ned asked.

"No, what?" Both Leo and Lilith turned to look at the edge of the woods behind them.

"I hear something."

"What, an animal? What kind?" Leo asked, realizing that he had failed to bring a rifle.

Ned screwed up his face and sniffed. "Actually, it's a person."

"Really?" Leo said. "We don't have any crew out here. It's probably a perimeter security patrol. We're quite near the fence."

"Could be," Ned said. "But don't they always work in pairs? This is only one person. Over there, behind those rocks. And he's watching us, I can tell."

Leo stood up. "It's probably nothing, but better to be safe. I want you kids to get in the boat and row out into the lake, as far away as you can, and stay there until I say it's OK."

"No, Dad. Lilith can go. I should stay here with you."

Lilith grabbed his hand, pulling Ned toward the beached boat. "Ned, come on. Don't be a jerk. I want you to come with me."

A moment later, a man emerged from behind the rocks. He was short, not much taller than Ned. He wore black pants with a khaki shirt and red cap. Leo could not see his face. For a moment, Leo thought he might be a hunter, until he saw the Glock semiautomatic pistol at the end of his outstretched right arm. A second holstered gun hung on his belt.

The man spent a few seconds taking in the scene, looking back and forth between Leo, who scanned the disrupted picnic for something that might serve as a weapon, and the two teenagers, who, unable to untie the rope from the stump, had clambered into the dingy and were paddling as far out as the still-secured bowline would allow.

"What do you want?" Leo asked.

The man removed his hat, throwing it to the ground. Oriental eyes, aglow with hate, glared at Leo.

"Shen!" Leo said. He had believed that the professor either had been executed by the Chinese or imprisoned for life. If he was here, it was because the Chinese government allowed it, and because someone inside Arcadia had again leaked the time and place where Ned would be most vulnerable.

"You destroyed me, Mr. Leo. You took everything I had. My work, my money, my reputation. So now I will destroy you."

"Leave them out of this," Leo said, nodding toward the two teenagers in the boat.

"I created him, Mr. Leo. He's as much mine as yours. And so before you die, you will watch me destroy my creation, who you call your son."

Shen walked slowly toward the boat, still aiming his weapon at Leo's chest. Arriving at the stump, he kneeled and with one arm started to haul in the dinghy by its bowline. Lilith tried to release the line while Ned paddled hard in the opposite direction. Their efforts were futile. As the boat floated closer to the shore, Shen dropped the rope and unholstered his second weapon.

Ned abruptly stood up in the boat, waved his hands, and started yelling. Distracted, Shen turned toward the dinghy, taking his eyes off Leo for an instant. Leo sprinted forward and launched himself onto the gunman. Just before Leo landed the tackle, Shen turned back and fired at the airborne body. The bullet emerged from Leo's side as he landed on Shen, knocking the smaller man onto his back, stunned.

Lilith screamed when Ned jumped from the boat and pushed forward through the chest-high water toward the shore and the two men on the ground. Shen struggled to free his arm and shoot at the approaching teenager, but Leo—although bleeding heavily from the wound in his side and gasping with the effort—managed to keep Shen pinned down.

"Hold on, Dad," Ned yelled as he crawled from the water and stumbled up the beach. When he reached the two men, he slammed his large foot down on Shen's exposed right shoulder and arm, causing the humerus to fracture with an audible crack. Shen screamed in pain. Ned quickly thrust his arm between the two bodies, wrapping his broad hand around Shen's smaller hand and the gun. With a brutal jerk, he forced the muzzle of the gun down into Shen's chest and squeezed the trigger. Shen's head fell to the side and blood dribbled from the edge of his open mouth.

Ned gently rolled Leo off the dead man and knelt over his father, putting one hand softly on his forehead. Leo's eyes, still open, focused on his son, and Leo managed a weak smile. A moment later, his eyes rolled upward and his heaving chest became still.

Lilith pulled the boat back to shore and ran up the beach to kneel next to Ned. She found it hard to look at the gaping black hole in Leo's chest, or his favorite fishing shirt, now bright red from the blood of both men. Lilith took off her jacket and placed it tenderly over Leo's face.

Ned's body remained rigid and his shallow breath was nearly imperceptible. Lilith did not speak. Finally, Ned's shock broke with a spasm and he started to sob.

"I should have stayed with him. I could have saved him."

"No," Lilith said. "What could you have done? Shen had a gun. We'd all be dead."

"When Dad jumped at the guy, he knew he would probably get shot and . . ."

"Yes."

Ned started shivering.

"Your clothes are soaking wet, Ned. Let's use the blanket."

Lilith took Ned's hand and led him along the beach out of sight of the bodies of the two men. She stripped off his wet clothes, wrapped him in the oversize blanket they had brought for the picnic, and held him tightly. After a half hour, he finally stopped shaking and opened his eyes, looking gratefully at Lilith.

"Better?" Lilith asked.

Ned answered by taking her head into his hands. They kissed solemnly. The blanket dropped from his shoulders. Lilith gently pushed him to the ground. Ned felt his back make contact with the cool damp sand of the beach. Both of Lilith's hands were on his chest. Then, the unforgettable sensation as Lilith slowly lowered herself on to him.

An hour later, for the first time in thirty thousand years, sperm carrying the DNA of a Neanderthal fused with the egg of a *Homo sapiens* and a diploid zygote began its dance with destiny.

Acknowledgments

I AM GRATEFUL TO MY colleagues on the advisory board of the Hastings Center, and to the leadership and staff of that distinguished institution, who introduced me to de-extinction and the ethical conundrums it presents.

Many people assisted with research, but I want to thank particularly Prof. Dr. Gerd-Christian Weniger and Dr. Bärbel Auffermann of the Neanderthal Museum in Mettmann, Germany, and the staff of the Gibraltar National Museum.

For their editorial advice and assistance, I owe a great debt to both Star Lawrence and A. J. Wilson. Ryan Quinn did a sharp-eyed copyedit.

Any errors that remain are the sole responsibility of the author.

About the Author

FREDERIC C. RICH IS the author of the dystopian political novel, *Christian Nation* (W. W. Norton, 2013), which warned that a demagogic populist, serving theocratic ends, could be elected president in 2016. His second book was a nonfiction exploration of environmental politics and philosophy, *Getting to Green, Saving Nature: A Bipartisan Solution* (W. W. Norton, 2016). Rich's interest in the genetic revolution grew out of his long career as an environmental leader and international corporate lawyer. He lives in Manhattan and the Hudson Valley of New York.